# INSIDIOUS VALOUR

## DANIEL MUNRO

Also by Daniel Munro:

Book 1) The Taste Beneath

Book 2) Diseased Intentions

Contact:

Email: authordanielmunro@hotmail.com

Instagram: author_danielmunro

Website: www.authordanielmunro.co.uk

Paperback ISBN: 978-1-99993786-5-3

Ebook ISBN: 978-1-99993786-6-0

*For Kevin, who smiled and fought throughout.*
*Loyal father, partner, son, brother, and friend.*

# PART I

## NO SIGNAL

Ryan staggered into Medical Room One, pulling the last metallic splinter from his left shoulder as he landed hard on the armchair, trying to steady his breathing and make sense of what happened.

He leaned forward, spitting blood on the floor. "What you saw..." he winced, talking to the semi-conscious stranger in the gurney, "...it was real. All real." A familiar glare threatened to take over his stare as he watched the person in front of him. *It's always fucking real.*

From the cafeteria, orders were yelled as positions and lookout points were delegated amongst the members of Penbrook Vineyard and the newest batch of survivors.

"We've faced them before," Ryan continued, attempting to cover the fresh gash that ran down his left bicep. "They're called *Termites.*" He paused, replaying the image of the swarm that had just tried to ambush them. "That's what they were nicknamed by their captors—Termites—a workforce designed to do nothing but build, work, fight, then die."

A box of ammo clattered across the corridor floor outside of the room. Two people rushed past to fortify the winery's western fire exit.

"And the speed you saw them run... it wasn't your eyes playing tricks on you. They're strong. I've seen them throw wooden spears through metal barriers." Ryan winced, sitting forward while massaging the nubs on his left hand where his ring and pinkie fingers used to be. "This power they possess is the result of adrenaline build-up, and the only thing that keeps that from being released into their system is the consumption of human meat..."

The stranger on the bed tried to open their mouth, and a croak escaped their bloody, bruised lips.

"Don't talk. I'll ask the questions." Ryan sat forward. "Use your eyes. Blink once for yes. Twice for no. Do you understand?"

One blink.

"Good." Ryan exhaled with relief, then asked, "Do you know who sent this wave of Termites after you?"

# 1

---

Six Weeks Earlier.

"I've got it!" Drinker shouted from inside the boiler room's dark space.

"Okay, tighten it," Ryan acknowledged through gritted teeth. His thick gloves provided virtually no protection against the ice-cold copper piping. One of his blond dreadlocks got caught in his grasp as he tried to hold the foam in place. There was a quick ripping of duct tape as the foam insulation tightened around the water pipe.

Ryan released his grip and stepped out from the cramped space, taking his gloves off and rubbing his hands together for warmth. On his left hand, the space where his little and ring fingers should've been screamed at him in some kind of phantom pain.

Drinker exited the boiler cupboard, looking comfortable in his usual black T-shirt and urban camo pants. "I can tell you've never spent winter in Scotland," his Glaswegian accent teased with rhetorical sarcasm.

"I wouldn't go to Scotland in winter even if I was on the run from the law," Ryan replied, rubbing his green eyes. He shut the door and looked up to the ceiling, seeing the damage they had caused to the medical corridor to insulate the water pipes. The whole of the winery was being prepared for the extreme winter conditions. "How much is there left to do?"

"Just the medical rooms left," Drinker said, scratching his dark goatee before rubbing his newly shaved head. "Then it's a case of solving the new problem."

Ryan nodded silently, kicking some of the ceiling debris across the tile floor before placing the scissors and duct tape on the medical trolley and wheeling it down the corridor. He was raging inside, beyond pissed off with everything life was throwing at them.

In the wake of an assault the previous month, part of the winery's ceiling had collapsed during repair, crushing their reserve supply of corn oil. They barely had enough for the people the winery already accommodated, but with the arrival of more survivors, they were doomed to run out before the next batch was pressed, filtered, and then mixed. Without corn oil, they wouldn't be able to run their generators or boilers, and the winter was only getting colder with every passing hour.

Ryan stood still, gripping the trolley tightly with his remaining fingers. Frustration burned deep inside of him.

"You okay?" Drinker asked, stopping beside him.

"Yeah." Ryan sighed, letting go of the trolley and taking a deep breath. He nodded to the final stretch of pipes above them. "You okay to make a start on these? I just need to go for a smoke."

"Aye. Nay bother."

"Thanks."

Ryan walked back through the medical corridor and pushed the door open to the cafeteria, which was eerily empty compared to normal. He grabbed his white parka coat, tied his dreadlocks back, and pulled the hood up, heading straight through the canteen kitchen and out the fire exit.

Nearly a whole foot of snow covered the vineyard's grounds, and the soft downfall didn't look like it was stopping anytime soon. Gazing into the ocean of white, the only company Ryan had was the taunting reminder that he was losing his fight to keep everyone safe—a responsibility he had taken on himself since the very first day of the war. His eyes felt compelled to look towards the graves of their most recently lost loved ones, but his shame wouldn't let him acknowledge their existence.

"Fuck!" he bellowed, leaning back against the wall and sliding down to a sitting position. He could've used a cigarette at this moment, but mostly, he needed to get away from his tasks and let the angst out of his system. The outburst echoed well into the distance, and then the silence came back; he sat alone in the lifeless void that was his world now.

His temples felt like they were being compressed into his skull, and his heart rate pushed blood around his body so hard that his hands were paralysed from the anxiety. Everything inside him screamed to the point where he wasn't sure if he was already in hell or if God was laughing at them.

They were running out of corn oil, expecting more survivors who they had to feed, and preparing for the next attack, which could come at any moment. An attack from an unconfirmed amount of mindless drones, all under the command of the former SAS commander, known as Admiral Caven. They would tear through the vineyard's defences and take everyone alive—for one of two purposes. Reproduction or sustenance. If the rumours of this army's size were anything to go by, it would be a clean sweep, no matter the defence they put up.

There was only one bargaining chip the vineyard had, and they currently held her captive in the winery's basement. Admiral's daughter, Hannah—the woman who killed Ryan's nephew.

Every passing day and the simple task of just feeding and keeping her alive was like a slap in the face. The bitch knew how to wind people up, knowing she was the only reason that Admiral wouldn't just decimate the vineyard when it came to it. She was the key to finding a solution for peace, but that peace would be based on a lie. Ryan would never let them live. None of them. He knew the peace would only last until Admiral's men had regrouped and attacked the vineyard again. *How many more of us have to die before I learn?* Ryan taunted himself, pounded mentally into the ground by his decisions and the loved ones lost.

He sat for minutes, blank, smothered by the nothing that was life now. Snow fell in silence around him, but nothing was peaceful or serene about his thoughts. A part of him died when he buried his nephew, Lyndon. It was the part of him that allowed him to mourn.

He was running on fumes and nothing but pure determination to keep everything functioning and his people safe. His soul may have been broken, but his will to keep fighting was his main source of energy. He turned his head right towards the front of the vineyard's grounds. The most able-bodied of the community had worked through the morning snow, erecting gazebo structures over the vegetable patches, but all had paused and looked in his direction after his vocal stress relief.

*Do not let them see you like this,* he encouraged himself and stood, waving to the workers before stepping back inside, gearing himself up to finish insulating the pipes. As he opened the door, his intrusive thoughts begged the question that was really taunting him.

*Did I bring this on us?*

———

Ryan's footsteps were slow and heavy as he climbed the stairs to the top-floor restaurant with a fresh cup of tea in hand to begin his all-night security shift. He zipped up his jacket and walked to the window that surveyed the front of the vineyard's grounds. He wiped the snow off the nearest table and looked out into the night's darkness, taking in the newest change in colours to the sky. Everyone had long grown accustomed to the multi-coloured sunsets of purple, red, and orange— but it was the night sky that displayed something different now. Shades of vibrant red flickered across the jet-black clouds with small tinges of green. Just another natural phenomenon since the war ended with no viable explanation.

After pulling a chair out, he reached into his pocket and took out his smart radio, a newer device similar to that of a smartphone from before the war. It was a gift from Drinker's former commanding officer, Lieutenant Adam Harper. The former marine served as the vineyard's direct correspondent to the European Alliance, a newer central government that was trying to rebuild the continent, and claimed it would help defend the vineyard when Admiral came for them.

Ryan tapped the smart radio's flat screen and checked the time. *19:35.*

Two of the generators powered down, leaving only the exterior spotlights to light up barely fifty metres of space on the outside. The restaurant fell into darkness, and the outside illumination was hampered by the continuous snowfall.

Ryan slowly sipped his tea and gazed out into the hypnotic downpour, hoping the snow would pass quicker than it suggested it would. At least, he was trying to focus on the snow. The problems inevitably came rolling back and bogged down his thoughts, playing like a broken record. Corn oil. Hannah. The new survivors.

What made all this worse was that they were keeping Hannah's imprisonment a secret from the European Alliance. It had to be kept quiet so Ryan could play his hand when Admiral Caven came for revenge. That decision presented another problem: did they tell the new survivors about their prisoner or keep it a secret?

On the one hand, they risked one of the new survivors telling someone in the European Alliance, of which Ryan knew Admiral still had people on the inside. On the other hand, if they kept it a secret, and one of the new survivors found out... there would be no trust, and chaos would follow. He was reluctant to both decisions.

*One problem at a fucking time.* Ryan leaned forward and held his face in his palms.

His heart jumped when the smart radio started vibrating with an unknown number flashing on the screen.

"Who the fuck?" he stuttered while his brain raced. He snatched the device and answered, "Who is this?"

"Ryan?" a familiar American accent replied.

"Harper?" Ryan exhaled heavily. "Why is your number withheld?"

"Sorry. All our devices were rebooted last week. It was an attempt to see if anyone else here had the hardware to hack our systems."

"I see." Ryan sat back again. "Did you have any luck with that?"

"Everyone's clean," Harper confirmed. "How are you coping with the weather?"

"Everyone's working hard to keep everything functional. We've done what we can for the animals, crops, water, and heating. We don't know if we have enough corn oil for when the other survivors arrive."

"Well, that's what I'm calling you about."

"The weather?"

"No, the new arrivals. They won't be with you as soon as we'd scheduled. We've relocated them to our three strongholds, where our aid workers will keep them secure during the winter," Harper reported. "We're recalling all our infantry and armed forces from the relocation programme."

"Recalling... For what? What's going on? Is Admiral coming now?"

"He isn't coming for you. We're going for him. We've found his supply ship, a Venezuelan cargo vessel off the coast of Portugal. We have his location. We're preparing to capture or kill them. We're going to end this."

"Wha-er, how?" Ryan asked, stunned. "When?"

"That part is classified. I'll keep you informed as much as I can," Harper explained. His tone was firm and determined. "This is just to let you know that you don't have to build up your food or energy rations just yet. Take care, my friend." He disconnected.

A dumbfounded Ryan stared at the smart radio, unable to move. Seconds blurred into minutes. Minutes blurred into hours. He didn't want to believe any false hope. He couldn't be that naïve. That kind of blind ignorance could get you killed. Yer, against his own better judgement, he felt lighter, the constant knot of his stomach had eased, and the room didn't feel as dark.

*They can end it?*

He refused to validate the happiness that dared to surface. A thought that terrified him.

The happiness that attempted to gnaw at his protective shield wasn't due to the fact that the end of the fighting might be in sight or that they didn't need to start spreading their resources just yet. It was because, should Admiral be defeated, Ryan could kill Hannah without consequence.

The notion should've made him sick. Until just over a year ago, he'd never killed an unarmed prisoner, but now, after he'd been forced to pull himself off shifts watching her in her cell through fear of losing his cool and putting a bullet in her... now he wouldn't have to worry about doing something stupid. Now, the tables had turned, and soon, he might not have a reason to keep her alive.

*I am a monster.*

He knocked the thought from his mind, wondering what he should tell his people. After swallowing a mouthful of cold tea, he sat the smart radio on the table and picked up a handheld radio—it was a more traditional-looking device with an antenna and number keypad.

"Drinker? Can you get everyone ready for a meeting before they go to bed? I've just received some news from Harper."

## 2

A thick cloud of steam and the aroma of basil soap greeted Ryan as he entered his family's private quarters. He was puzzled as he wasn't expecting anyone to be in after breakfast. His fiancée, Cassy, was supposed to be guarding Hannah while both of their children were being looked after in day school.

To the right of their bedroom, the bathroom was open. He closed the main door behind him and spotted Cassy's clothes sprawled across the floor. The sound of scrubbing became apparent as he approached, even above the pouring water.

"Can you chuck me the towel?" Cassy asked from inside the shower.

"Yeah. Hang on," he answered, walking around the queen-sized bed and entering the bathroom. He took the orange towel and stood next to the shower door, waiting for her to finish. Once the water was off, her hand appeared through the door's opening and took the towel. "Enjoying your last shower before we have to reduce to one a week?" he asked.

"Not really." Cassy rolled her eyes while drying her skin. "I just wanted to wash off whatever that bitch breathed on me."

"How was your shift in the basement?"

"The usual. She's still trying to get under everyone's skin."

"She wants a rise out of us," Ryan guessed. "It seems like she wants someone to attack her."

"Why would she want that?" Cassy asked, stepping from the shower with the towel wrapped around her brown hair. She made her way into the bedroom, pulling on the trousers and jumper she'd left on the floor.

"If we take her out, we have no trading card for when Admiral comes calling," Ryan said, closing the bathroom door and wiping some condensation off the bedroom's red wallpaper. He opened the window to get some fresh air in before the dry winds forced him to shut it immediately. "I can easily imagine her being a martyr so her dad could launch an assault without hesitation."

*Maybe I should have said something...* A twang of guilt hit Ryan as he spoke, the result of not telling the full truth during the community meeting the night prior. He had mentioned that the relocating of the other survivors had been halted but didn't say why. The ability to say the words 'it could be over' wasn't in his system. He couldn't do it. He couldn't build up their hopes just for something else to come along and smash them down.

"Well, whatever she wants, it's not happening," Cassy said as she dried her hair.

"Good."

Cassy approached him and took his hand. "Was that you I heard yesterday? Someone shouting *fuck* so loud that it actually startled the chickens?" Ryan couldn't bring himself to answer, but his eyes told the truth. "You can't punish yourself for any of this. You've been through enough."

"So have you." Ryan brushed her cheek, looking into her large, brown eyes. "So has everyone." Their bond was almost telepathic now. Cassy knew that Ryan was holding onto something that clawed away at him.

"We all know you've been keeping strong for our benefit, but you're allowed to let it out."

"I don't have time to let it out. Not while everyone's working hard to keep what we have here working."

"I should've expected that stubborn answer."

"You could've said no when I asked you to marry me," he joked, feeling better in her presence. "We can put someone else on Hannah's wash shift if you don't want to do it."

"You don't have to worry about me." She kissed him. "I'm going to get our Maisie and Alfie. I'll see you later for dinner."

"Okay."

Ryan watched his beloved leave the room and close the door behind her. The few moments of peace he found had always come from her. Cassy could make the screaming in his head evaporate just by looking at him, nulling the pressure of every decision and every choice he'd been forced to make over the years.

He turned to the desk at the foot of their bed and picked up the crayon drawing Maisie had drawn of their family. Ryan and Cassy were holding hands, while Maisie was holding Alfie, her five-month-old stepbrother. He knew he was smiling as he stared at the picture, but it wasn't long before the dark depression came back as he stood alone in their family room.

He placed the drawing down and pulled his desk key from his pocket, unlocking a drawer and freezing at what he saw. He had to check twice, his eyes widening and his throat drying. His Glock.17 pistol, which he used and stored the same way every single day, was facing the opposite direction from how he always kept it.

He was done believing he was losing his mind and knew only one person had the key to the drawer. *Cassy's arming herself when she's watching Hannah.*

His rear hit the bed as he stared at the gun, and shivers slid over his body, which slowly burned into anger. His anger wasn't with Cassy but the world that put her in a position to arm herself. She hadn't taken a single life since The Fast War. She still had her innocence—for now. His angel among the demons was willing to throw away her wings to join his world.

*Have I failed her?*

He considered forcibly pulling her off guard duty, but that only made him feel guilty, like he was denying her something—he just didn't know what.

*Don't let her become you. Don't let her become that monster.*

He took the pistol and locked the cupboard, holding the cold metal in his hands. Ryan knew the best alternative was to keep it on him until he'd thought about how to talk to her about it in what felt like the dirtiest double standard he wanted to uphold.

He sat in his absorbed tornado of conflicting thoughts and emotions, unaware that he'd fallen backwards onto the bed and allowing exhaustion to overtake him. His phantom fingers ached as his last thoughts repeated while his eyes began to close.

*Don't let her become you. Don't let... her... become...*

———

With the heaviest eyelids, Ryan forced himself awake and rolled to the side, making sure he fell out of bed. He hit the carpet hard enough to pull him out of his deep sleep. The chipped bones in his right forearm protested with a sharp jolt, and he sat up sharply to take the weight off.

It was already dark outside, bathing Ryan in guilt that he'd slept through the whole day. He'd managed to undress himself before he'd crawled under the covers and left the Glock on full display on the bedside table.

*How do I talk to Cassy about this?*

He groaned while pulling on his jogging bottoms and two layers of hoodies. The time on the smart radio read just after five in the afternoon, and he was feeling the effect of missing two meals. After tying his shabby, white trainers, he left the family room and met Cassy, Maisie, and Alfie in the cafeteria.

Maisie still wasn't talking. She hadn't said a word since she saw Lyndon's death, but fortunately, she had finally started eating properly again. Ryan made sure he put on his bravest face around his adoptive daughter, hoping any of his strength would rub off on her.

"Are you on an all-night shift again?" Cassy asked, taking the empty plates over to the hot counter.

"Another three in a row," Ryan answered, repressing a yawn as he cradled Alfie.

"I'm worried about you."

"I'm worried about you too," he said back, not realising how sharp the reply was.

"What do you mean?"

"Can we talk... later? Or at least, not near them?"

"Why? What's going on?" Cassy demanded, taking Alfie in her arms.

A thundering boom came from the basement, making everyone in the cafeteria jump.

Ryan drew his gun. "Who's watching Hannah?"

"Drinker," Cassy said as she consoled Alfie, who'd woken and started wailing.

Ryan ran down the stairwell, unlocked the basement door and jumped inside. He swung his aim to the right, where he found Drinker standing outside the cell door, holding his ears.

"It's not come from us," the Scotsman said, pointing towards the open passageway into the other half of the basement, where a thick cloud of smoke billowed out from inside.

To Ryan's relief, neither of the chemical cupboards looked disturbed as he rounded the corner into the open part of the basement. He skidded to a halt and took into the devastation before him.

Generator two had backfired, splitting apart two barrels of corn oil underneath.

———

Though Dominic believed the generator was saveable, the supply of corn oil it was attached to had burned beyond use, leaving them with only one drum left.

"One barrel will last us four days at our current usage," Ryan explained to everyone in the cafeteria. "We're going to have to reserve all electricity for the freezers and stoves. Wrap up extra warm at night and use candles at all times. We'll have to bring out the stockpots and

boil water for all cleaning purposes... like in the first year of the war."
He paused, sparking a cigarette indoors, which was something he never
normally did, but he wasn't bothered as the realisation of doom hit
him in the face. "We can't rely on a backup supply from Rennes, so we
need to start thinking about what to do when we run out of fuel."

# 3

Storm *Carmichael* had been tormenting Northern France, forcing the rough seas against the small coastal island of Mont Saint Michel. The blizzard was on its second and most violent day. The snow-covered castle's roofing crumbled from the turbulent winds, sending rubble tumbling to the ground and smashing against the sea wall. The salty ocean air turned the snow to mush along the coastline, and the freezing winds were as deafening as the waves that raged against the beachfront.

The relentless battering and collapsing structures loosened the rocks of the shoreline, dispersing the body that had been buried there two months prior. The naked and bloated corpse tangled against one of the bridge's security wires, flinging it violently upwards and crashing in the middle of the access road with a disgusting splat. What remained of the decomposed organs and muscles leaked out of every orifice in the form of muddy brown and green sludge.

Decapitated. Hands and feet removed. The murderer wanted the body's identity hidden. For all the European Alliance knew, this body could've been on the top of their most wanted list.

———

There was a flurry of callouts and orders coming from the open square of Rennes town centre, followed by the high-pitched whining of an engine starting. Mikey's eyes shot open, alert to the commotion coming from outside. Throwing the duvet off, he slapped his bare feet on the cold, wooden floor and ran to the window, wiping the condensation off and peeking through the clear spot.

His eyes focused on two units of fully geared soldiers hurrying across the town square, filing into the open ramp of a Chinook helicopter. He recognised General Woodburn and Lieutenant Harper following behind them. Within minutes, the chopper was airborne, and to Mikey's surprise, it wasn't heading towards England.

"That's different." He wiped the window to follow the chopper before it disappeared west and out of sight.

He sat back on the bed, pulling on some black jogging bottoms and a pair of socks. He opted for a long-sleeved T-shirt as he stood in front of the wardrobe mirror, running his fingers through his thick black hair and scuffed it to the left. He was used to doing his hair by hand since he'd left his comb at Penbrook Vineyard.

He'd left a lot behind. It wasn't an easy decision for him to leave. It was a necessary decision.

His partner, Jen, was pregnant with their first child, and Rennes had more medical facilities than they had back at the vineyard. Even though Mikey had helped deliver four babies in six years, the thought of delivering their first child in safety was a key factor in their move across the English Channel.

It wasn't the main factor for the move, though. In fact, it was more of a demand from the European Alliance. Jen being able to live there with him was one of the perks that Mikey negotiated.

The reason for his conditional stay at the home of the European Alliance was simple. Mikey was sick. Terminal, but not with anything once feared in the world before. He'd been subjected to a weaponised version of Kuru—the human form of Mad Cow Disease, normally obtained through eating meat. Human meat. The European Alliance had produced a serum to counter the effects of Kuru, and Mikey had been supplied with the drug while under observation, not just saving his life but also stopping him from turning to cannibalism should he lose all self-control.

Kurustovia45, as it was officially being called, had been designed to eat away at muscles and the prefrontal cortex of the brain, which was the area that allowed for free will and decision-making capabilities. The only way to slow the tissue's degradation was to ingest or consume the same proteins. If someone with the disease was deprived to the point where the cortex began to shut down, they could be fully manipulated into obeying anything. The most notable side effect of Kurustovia was the huge spike of cortisol whenever their pulse increased, triggering a rise in aggression. If the cortisol was secreted, and the body produced lactic acid, it formed a toxin in the muscles—a drug-like chemical that didn't require oxygen to circulate around the body. The reaction results included extra strength, speed, and the ability to swim underwater without surfacing for air until the toxin wore off.

"What the fuck was all that noise?" Jen asked, stepping out of their bathroom with a toothbrush in hand.

Mikey turned to her, not trying to hide his confusion. "Harper and Woodburn just left on one of those big fucking helicopters. Took some soldiers with them."

"I didn't think they had an excursion until they were going after Admiral?"

"That's what I thought." He shrugged, then smiled as he looked his girlfriend over. At seven months pregnant, and despite the harsh winter, her Caribbean skin glowed.

"I've told you to stop staring at me like that. Weirdo." She scowled, throwing a scarf at him. "Wrap up warm this time. It's fucking cold out there."

Mikey wasn't sure if his infliction of Kurustovia had messed with his inner thermometer, but recently, his body wasn't registering the winter chill. Jen had to resort to talking to him like a child just so he'd wrap up properly.

"You already sound like a mother," he said and winked with a grin.

"That's because you've always been a man-child."

Mikey grabbed his puffer jacket and wrapped the scarf around his neck. Jen pulled a beanie over her dark, curly hair and opened the door, motioning for him to hurry up.

"Come on! I wanna find out if we're having a mini-me, or a muppet like you!"

A few inches of snow covered the ground as the couple walked hand in hand to the hospital, with the southernly winds seeming to try and knock them over. The roads had been paved of the previous downpour, and Christmas music filtered from one of the open windows as they made their way through the town. There were rumours that the next year might potentially have a Christmas market. It was all hearsay but positive, nonetheless. Anything to keep people's spirits up in the wake of the whole continent nearly being wiped from the map.

Mikey jumped into the snow and made an angel; all the while, Jen laughed, embracing the fact he was getting ready to be a father. The journey took fifteen minutes by foot on a good day, so it was no surprise when they eventually made it to the hospital's front doors in just over half an hour, though they did stop for five minutes by Vilaine River, holding hands on the bridge. The hospital was a three-storey building with dark grey paint riddled with the familiar bullet holes of The Fast War. It could've been mistaken for a school had it not been for the signs outside.

Mikey and Jen were greeted by the overly enthusiastic receptionist who never seemed to take a day off.

"Madam Jen and *Garcon* Mikey," Greta teased as she slowly stepped from behind the desk. The sixty-two-year-old was taller than him by a clear foot. Her smile exposed her yellow teeth, a contrast to her pale skin and short hair. "Finding out if we have a baby boy or girl today, oui?" Her thick French accent always had a joyous ting to it.

"Yes," Jen answered, trying to hide her excitement.

"Well, if it's boy, hopefully he might grow taller than him, no?" Greta said, nodding at Mikey.

"I can see you're in a good mood today," he pointed out while rolling his eyes, reaching inside his jacket and pulling a cigarette out. "I'll let you two catch up for the next couple of minutes." He turned back towards the main doors.

"Smoking is not good for growth!" Greta called as he stepped outside.

"Very funny," he groaned, though smiling and pulling the lighter out.

To most people, it would have looked like an innocent cigarette, but only he and Jen knew why Mikey would always walk straight back out after arriving. Other than Jen's pregnancy and his illness, there was another reason he agreed to move to France. He was doing undercover work.

After two Admiral sympathisers had managed to infiltrate the European Alliance's outreach programme and get to the vineyard and a mole had managed to infiltrate the security network, it became apparent there was every chance there could be more working on the inside. Mikey was going to find them, and fortunately, he had someone working on the inside, too.

He walked left out of the hospital and followed the path to a fire exit, smiling at the same teenager who delivered pastries and bread every morning. He smelled them from where the boy was and wanted to steal one from the back of the unattended van. He walked until reaching the fire exit, leaned back against the wall and tapped the door twice. That was his prearranged meeting time with Sergeant Kieron Rook, his undercover friend within.

"You hoping for a boy or a girl?" Rook asked as the door creaked open, and the well-built soldier stepped out. His rusty-coloured pony-tail stuck out from under his beanie, and he wore all-black winter gear. His smile reached out to the scar on the left side of his face, which ran all the way up to where his missing ear would be.

"I'm happy either way, just as long as they don't have their mother's attitude." Mikey chuckled, then asked, "Anything to report back to Ryan?"

"Harper and Woodburn have been called out. One of our Navy vessels intercepted a rogue supply vessel from Venezuela."

"Oh, so that's where they were headed."

"You saw them leave?"

"Was hard not to. They looked in a rush." Mikey stubbed the cigarette out against the wall. "Anything more before I go?"

"Not that I'm aware, but everyone's being really tight-lipped around me."

"Everyone still giving you shit for knocking out that guard?"

"The prick shouldn't have called me a redneck." Rook shrugged.

Rook had been framed for stealing syringes two months before, only due to the fact that where he once served had a high rate of drug abuse among its soldiers. Though he'd been cleared as innocent and the syringes confirmed to have been taken by the Admiral's sympathisers, many of the French servicemen still didn't believe Rook's innocence. More so, they didn't want to believe it was one of their own who had been helping Admiral and held a scapegoat style grudge against the American.

Rook's shoulder-mounted radio crackled. *"Private Rook, are you there?"* a whiny French accent asked.

"It's *Sergeant* Rook, and yes, I'm here… if you're referring to your mother's bed," he replied coldly.

Mikey did his best not to laugh but couldn't hold out.

*"Very fucking funny, inbred. We've had a body wash up near Mont Saint Michel. Make sure the medical examiner is ready for us in fifteen minutes."*

"What if he's already doing another autopsy? You want me to pull him out of that?"

*"Don't ask questions and just fucking do it."*

"Copy." He took his finger off the receiver. "Fucking asshole." He turned to Mikey and said, "Wish you the best for today, bud. Send my love to Jen."

"Yeah, will do, man." Mikey bumped his fist, then turned back towards the hospital's front entrance, laughing to himself the whole way. He made sure to rush through the reception area before Greta had a chance to make another jab at his height.

He saw the elevator doors close at the end of the main corridor and let out a groan. Instead of waiting for the next one, he pushed open the door to the right and climbed the stairs. He reached the second floor and stepped into the maternity ward, overcome by the smell of disinfectant. He knew the room Jen would be in, which meant he didn't have to wander the long, white corridors or ask for directions.

He opened the treatment room door, finding Jen lying on her back in a pregnancy gown with her legs in stirrups, her stomach exposed, and the ultrasound switched on.

"Where's the doctor?" he asked, pulling out the chair next to her bed and holding her hand.

"She'll be back in a minute. I requested to have another pillow as these hospital beds fucking suck," Jen said with a wince. She lowered her voice to a whisper and leaned closer. "Did you speak to Rook?"

"Yeah. Not much going on, and the Euro-Military is still giving him shit."

"They still want to blame Rook for what Francesco and Alessandro did? Or just in denial that it was their own that was corrupted?"

"Fuck knows. It looks like he's having fun winding them up with it, though."

"Good," Jen said, trying to sit up, "He doesn't deserve the shit he's been getting."

The door opened softly, with Doctor Lizarazu stepping in. Her crisp, white overalls nearly made her blend in with the walls. She lowered her glasses and lent a friendly frown. "Miss Jen, you need to stay lying down," she said, and before Jen could open her mouth, she was placing another pillow behind her. "Now, let's find out if it's a baby girl or boy."

Mikey stepped out of the hospital reception with a spring in his steps, ecstatic that he and Jen were expecting a baby girl. He dialled Ryan's number with haste, ready to share the news.

*No signal.*

"Fucking again?" Mikey growled out loud as he lit his second cigarette of the day, thankful he wasn't surrounded by the overpowering sanitisation inside. Since being infected, his sense of smell had altered, making the usual scents he used to tolerate unbearable now. It wasn't just his nose but his hearing, too, which seemed to have improved tenfold.

"You're one of them, aren't you?" a thick Slavic accent asked from Mikey's left. A man approached. Tall, slender, pale, blotchy skin, and thin, buzzed cut hair. His tracksuit stuck to his skinny frame.

"One of who?"

"The vineyard scum." The man's bright eyes narrowed in, and his tone was clearly hostile. "The preachy, weak, Muslim lovers."

"Who the fuck are you?" Mikey threw the cigarette down and faced up to him. An overbearing stench of spirits drifted from the man's breath.

"I don't like you people. You house the terrorists," the man said, towering above and staring him down.

Up until two months ago, Mikey would've tried to talk down the situation, but with Kurustovia's hooks sunken into his brain, adrenaline began to take over.

"Oh really?" Mikey asked, looking down at the floor and then back at him. The man didn't have time to react before Mikey shot out his hand and grabbed him by the throat, throwing him against the wall. "We've done more to rebuild this world than your drunk ass ever will," he snarled, drooling already. "You ever talk ill of my people again, I'll fucking string you up by your balls and leave you outside whatever fucking camp it is you're holed up in."

With eyes beginning to roll to the back of his head, the man was about to pass out before someone pulled on Mikey's arm.

"Drop him now!"

Mikey recognised Rook's voice, and he released the man, letting him crumple to the floor and gasp for breath.

"What happened?" Rook stood over the man and then looked at Mikey.

"This prick came out of nowhere and asked if I was one of the vineyard people. Said he didn't like us," Mikey answered as he straightened his jacket.

"I think he's been drinking."

"Don't care. What a prick."

"Are you okay?" Rook eyed Mikey over, who appeared more like an enraged drug addict than his usual calm demeanour.

"I'm fine."

"Where's Jen?"

"She's inside. Saying goodbye to the others."

The man on the floor laughed and raised his hand in the air, waving at someone in the distance.

"Shut your ass up," Rook said, picking up the man and securing his hands in place with a zip-tie. "I'm taking him in. Sorry this happened."

"Don't sweat it." Mikey brushed himself off and added, "I'm more concerned that he knows who I am and where I'm from."

"I'll get to the bottom of it." Rook carried the man to his patrol car and pushed him in the back seat. After slamming the door shut, he turned back to Mikey and put his hand on his shoulder, leaning in to whisper, "I'll be over to see you later. Something else has happened."

# 4

Mikey and Jen weren't the only members of Penbrook who Rennes had taken into its protective custody. Two more occupied part of the hospital's east wing, the most heavily guarded patients of all. Mikey looked through the small window of the first door and into the dark room. His heart sank for the heavily medicated woman inside.

Steph. Ryan's sister.

She'd been seriously injured during the attack that killed her son, Lyndon, and had to be evacuated to Rennes for emergency surgery. The back of her head was shaved for the operation, and the stitches were visible under the gauze that covered her head. What remained of her blonde hair had turned stone white in recent weeks, almost like she was a ghost.

At first, Steph had been kept in the apartment next to Jen and Mikey during the recovery stages after surgery, but once she had awoken and learned what happened to her son, the suicide attempts started. Mikey had been fortunate to intervene both times before the chief of medicine declared her unfit to be out of twenty-four-hour care and placed her in the hospital's high-security wing. Constantly under surveillance and heavily medicated, she wasn't allowed to feel the pain she was in and had to be fed by an orderly on most occasions.

Mikey visited her every night during his medically recommended walks, and it sparked something inside him every time he saw her like that. She was Ryan's sister, which practically made her his sister too.

"Night, Steph," he whispered, resting his palm against the door. Sometimes he felt it was better that Ryan didn't see her like this. Mikey knew he'd kill Hannah for sure.

He walked on to the next room and opened the door. The beeping of a heart monitor was the only noise. On the singular bed lay Rich, the first to be unknowingly infected with Kurustovia45 two months before. During the disease's first rampage against his body, he'd been put into a medically induced coma to calm him down. Back then, no one knew what he had; some even theorised it was rabies. While he was under, he lost all self-awareness and freedom—including his own ability to wake up. He'd been in this state since then and was brought to Rennes, where he could be monitored and fed intravenously.

Mikey looked at the chart at the end of the bed. No improvement. He dropped his head and sighed angrily, making sure he controlled himself. Steph and Rich were daily reminders of why he was here, and the people responsible for their conditions were going to pay, even if Mikey had to go behind the European Alliance's back.

Solemnly, he left the east wing and headed for the hospital's main entrance, saying goodbye to the staff as he did. A squad car pulled up, and the passenger door opened.

"Wanna lift?" Rook asked from the driver's seat.

"Yeah, cheers," Mikey said, getting in and closing the door. The small action was designed to seem like a friendly gesture, but in reality, it gave Rook an excuse to head over to Mikey and Jen's place without arousing any suspicion. "So, what's happened?" Mikey asked.

"Remember when I got that call about a body being washed up?" Rook explained, turning out the hospital's driveway and taking the long way round to Rennes' town centre. "It's a murder. The head, hands and feet were removed. Someone doesn't want us to identify them. It's been in the water for a couple of months at least, according to what the medical examiner had to say regarding the level of decomp. All we have to go on is that this person has metal plating in his arm."

"Anyone in the missing persons files that has metal plating?"

"That's where an issue lies. The logs were updated three weeks ago when the mole was still here."

"So, the mole could've covered up a murder or edited the files before they left?"

"It's plausible. In fact, it's more than likely. They had access to the rotas, defence mechanisms, and even the fucking security doors. It's likely someone was onto them, so they killed them and erased them from the records."

"Fucking shit."

"Yeah, it is." Rook slowly pulled up to the entrance to the civilian quarters. "Do you still have that rifle in your room?"

"Yeah."

"Here." Rook handed him some bullets. "Load it. If there is some kind of uprising against you from within the refugee camps, you need to defend yourself. That drunk asshole today... Someone's been slipping information about you to him. Someone who is trying to get the general population on Admiral's side."

"Can you bring him to me? I'll bleed whatever information I need from him."

"I'd love to, but we can't expose that we're onto them. I'm going to focus on that body we found. If we can identify it, we might be able to find out what else they discovered about Admiral. With any luck, we can find who's behind all of this."

# 5

Ryan sat at the end of Maisie's bed, pulling a jumper over her head and tying her ice-white hair back. "Do you want to wear your gloves today?" he asked, his breath misting in front of his face. Maisie nodded, so he fitted the gloves over her hands and led her into the main bedroom.

Cassy sat on the side of the bed, feeding Alfie. She looked up and caught Ryan's eyes, which might as well have been an artist's colour pallet. "Are you getting more sleep during the afternoon?" she asked with concern.

"I can't today. I've got to get a plan of action ready for when we run out of power," he answered, opening the door and letting Maisie step out. "Can you come see me after you've dropped Alfie off at daycare?"

"Okay."

Ryan smiled and closed the door, taking Maisie to day school before heading upstairs to the restaurant and taking over Drinker's security shift. It felt like the top floor was his home now, and a pang of self-loathing came from how much he'd been neglecting his family.

He entered the galley kitchen and opened the bench fridge, taking out one of the newest pistols in their inventory. It looked like a carbon copy of the Glock.17 he used, but according to an avid gun collector he'd met a few months ago, this one was an original model of the pistol brand. The versions that the vineyard had were a newer prototype, tested by the British Armed Forces just as The Fast War started.

This avid gun collector was an undercover agent of Admiral, who got inside the vineyard and tried to take Ryan down. They had failed but left Maisie traumatised in the process.

Ryan took the gifted 'original' Glock and sat it on the table next to a notepad and a flask of boiled grape water. The smart radio buzzed in his pocket, making his heart jump again. He saw Mikey's number on the lock screen, staring at it for a few seconds. He wished he had him here now to help with this situation. Ryan stood the device against an empty wine bottle and pressed the video icon to answer the call.

"Finally! A fucking call has got through." Mikey's face took up the screen. "You alright, bruv?"

"Been better," Ryan admitted, leaning elbow first on the table.

"You look like shit."

"Thanks. It's all these fucking nightshifts."

"Well, this might cheer you up. Got a bit of news for you."

"Go on then."

"We're having a baby girl!"

"Oh shit! That's, er, that's amazing." Ryan laughed and said, "I'm happy for you both."

"Why did that sound sarcastic?" Mikey could see the look on his friend's face. "What's wrong?"

"Nothing you need to worry about. I'm happy for you."

"Don't give me that shit. What's happened?"

"Fine," Ryan huffed. "We've only got four days of corn oil left."

"What? How's that possible?"

"Our reserves got damaged during the repairs. Last night, generator two backfired into its own supply. We have one drum left."

"Well, that's not entirely true, is it."

"What do you mean?"

"There's more corn oil out there."

"Where?"

"The same place where there is a whole armoury waiting to be found. One of the many places we've kept quiet."

Ryan sat up straight. Mikey was right. The community they once had a trading deal with.

*The prison in Lewes.*

Only a month before the prison had been attacked by Admiral's people, Mikey had taken a winter batch of corn oil down in a trade for ammunition.

"You're fucking right!" Ryan exclaimed, tapping the table with his fingers. "Wouldn't it have been taken after Admiral's men attacked them?"

"Why would they have taken it? Their vehicles ran on petrol, and the whole armoury was untouched. The only thing they went there for was... meat."

Mikey's screen froze, then started to lag with a few moments of brief clarity before the connection cut off. Ryan tried to call him back, only to be greeted by a notification that said the user was busy. He sat the smart radio down and waited, but there was no call back.

"Shit," he cursed himself, annoyed he hadn't congratulated or shown as much enthusiasm for their baby's gender reveal or asked how his sister was recovering. He knew he was happy for Mikey and Jen and wanted to know if Steph was getting any better, but his thoughts had been elsewhere.

On the brighter side of things, Mikey had just taken a huge weight off his shoulders. Ryan knew exactly where the boiler room and armoury were in the Lewes prison, and Mikey's theory made sense. Admiral's people did use petrol, but didn't seem to have anywhere near as much ammo to take the fight to the vineyard during their first encounter, which wouldn't have been the case if they had found all the weaponry.

"You wanted to see me?" Cassy asked, stepping into the restaurant.

"Yeah." Ryan turned from the smart radio, smiled softly and placed his Glock on the next table. "Do you want to tell me what your intentions were with that?"

Cassy crossed her arms, and her eyes narrowed. "You know what my intentions are."

"Do you think you're ready to step into my world? My world of having to take lives?"

"I'm already in your world," she answered carefully but firmly. "Every time you go out there and I don't know if you're coming back. Every time I look at our daughter and see what they've done to her. Every time I see you go out to the graves and stand in silence because you blame yourself for the situation we've been forced into. Every time I'm on shift watching that bitch downstairs. I'm already in your fucking world."

"This wasn't meant to be an argument." Ryan raised his hands, trying to defuse any negativity. "It's not a lecture. It was a genuine question."

"Why?"

"Because you can't have my weapon. I've grown to know it inside and out. I'm not giving it away, even to you." He reached for the other table and picked up the older model Glock. "This is pretty much the same as mine." He held the pistol in front of her and unloaded it, demonstrating the safety mechanism in the trigger. "Take it."

Cassy held it in her hands, looking back up with a tear in her left eye. "Aren't you mad that I've been taking yours?"

"No. I know why you did. I only have two requests."

"Which is?"

"Keep it locked as it should be, and only use it if she's a direct threat to you. Don't use it just because she's saying bad things."

Cassy seethed and said, "I hate her."

"I know." Ryan hugged her, hoping to nullify her pain. "It would only be fitting that you killed her with a weapon supplied by one of Admiral's men. However, we need her alive. Okay?"

"I know."

"Can I trust you not to kill her when we have to go out?"

"Go out?" Cassy pulled out of the hug. "Where are you going?"

"Lewes... Mikey reminded me that we sent a batch of corn oil—a big one—only a week before they were attacked."

"How can you be sure it's still there? Or hasn't been damaged?"

"They stored it below the yard, near the ammunition cache... which was untouched. If they missed that, they missed the corn oil."

"That's a big 'if'. How can you be certain?"

"There's only one way to find out. We have to go and see for ourselves."

"When did Mikey tell you this?"

"About five minutes ago. We had a small window to talk before the connection cut off... He's also got some news for everyone. They're having a baby girl."

———

Ryan called for Dominic and Drinker to meet him upstairs so they could plan the newest excursions.

"Afternoon, *boss*," Dominic addressed Ryan as he walked to the table and pulled out the chair opposite. His black hoodie and jogging pants were only a few shades darker than his weathered skin. Ryan had given up on asking Dominic not to call him *boss*, as it only seemed to fuel the former school security guard even more. Even if it was an annoying nickname, it was good that his people still had their own forms of humour in the dying world.

"Afternoon, Dominic," Ryan answered while rolling his eyes. "How's everyone downstairs?"

"Cold."

"Understandable. Drinker will be joining us in a bit."

"Already here, gentlemen," Drinker announced, stepping in with wine bottle. "Relax, it's tea. I couldn't find a clean cup."

"I wasn't judging," Ryan said, tapping the notepad with his pen and leaning forward. "So, this is the task. Now, when the snow has finally stopped, Me and Drinker will go alone on the first morning. We'll take whichever of the two eighteen-wheelers is charged up the most." He pointed out the window to the two electric lorries that had been found during the most recent supply run. Both were parked outside the crumbling sewage plant opposite the vineyards grounds.

"How long to get to Lewes?" Drinker asked.

"With this snow on the road, about an hour each way," Ryan said. "Jen showed you how to check the battery percentage on the lorries when you found them?"

"Yeah."

"Good."

"What happens if you get in trouble?" Dominic wondered.

"We'll communicate with the handheld radios. Lewes is in range." Ryan picked up three chunky military devices and placed them on the table. "Dominic, you'll be on guard up here throughout. Cassy and Ted will take turns watching over Hannah."

"One radio for you. One for me. One for downstairs?" Dominic tapped the top of the radios while numbering them.

"Exactly. Now, on the off chance we get attacked or have vehicle troubles, you go into full lockdown until we have it sorted. The heavy machine guns are loaded and ready to move. If at any point communication breaks, again, assume lockdown."

"You got it, *boss*," Dominic nodded.

"How much corn oil have they got in Lewes?" Drinker asked.

"Around twenty-seven drums," Ryan answered. "That's nearly three months' worth of power."

"That's worth the risk in my book," Dominic added, with Drinker nodding in agreement.

"Okay. The first morning without snowfall, we go."

# 6

Drinker opened the door to the galley kitchen and, ticking off on his notepad, reported, "All guns are accounted for."

"Good," Ryan huffed, standing by the window with his SIG716 assault rifle. The weapon had become more or less an extension of him when he was in defence mode. The first time he'd used it had been on a one-off mission to take out a stronghold of Admiral's second-in-command. Ever since then, the unique fore grip, ACOG scope, and long barrel suppressor felt natural to use instead of the previous, short-nosed G36C assault rifles. Just two of the wide range of salvaged weapons over the years.

The early dawn sky was clear, and it hadn't snowed since the previous afternoon. They were gearing up to leave.

"Something on your mind?" Drinker asked as he loaded his G36C.

Ryan turned, pointing at the Glaswegian's weapon. "That's Mikey's favourite. He'll go nuts if you break it."

"We could just not tell him?"

"I couldn't if I wanted to anyway," Ryan sighed, tapping the smart radio before slipping it into his pocket. "Signal has been shit for two weeks."

"Aye, it happened before, man," Drinker said, pulling his white parka on. "Last time we had a security breach, General Woodburn ordered a cleansing of the system. Took about a month before the uplinks reconnected properly."

Ryan sighed, pulling the chair out and looking back out the window. He thought he was done with having to leave the grounds—or at least he'd hoped. He'd once been promised that the only life out there was other groups of survivors until they'd found out the hard way that Admiral's people had been hiding underground, avoiding the thermal scanners aboard the European Alliance's surveillance drones. What terrified him most about the whole situation was the lengths people would go to survive or what levels of insanity the broken world drove them to.

Ryan shook his head. "It still shocks me that this is what we do now. Our version of *shopping*."

"What do you mean?"

"A little over seven years ago," Ryan paused, placing his rifle on the bar, "being in possession of these weapons was a crime. Now, it's a necessity."

"Aye," Drinker agreed.

"Some of the people I've seen, or even some of the people you've seen—people who were once like us—imagine what they've done to survive this long. You could bet good money they have at least one kill under their belt. The world was broken before the war, but trying to fix it now..."

"Would be like trying to plaster over a cracked shark tank," Drinker said out loud.

"Pretty much." Ryan chuckled at the analogy, picking up his gun off the bar and zipping up his coat. "Ready to go back out into that world?"

"A chance to bump into another fucking looney? Fucking sign me up!"

They walked quietly but with pace down the vineyard's main drive-way. To their left, four recently erected, industrial-sized gazebos stood over their vegetable patches, protecting the lifeline of the community. The metal frames rattled in the rapid winds, though they were well anchored to each other and the ground.

"Still boggles my mind," Drinker said, looking towards the protective perimeter that encircled the whole vineyard.

A one-hundred-metre-deep maze split into twenty-six sections clockwise with one-hundred and thirty possible routes, but with only one actual way through. It had previously been armed with random acidic salt traps hidden throughout until the European Alliance had politely asked the vineyard to remove them. Instead, fire extinguishers were now rigged in random locations inside. It was the closest thing they had to a burglar alarm.

Dominic provided cover from back in the restaurant as Ryan and Drinker pulled away in the electric eighteen-wheeler, moving slowly over the thick snow.

"We'll be back before sundown," Ryan confirmed into the handheld radio.

"We'll be waiting for you, *boss*," Dominic replied. "Drive safe."

"Got it. I'll call in once we've arrived." Ryan tossed the radio on the dashboard and sat up straight, keeping his eyes peeled on his side of the vehicle.

Drinker tapped the steering wheel as he hummed some kind of jaunty tune, which Ryan couldn't identify.

"You've been cheery since we decided to go on this trip," Ryan pointed out.

"Aye," Drinker acknowledged, turning carefully at the top of the carriageway and manoeuvring through the car barricade. "I've been looking forward to going back out."

"After all the shit you've seen... you're excited to go back out? Are we that bad company in the vineyard?"

"It doesn't have anything to do with you," Drinker said and cackled softly. "Maybe being on patrol with Harper for five years changed me."

"Can't stay focused in one place?" Ryan asked.

"It's nothing like that. I'm happy and grateful you took me in. The security shifts definitely keep me occupied. I just look forward to going back out."

"It's appreciated. You're good at it. It's kinda the same situation we had with... Sam."

"Sam? Was he... one of the... people when we first met you?"

"Yeah." Ryan nodded, quickly sparking a cigarette and making sure he blew the smoke out his nose. He wanted to forget that day, but even the smallest mention would bring the memories back. The smell of Sam's burning flesh threatened to overtake the cigarette smoke.

"I'm sorry. Didn't mean to bring it up like that."

"It's fine," Ryan lied, puffing again, trying to savour the smoke. "He was like you."

"I've heard he was good at distance shooting. I'm crap with those snipers."

"I didn't mean like that. I meant dedicating his time to security to take his mind off something. I could tell it was hurting him, but he always put on a brave face and did his duty."

"What was hurting him?"

"Loneliness. Depression... He didn't have anyone. He was gay."

"Oh," Drinker said in a surprised tone. "I see." He carried on down the A25. "Wait, you don't think...?"

"You do like the same wine as him."

"I'm not fucking gay!"

"Of course not, sweetheart." Ryan winked and pouted a kiss.

Even Drinker laughed, realising he was the butt of the banter for once.

Ryan enjoyed the small moment, remembering Sam and how great a person he was and then how his life ended way too soon. *I couldn't save him.* He took another heavy drag of the cigarette.


Something that had stood out above all else over the previous twelve months was the amount of wildlife that had come back to the surrounding areas. After years of them having been thought to have either completely abandoned the county or been hunted out of existence, there were tell-tale signs of life beginning to thrive in the south-east of England. A few packs of dogs ran across the road into bushes, startling birds and causing them to fly away. Different shapes and sizes of hooves were made in patterns across the opening of Surrey Golf Club.

It had been previously theorised that the mass grave under Maidville's schools' rugby pitch had warned off animals, or even the possibility that the town was close enough to London after the nuclear bomb that it had a low level of radiation, which the animals could sense. No one had an answer for the nonexistence of wildlife, but Ryan didn't care. He was just happy to see life back.

They passed towns that Ryan knew and had grown up near. They drove past a cow that had collapsed on the other side of the motorway by Gatwick Airport; covered in snow and non-responsive to Drinker honking the horn, they guessed it must've frozen to death. Of all the ways to go in this decedent world, it was a sobering notion to know that hyperthermia wasn't the worst.

Ryan and Drinker spoke about the possibility of having some kind of animal sanctuary in the future, tossing ideas back and forth until the realisation that if they kept predators, they would have to feed them. Both men had killed people, but neither could agree on killing an animal for another's food. That halted the conversation as they reached the outskirts of Lewes.

The lorry slowly skidded across the snow a few feet before eventually stopping as they pulled onto the main road leading into Lewes town centre. Ryan stepped out the passenger door and observed the car barricade before them, a match-for-match replica of the two Penbrook Vineyard had at the end of its main road. It had been Ryan who once showed the Lewes community how to do this with the abandoned vehicles outside the prison, both freeing up the road and closing off the end, creating an obstacle for anyone trying to get in.

Ryan walked through and found the hatchbacks that would have the brakes cut. He whistled for Drinker to come and join him. His arms hadn't recovered fully yet, making even the normally simple task of pushing a burned-out car with its brakes cut a painful job.

"These folks get this barricade idea from you?" Drinker questioned as they pushed the last car out of the way.

"Yep," Ryan huffed, trying to hide the sheer pain coming from his right forearm. "Wasn't just materials we traded."

After ten minutes, the two men created a gap wide enough for the eighteen-wheeler, and Drinker slowly drove through with guidance.

"It's literally five minutes down this road," Ryan explained, pointing ahead. "We'll have to turn around and reverse in, just in case we have to leave in a hurry."

It was just two years since Ryan's last personal visit, and he could still recognise everything along the road, even under the thick snow. All the destroyed houses, the torn apart petrol stations and shops. The town took a much harder hit than Maidville had during the war. The prison community had thrived well, using the courtyard to grow and harvest crops while trading ammunition for the grape water that the vineyard could produce on a much larger scale compared to them.

Ryan hadn't been back to the prison since a survivor managed to get to the vineyard and the beginning of the fight with Admiral started. He didn't know what conditions would be waiting for them.

"Here." Ryan motioned to the left, and the lorry began to slow.

Drinker reversed into the visitor car park, which ran alongside the road and parallel to the prison's southern wall. A loud pop came from under the front left wheel as he pulled in, "Shit!"

Ryan jumped out and looked back to examine the situation. Dark green and brown liquid oozed out in a thick sludge. There were a few thick, pale shards under the snow, and his heart sank when he saw what was left of an arm. The vomit was inevitable as Ryan emptied his breakfast of corn and soda bread onto the snow. After rinsing his mouth with grape water and spitting it out, he approached the passenger door. "It wasn't the tyre," he said with a heavy breath. "It was a skull."

"Sorry, man. I missed it under the snow." Drinker dropped his head.

It wouldn't have made much difference. They had to have been dead for over a year now. "Back up and point the truck back out to the road. Those are the main doors right behind you."

"Aye," Drinker acknowledged, looking in his wing mirror. "I'll try and be careful."

"You've got us down here in one piece," Ryan said, trying to lift the mood. "It's all good."

Drinker manoeuvred the vehicle back around and jumped out,

making sure to take the keys with him as they locked up. He met Ryan
round the back of the lorry and opened the large double doors to the
delivery section. He looked the front of the building over. "You said
there was some kind of fight here?

"Yeah."

"A secure location, a fight, yet the building looks intact."

"That's because they had someone who let them in," Ryan
answered, pulling his assault rifle up. "Someone who sold them out.
They were never meant to be harmed but instead... harvested. This
was a food stock-up before they planned to attack us."

"The more I hear of these people, the more I want to kill them."

"You and me both. Let's get what we need and get the fuck out of
here."

Ryan led them with a torch as they pushed down to the sub-basement
and through the boiler room. Stale water tinged the air, and the unkept
water pipes had blown at some point, letting moss grow and decom-
pose through the course of the year.

Drinker kept his G36C tight to his shoulder, aiming wherever the
beam of light was. Ryan pushed a double door open into a wide space,
which he knew was where the generators were.

"Similar set-up to what you've got," Drinker said, following Ryan
inside.

"A few of our friends showed them how to rig it up," Ryan
explained, approaching the generator in the middle of the room. "They
mainly used solar panels on all the roofs for their basic electricity, but
the generators are powerful enough for their hot water supply." He
shined the torch further inside and against the back wall, illuminating
stacks of corn oil drums. "Thank fucking fuck, they're here."

Drinker lowered his gun. "I'll drop flares back along the corridors,
just so we don't have to rely on the little light in your hand."

"Good shout." Ryan nodded, wiping his nose. "Why the fuck does
it smell like wet dog in here?"

"Fuck knows." Drinker shrugged, popped a flare and dropped it in the middle of the basement. "All I know is we need to thank Mikey for bringing this to our attention."

"No doubt. I'll call him the second the signal sorts itself out."

"He's probably enjoying the peace of being away from you," Drinker teased.

"Fuck off," Ryan snorted, though he knew that Mikey not having to deal with Ryan's burdens was probably a good thing for him.

*He's probably having the time of his life in Rennes.*

## 7

For the second time in three days, Mikey had been awoken by thundering helicopter blades, though that time, they were descending. Instead of running to the window, he pulled on all his clothes from the previous night and ran out the apartment door, making his way downstairs to the front entrance.

He wanted to be outside before the Chinooks landed, to appear that he was already there and enjoying nothing more than an early morning cigarette. His mind raced for days, considering what they could've found, and he hoped Lieutenant Harper would share at least some information worthy enough that he could pass back to Ryan.

The town centre's open plaza had heavily guarded and fenced-off helipads in the centre, with direct access to the central hub of the European Alliance Governing Board—the opera house. Though he kept it discreet, he focused on the men and women who seemed to rush inside, like some kind of emergency conference was called upon the squad's return to Rennes.

Mikey shielded his face from the harsh gusts and watched the two choppers land, both of which had their exit ramps aimed towards the town hall. He only saw the back of Harper's head for a second before the returning team was escorted into the building and out of Mikey's vision.

"Shit," Mikey hissed, flicked the cigarette into the snow, and headed back inside.

Two laundry ladies were outside his door, waiting for someone to answer after continuous knocking.

"Ah, sorry," he said awkwardly. "Girlfriend is in the bathroom."

Both maids stared blankly, confused. He realised they didn't speak English, so he held his hands in the air and opened the door, letting just himself in. "One minute. Un *minoto*." He had no idea if that was the correct translation.

The dirty towels and bed sheets were packed in bags by the sofa, which Mikey placed into the maid's basket and gratefully accepted the fresh laundry. After closing the door, he headed back into the bedroom and started to make the bed.

"Fresh sheets day," Jen said, stepping out of the bathroom as Mikey struggled to attach the corner of the bed sheet to the mattress. "It's like being in a hotel."

"A hotel where you have to make your own bed," he complained, letting go of the fabric and quitting on the spot. "Fuck it. I'll do it when we get back."

"Did you get a chance to speak to Harper after he landed?" she asked.

"No. Hopefully, Rook will have an update on the body."

"Is he on hospital duty today?"

"Starts at midday, I think. We'll be there about half an hour before him," Mikey explained while picking up his jacket and scarf and opening the door to the hallway. "After you."


Mikey made sure they took a slightly different route to the hospital every morning since his run-in with the drunk at the beginning of the week, being aware of who could be watching or following them. Nothing seemed out of the ordinary, but they both knew not to trust the appearances of their surroundings.

He nearly tripped when he saw the bakery's delivery van. Craving was an understatement. He was determined to try one of the pastries. "I'll see you in there." He kissed Jen by the hospital entrance and let her go inside. He wasn't ready to face Greta's enthusiastic jibes just yet.

The pastry delivery boy smiled as he carried a tray of almond croissants past him. The sweet aroma was too tempting, and he decided on the spot he'd be grabbing one before joining Jen in the east wing, even if it meant taking one from Greta's desk.

After a couple of minutes, the teenager came back out with a pastry and tapped Mikey on the shoulder, offering it to him.

"Merci," Mikey said, trying not to feign a clunky French accent for the second time in an hour.

The boy nodded and trod across the snow towards his van. There was a loud bang... a gunshot. Red mist exploded from the back of the boy's right shoulder, flinging him forward, face first in the snow.

Mikey dropped the croissant, turning behind to see where the shot came from. About fifty metres away, peering around the side of an ambulance, an AK47 pointed at him. He dropped to the floor as the first barrage of bullets shattered the hospital doors. He crawled to the boy, quicker than his attackers expected, as they struggled to keep up with his movements until one of them hit a lucky shot straight through the bottom of his left foot.

The cortisol kicked in before he could vocally react. He picked up the boy, charging shoulder-first through the fire exit, falling to the floor as he did. Using his good foot, he kicked the door shut and stood on one leg, grabbing the fire axe by the exit.

The shooter's footsteps were clear as they ran to the door. Mikey pulled the boy away as a volley of bullets thudded against it, but none made it through. The door kicked open, and Mikey swung the axe with all his rage, connecting with the shooter's torso. The tip smashed completely through his rib cage and cut all the way through to the spine, coming out the back of the attacker. There was no scream, just instant death. Mikey pulled the axe out and brought it back down on their head, obliterating their skull with the inhumane power he now had. He dropped the axe and limped back to the boy, checking for a pulse. Nothing.

"Fucking hell!" Mikey growled. His chest heaved as he stood over the young, innocent life.

There was more gunfire coming from inside the building now and from every direction. There were multiple shooters. Screams echoed down the stairs from the hallway, with people running for their lives.

"Jen!" Mikey took the axe and picked up the AK47, strapping the latter over his shoulder as he cautiously stepped back outside the fire exit. A wave of people burst from the main entrance. Horrified. Some covered in blood. "Jen!" he called, not seeing her among the escapees.

Driven by anger and desperation, he tried to run before his foot gave out. Despite not feeling the pain, it was incapable of functioning at its full capacity. He steadied himself and began limping as best he could before slipping on the snowy pathway.

Two more gunshots rang out from nearby, and he crawled to see inside the reception area. Trolleys and beds were tipped over, and two more bodies sprawled across the middle of the corridor. He felt the smallest relief that neither was Jen, but the horror was still real. More screams gave him the surge he needed, encouraging him to get to his feet by using the axe as a cane.

He made it inside and to the end of the corridor, looking left towards the canteen first. It was a bloodbath, with at least a dozen bodies crumpled across the floor and tables. None of them Jen.

"Come on," he whispered to himself, keeping focus. "Where would she go?"

Someone was shouting orders on the other side of the canteen. A language he didn't know but recognised. *Slavic, or Baltic. Polish?*

"Non!" a female voice cried out, begging for her life. A single gunshot silenced her cries for mercy. Footsteps echoed from the direction of the shot, making their way across the dining area. Mikey caught their reflection against the door window, seeing they were heading towards him. He'd be spotted easily trying to cross the corridor to the stairwell, so he picked up a pedal bin and threw it against the canteen door, which was followed by the predicted gunfire as the shooter took the bait. He used the distraction and bolted towards the stairs, hopped three at a time and swung around the bannister. Mikey pointed the AK back down the stairs and rested it on the handrail.

This shooter didn't know what hit him as two controlled shots entered his neck and face. Mikey watched him drop to the floor, and more blood splattered across the hospital's pristine, white walls.

Another two voices followed, angered and approaching fast.

He gripped the handrail and pulled himself up the next set of stairs onto the first floor. There were bodies everywhere, and every treatment room had been kicked open and torn into. Windows were broken, and the shards littered the floor alongside the bullet casings.

Mikey took everything in, followed the blood trails and bodies, which led up to the next set of stairs, and headed towards the maternity ward.

One of the other shooters started to climb the stairs from below. Mikey ran to the nearest hospital bed, got behind it and pushed back towards the stairwell, carefully peeking his head over the foam mattress. As soon as the attacker rounded the corner, he shunted the bed down the stairs with all his strength, pinning them against the wall from the stomach down. He raised the rifle and fired the last of the magazine into them before throwing the weapon to the floor.

"Mikey!" he heard Jen scream from the 2nd floor. The cortisol soared. The hatred lit on fire. He jumped the stairs one-footed, leaping around the bend and up the next set. Halfway down the corridor in front, a man held Jen against the wall by the throat. Her attacker lifted his hand back with a knife, aiming for her belly. It felt like time had slowed. He only had one option.

Mikey sprang, covering the distance in barely the blink of an eye, making sure he got to the knife before anything else, squeezing the man's wrist and pushing it away as he rammed his shoulder into his ribs. Jen fell from the attacker's grasp, slumping to the side as she held her neck. She had a lot of fight in her, but the pregnancy took a toll on what she was capable of doing.

One-handed, Mikey picked the man up by the crotch, squeezing both testicles until he heard a pop. A gut-churning scream echoed throughout the whole hospital, and then Mikey threw him to the ground, cracking his face against the flooring.

The attacker tried holding their crotch, curling up into a ball.

Mikey couldn't control himself. He'd exerted too much. Now, lactic acid mixed with cortisol, forming the unwieldly toxin that pumped through every vessel in his body. He took the man by the back of his hair and began slamming his face into the floor. Once. Twice. Three times. It became a blur, over and over again, until there was nothing left to smash apart from the scruff of hair that remained in his hand.

Jen put her hand on his shoulder, and Mikey turned quickly, eyes white. The drool lathered down the front of his jacket, frothy and white. He looked like a rabid dog.

His chest thumped, and his limbs felt like they needed to run their own marathon. He glared into Jen's eyes, his body heaving and full of hate. She held her stomach, and tears swept down her cheeks.

The sickening smile faded, and his wheezing calmed before his face dropped. "Are you okay?" he managed, forcing himself to snap back to where he needed to be. "Are you okay? Is the baby okay?"

"We're okay," Jen confirmed, hand still on her belly.

"God, I'm so sorry. I shouldn't have left you." The sentence came out still angry, but behind the overbearing Kurustovia, he was more concerned than his crazed expression suggested.

"Not now." She held his face. "We have to get out of here."

———

"We have an unknown number of shooters in the hospital," Rook explained into his shoulder-mounted radio as he leaned behind his patrol car, pistol in hand. "I repeat, an unknown number of shooters."

"*Do you have eyes on them?*" the dispatcher asked.

"Negative. They came through the main and west wing entrances. Multiple causalities. Requesting permission to advance inside."

"*Are there any hostages being taken?*"

"How the fuck can I tell? I've just said I don't have eyes on them."

"*We need you to calm down, Private,*" the dispatcher condescendingly replied. "*Do not engage until backup has arrived.*"

A huge roar of gunfire broke out from the east wing just as Mikey limped out with Jen.

"Over here!" Rook called, waving them to safety as he covered the windows behind them.

Mikey fell back against the car once he'd rounded it and sat, trying to control his breath. Rook looked over his injuries before Mikey swatted him away,

"Don't worry about me," Mikey protested. "Make sure Jen's okay."

"You're seriously hurt," Rook pointed out behind another burst of bullets being fired. It sounded like there was a siege in one of the wings.

"Where's that coming from?" Mikey asked, looking over the bonnet.

"East wing," Rook answered as he turned his attention to Jen.

"I'm fine," she said, though she looked shaken.

"East wing?" Mikey huffed. "Steph's wing?" He envisioned the man who attacked Jen and the knife thrusting towards her, then pictured the same for Steph, alone and helpless.

Rook tried to hold him back, but Mikey pushed himself up and free from the grip, limping back towards the hospital faster than most people could run. Jen's screaming was drowned out as Mikey homed in on the gunfire, hopping back towards the danger.


"Lachez vos armes!" a lone security guard called out as Mikey peeked around the corner to the secure ward just before one of the shooters fired a round without hesitation.

Steph's room was in the middle of the corridor, with the assailant approaching from the far end. Mikey knew he could run and get there before him, but it was too risky with his limp and the bodies that littered the floor.

He hoped the shooter would walk past her room and towards him, where he could catch them by surprise and overpower them, but all hopes dropped when they kicked in the door to Rich's room and fired indiscriminately. Mikey's hypersensitive hearing picked up the heart rate monitor flatlining. "No. No." Mikey fell back, landing against the remains of a water cooler, which slammed against the floor.

The shooter jumped out and glared at Mikey, firing instantly. Mikey dove behind the corner just in time as the bullets thumped into the wall and ceiling around him.

"Jej krew cie wkyoncy!" the shooter taunted, over excitedly and full of contempt.

Mikey didn't know what it was that he shouted, but he had to take a quick glance after he heard what he thought was the sound of a gun hitting the floor and then a door opening. The AK47 lay amidst the blood and shattered glass, abandoned by its user. Suddenly, his eyes spotted it.

*Steph's door is open!* He crawled quickly to the gun, pulling it up to his shoulder and opening Steph's door wider. The shooter sat beside her, a syringe sticking out her arm with the contents pumped in.

"What the fuck is that?" Mikey shouted. He pressed the barrel hard against the shooter's head.

The shooter laughed softly, like he'd already accepted his death. As if this was what he was here to do. "Kurustovia," the man cackled.

Mikey heard it, tried to disprove it, and then felt the look in the man's eyes. He wasn't lying.

Another syringe on the floor was full of blood, and the laughing became almost demonic. Without thinking or having to command his body, his finger squeezed the trigger.

# 8

Ryan lifted the last oil drum into the back of the lorry, heaving as he dragged it further inside and placed it next to the rest of the supply. Pulling on one of the interior cables, he fastened them to the backboard, making sure they were tightly held in place for the journey home.

He jumped back out and onto the crunchy snow, looking around the empty car park. He heard a seagull in the distance, a sound almost forgotten in his memory bank. Other than the cawing, Ryan and Drinker's footprints were the only signs of life that the prison had seen after its abandonment. He pulled the handheld radio up and clicked the receiver.

"Dominic?"

"Here, *boss*."

"Everything okay at home?" he asked, itching his right arm.

"No disturbances," Dominic reported.

"Good. We've got the oil. It'll take about an hour to clear the armoury, and then we'll be heading back."

"We'll see you then. Out."

Ryan put the radio in his pocket and headed back inside the prison, following the winding corridors into the basement, lit dark red by the flairs. Drinker had already filled two holdalls with ammunition cartridges, hoisting them over his shoulder.

"We'll identify each kind of round when we get back," Ryan said, taking an armful of assault rifles from a cupboard. "We've got about two hours before it starts getting dark."

"Aye. Smash and grab this place, then get back for a wine!" Drinker laughed, and then his face dropped. "I didn't mean disrespect for... here."

"I don't think they would've minded. We're definitely not the worst people to have been here."

They made five trips carrying various rifles, shotguns, and ammunition back to the vehicle with relative ease. It would be the final journey that would be the slowest and most carefully taken—the transportation of the explosives.

Ryan carefully picked up a case of grenades, taking each step slower than he ever thought possible. He felt like his feet wanted to slip, and he stared down at the dark green balls of destruction, begging them to behave. With each silent step, it felt like the trodden snow was getting louder and icier from being compressed under their feet. Water dripped beside Ryan's feet as he slowly climbed the stairs, his shoulders aching and hands tensed, not daring to wobble.

Drinker was only a few metres behind, hoisting three Rocket-Propelled Grenade Launchers over his shoulder. He was moving just as slow, even swearing under his breath as he accidentally caught the butt of the launcher on the pipe.

They emerged out into the daylight, both visibly relieved that they hadn't just turned themselves into flying mince. Ryan hoisted the box of grenades onto the back, and one fell out, rolling slowly towards the corn oil.

They watched as it bounced, hit off the side and nestled against the first drum. They knew the pin was in when it started rolling, but the small chiming of metal against metal caused their hearts to stop.

Seconds later, nothing happened. They waited longer, anticipating for it to detonate. Eventually, Ryan pulled the box out and sat it on the ground, then jumped up and slowly walked to the grenade. *Yeah, this is fucking stupid.*

"Do you think..." Ryan began to ask, "...that carrying a shit load of explosives..."

"In a truck full of ammo and much-needed oil is a stupid idea? Aye."

"Yeah. Good."

"What do you want to do with them then? We can't leave them here for everyone and their mum to find them," Drinker said, hands on his hips.

Ryan grinned, almost like a child.

"Here should do." Ryan tapped the dashboard, signalling for the truck to stop about a hundred metres up the road. He jumped out and jogged back to where he'd left an RPG by the side of the road, picking it up and resting it on his shoulder.

"You sure this is wise?" Drinker asked as he caught up.

"You have wine. I have this," he replied, aiming for just inside the prison entrance, where the rest of the explosives had been tucked away.

The sight of the prison haunted Ryan since their arrival. It looked too clean. Too safe for the hell that had befallen the people here. It felt like it was mocking them. The only evidence they'd found of foul play was a body hidden in the snow. The screams that would've come from here were real. The laughing of Admiral's men as they taunted them. The hyena-like laugh of the Termites. All real.

Drinker loaded the projectile in the front and stepped away. "Are you sure you know how to use that?" he asked.

"I had to use one at the beginning of the war. Could've been beginner's luck that I hit the target then. If I miss this one, you can have the last shot."

"Alright then." Drinker shrugged, watching the target. The rocket left the barrel with a high-pitched release of air, hurtling towards the prison's open door. To his amusement, it missed, exploding about twenty feet short. "Well, that was aw..." he commented, turning only to see Ryan lying on his back and about five feet behind where he'd been kneeling before. "I'll guess it was beginner's luck then." He chuckled, helping Ryan up and taking the weapon.

Drinker had used the weapon multiple times while serving under Harper's command. He loaded and shouldered it, letting it rip. Two seconds later, the front entrance of the prison exploded, bringing down the watch tower atop it and setting off the other grenades inside.

"Fucking-shit-the-bed," Drinker exclaimed, slapping his knee. "That shot is deserving of a wine."

"Alright, fucking show off." Ryan took the launcher and tossed it in the bushes opposite. "Let's get back home."

As the front of the prison collapsed in on itself, it felt like the fitting way to say goodbye to what used to be their last trading community. For what had caused the prison to be abandoned came with a deathly presence. Ryan never wanted to see the place again, and he didn't look back.

———

Ryan watched the world go by as the eighteen-wheeler trundled carefully across the snow, passing towns he once knew and had visited more than he could count. Places that seven years before could not have predicted how they would've ended up and were now just as decayed as his memories of them. The rotted remains of undisturbed bodies still littered the pathways of the suburbs and villages, and what buildings still stood were crumbling as the years passed by, eroding floor by floor.

"Kinda harsh that we couldn't bring the explosives with us," Drinker said, interrupting Ryan's moment of reflection. "They could've come in handy."

"It's not the end of the world," Ryan said ironically as they passed what remained of a furniture superstore. "We have our own."

"What do you mean '*we have our own*'? I've never seen any on the inventory or in the weapons storage, for that matter."

"That's because we hid ours when the European Alliance asked us to take our traps down," Ryan said coldly. "Just in case they decided it would be unlawful for a community to be in possession of such weapons."

"And the inventory?" Drinker asked, almost offended.

"We altered that two days before you moved here," Ryan admitted. "Are you seriously going to get pissy that we took measures to guarantee our arsenal?"

"You thought you couldn't trust me?"

"We didn't know who to trust. Look what happened with the twins."

Drinker huffed loudly with displeasure, turning slowly onto the next carriageway. "Where are they hidden then?"

"They're not in the vineyard." Ryan turned to look at him. "They're in the barricades at the end of our road. Happy now?"

"I suppose."

"Good girl." Ryan winked before turning back to the window. "It's actually easier to wind you up than I would've thought."

"You were winding me up this morning, too, weren't you?"

"Winding you up about what?"

"Your friend, Sam, being gay."

"No," Ryan said factually, sitting up straight. "He was gay."

"You never mentioned it before," Drinker pointed out.

"Never had to." Ryan leaned forward, squinting to see something in the middle of the road. "Not even Sam bought it up." He focused harder and then made out the blood trail in the middle of the motorway. "Stop."

The brakes screeched, and the tyres skidded across the snow before eventually coming to a standstill in front of the mutilated corpse. Both Ryan and Drinker jolted forward before hitting back against their seats.

"What is it?" Drinker asked, unclipping his seatbelt and opening the door, rifle in hand.

Ryan followed, pulling his SIG up and jumping onto the snow-covered road, walking towards what was left of the body. Ryan checked the surroundings and confirmed they were just outside Gatwick. "This is the cow we passed earlier."

"Something has been at it recently, then," Drinker said,

approaching round the other side of the open wound. A mixture of ripped and torn organs spilt from the belly. "Whatever it was, it went that way." He pointed behind Ryan, where the blood trailed over the hard shoulder and down to what was left of a roadside café.

Ryan saw paw prints in the snow. Multiple sizes and patterns. "Let's not wait to find out what the fuck it is."

Drinker nodded in agreement, turning back towards the truck and shutting himself in the cabin. Ryan leapt into the passenger seat and was about to shut the door before a howl rang out.

A howl that sounded like a laugh. A Termite laugh.

He didn't need the winter weather for his blood to freeze and force him to slam the door shut. He watched intently out the window, both men silent.

Slowly marching out the front door of the café, a black dog with orange spots looked back at him, blood dripping from its mouth onto the ground.

"I never thought the day would come," Ryan said, his breath warm against the cold vehicle, "when a fucking hyena would be the lesser of two evils."

# 9

The serum's clear liquid slowly pumped into Mikey's left forearm, and Jen held a piece of cotton over the entry point. His hands untensed, his shoulders stopped shaking, and the air flowed comfortably into his lungs as his heart rate regulated.

"It'll be okay," Jen spoke up, kissing his cheek before she wiped away one of her tears.

"Are you okay?" Mikey asked, forcing the words out, trying to move from the hospital bed. His efforts were hampered by the straps that held his forearms to the railing. "Will someone let me out of these fucking restraints?"

"You need to calm down." She held his face. "I'm okay. Our baby girl is okay."

Above all else, he was truly grateful for their safety, but he couldn't let what happened slide. Rich was dead, and Steph... Steph was now infected.

*I have to tell Ryan.* "Where's the smart radio?" he persisted.

"I don't know. It's not in your pocket."

Mikey tried to think of when it could've slipped out. He ran the scenario back through his mind, picturing all the times he'd fallen. He counted five times in five different locations.

Rook opened the curtain, hushing them to keep quiet as he did. "Have you had your injection?"

"Yes," Mikey answered, looking at his arms. "Can you take these off?"

"I can't. I'm not even meant to be here. I've just come to check on you both."

"We're okay," Jen answered, holding her belly, then looking at Mikey's foot. Her voice sharpened. "Apart from his foot and two of our friends being attacked." Her voice sharpened.

Rook bit his lip, looking the wound over. A beam of sadness crossed his face like he was blaming himself. "I'll make sure I get whoever is fucking behind this."

"Can you contact Ryan?" Mikey's voice had every hint of concern in it.

"No." Rook shook his head. "I mean, I've already tried. Signal is still down."

"Shit."

"I've got to get back out there and help. There are hundreds wounded. When I get a break, I'm going to see the medical examiner about that body, see if she's picked up anything else," Rook said, closing the curtain and sneaking off.

Mikey lay his head back on the pillow, wincing as his body calmed. The pain began to scream in his foot. He closed his eyes and shut it all out, but all he could think of was the amount of death he'd seen. Hundreds, all slaughtered in what was a definite, targeted attack on them. He held Jen's hand, happy that he still could and that they would still be a family, but his trust in bringing their child into the world in Rennes had vanished. On the other hand, he couldn't leave Steph here by herself and definitely not in her condition.

He tugged at the straps once more but to no avail. His body was weakening, recovering from the unimaginable amount of hormones he'd burned through.

Jen gripped his hand. "You need to recover and be prepared for whatever conversation is going to await us later."

"Conversation? With the dickheads that have me strapped to a hospital bed?"

"They're terrified of you. They saw the remains of what you did."

"Good." Mikey smirked, though not happily. "Hopefully they'll find out that we won't play by their rules."

———

Four hours passed before the curtain reopened again. Lieutenant Harper stepped in and swiftly undid Mikey's restraints. "The staff shouldn't have done this to you," he apologised refutably, his Texan accent tainted with a seething rage towards the situation. He pulled a wheelchair into the room with him. His ginger hair hung in parts over the side of his face, and his beard had grown even more wild. "Get in. You're going back to your apartment."

Mikey slid off the bed and into the chair, and Jen pulled her coat on and moved around the bed. Harper wheeled Mikey out in front of two armed guards, who waited for them to leave, then followed down the corridor, causing the staff to move out of the way. There was chaos everywhere, with doctors running around.

They passed through the lobby, seeing the back of General Woodburn, who tore into the three security guards who had put Mikey in restraints.

"...ever treat them like that again. He did your job more fucking effectively than you did today. I don't care what your boss says..." was all they heard from Woodburn before wheeling right and towards the elevator at the end of the next corridor.

Every treatment room was full, and anyone with any kind of medical training had been called in to help. Mikey wanted to jump out of the wheelchair and put his paramedic skills to effective use, feeling guilty for leaving, but all his energy had been burned out.

The elevator doors opened, and Harper pushed the button to the underground car park. "General Woodburn is going to have their heads for how they treated you," Harper said coldly, "and for how this was allowed to happen."

"Are you close to finding out who did this?" Jen asked as they reached their floor.

"Not right now, but a full-scale investigation is starting," Harper said, wheeling Mikey out and across the car park concrete. Rook was waiting with his squad car, doors open. "I didn't want to say this to you, but it's reality now."

"What is?"

"Don't trust anyone. This attack was supplied by someone inside. Someone with access to our weapons lockers," Harper admitted, helping Mikey into the back seat. "I can't tell you too much, as it's all conjecture until we have proof. Someone still has control of our systems. That's why we can't contact Ryan. The system isn't down. It's been tampered with."

The squad car pulled up outside the entrance of the apartment block, and the security guard immediately stepped aside and opened the door. Mikey exited on crutches, taking each step slowly so as not to slip. *I've fallen enough today*. His shoulders finally began to awake to the torment he'd put them through.

Rook helped the couple upstairs and through their front door. Mikey scuffled over to the sofa and fell hard onto it.

"What's Steph's situation?" Jen asked as she took her coat off and placed it on the hanger.

"She was so drugged up at the time, it's like she hadn't noticed," Rook informed, closing the door behind them. "They're going to clear out the apartment next door and have her live next to you again." He pointed out the door. "General Woodburn organised that, and has put me on protective detail for you two. He's going to have some heads rolling for what's happened."

"Well, at least we have you guys on our side."

"It could get worse while he and Harper are gone."

"Gone?" Mikey sat up, carefully lifting his foot onto the coffee table. "Gone where?"

"A covert mission. The European Alliance won't give me any details."

"They're going to leave when all this shit just happened?"

"It's big, apparently, is all I know. Sounds like it could end all this shit."

"What if it doesn't? Or what if it's not in time before another attack?"

"Well, that's what I'm here for." Rook pulled a chair from under the desk and placed it in front of the door. "And, with me being here full time, I say we use it to figure out who we're up against."

"Let's do it," Mikey growled. "They fucking targeted us. Steph is now like me. Rich is..." his voice trailed, and Mikey actually absorbed the fact he was dead. Jen sat next to him, and the two hugged quietly, mourning for him.

Rich was the last survivor of his family, with his twin brother killed during the first encounter with Admiral's people. Rich had survived, stayed strong, and stepped up in the community, taking over agricultural duties and bringing in the crops. He'd survived only to be infected, pushed into a coma, and then shot in his bed. A coma Mikey had accidentally induced.

"What if I hadn't put him in that coma?" Mikey sobbed. "He could've done something. He could've defended himself."

"Don't talk like that. It wasn't your fault," Jen tried to comfort him but made sure she was stern. "You didn't infect him, and you didn't fire a fucking gun at him. Don't blame yourself for this. There is some cunt out there, and we need to fucking find them."

"She's right," Rook agreed from the other side of the living room, staring at the front door. "Someone has been trying to play us all, moving us around a chess board, and now they're going for checkmate."

"You think they know we're onto them? Like with that body you found?"

"Let's hope they think that." Rook turned around and added, "It means we're getting close."

# 10

Fourteen volunteers helped carry the corn oil from the lorry and take it back through the maze. For some of them, it was the first time they had stepped outside the safety of the walls since they had been put up five years prior.

Ryan and Drinker carried the weapons over four trips before parking the lorry outside the sewage plant and running back inside, locking the interior gate to section D1 of the maze.

They were greeted by an unexpected warmth as they entered the reception, closing the doors and walking through to the cafeteria. A fire burned in the middle, with two stock pots of water suspended above, boiling away. There were dozens of candles on the tables. Ryan spotted Cassy walking towards him with Alfie in her arms.

"Good work today." Ryan slapped Drinker on the shoulder. "Go get your wine."

"Aye, just a cheeky glassful for tonight. Sure you don't want one to take your mind off that abysmal shot with the RPG?"

"Ha, funny."

"Probably the happiest I've seen you for a while," Cassy interrupted. "Exciting trip?"

"A successful trip," Ryan answered, taking Alfie and holding him against his shoulder. "Drinker's gay, by the way."

"Oh wow!" Cassy exclaimed, looking at the stunned Scotsman. "You would've been perfect for Sam."

"That's what I said," Ryan added, turning with a huge grin on his face.

Drinker went to reply, cutting himself off and holding his middle finger in the air for a few seconds. "I'm not taking that bait," he said, trying to repress his smile. "I'm going to go get some of that red wine."

"Okay, sweetheart." Ryan sniggered before turning his attention to Alfie.

"How was it out there?" Cassy asked, leading Ryan back to the table where Maisie sat, eating cherry tomatoes.

"Eerie. Like really bad," Ryan said, sitting down carefully. "The prison didn't have a mark on it from the outside. It looked like there was never an attack." He stroked Maisie's hair. "It actually looks like the world is laughing at you. Like the snow is hiding all the real horrors that have happened."

"You got through it, though."

"I didn't have any other choice." He pointed at the boiling water. "We can't go all winter like that."

"Was all the corn oil there?" she asked, looking at the stockpots.

"Two had been used, one damaged but moveable. Armoury was untouched. What about you? How was it here?"

"We turned all electricity off apart from the fridge and freezer," Cassy explained, nodding towards the cafeteria kitchen. "Teddy thinks if they went down, we might not be able to get them back up. They haven't had a motor change in two years."

"Was a good idea." Ryan nodded and asked, "Who's mixing the first batch of oil?"

"Teddy is. He wants to help out. Said he feels guilty that he's not going outside or helping with security."

"He's raising a toddler, and his wife has only just started walking after being shot. He has no reason to feel guilty."

"That's what I said to him when we swapped over watching

Hannah," Cassy said, her voice lowering to a near growl at the very mention of her name.

*Hannah...* "How was your shift watching Hannah?" Ryan asked, concerned as his fiancée's face darkened with hatred.

"She's getting worse," she snarled softly, trying not to let Maisie hear the conversation. "She talks about what will happen to me when I'm captured. It's called the 'breeding programme', apparently. I don't even know if she's telling the truth, but if she is... those poor women." She wiped her nose. "That's what'll happen to me."

Ryan pulled her in and held her close. "I won't let anything happen to you."

"I know." Cassy kissed his cheek.

"Did you want to do it? To kill her?"

"I..." She hesitated and then said, "I did, but that puts us at a disadvantage if I followed through with it."

"I'm so fucking proud of you," he whispered, kissing the top of her head and passing Alfie over. "Can you take care of bedtime for these two? I need to see how Teddy's getting on before I go to bed." He stood and walked to Maisie. "You've been looking after Mummy while I've been gone?"

"I have," she said softly, not looking away as she picked at the bowl of tomatoes. Ryan smiled wider than he could've ever thought, and his heart melted on the spot. He'd missed her voice so much. "Can I sleep in your bed tonight?" she asked.

"Of course you can, smelly bum." Ryan held her hand and walked her to Cassy. "Keep my side warm for me. I'll be up in a little while."

As a proud dad, he waved good night as his family disappeared upstairs, ready to join them for a well-earned sleep before getting back to his security duties the next morning. He looked around the cafeteria at all the families huddled near the fire as they ate their thyme rice and soda bread.

It was the most basic of meals they had been forced to have for years, but a couple of nights wouldn't dampen their spirits until the generators were back up and running. They had two years of this before the power was restored and salvaged cooking oil had become their main supply until they sourced their own.

That's how it was at the beginning, and everyone at Penbrook Vineyard remembered it well. It was a long, hard learning experience of trial and error, but they were proud of their home and honoured their missing ones by keeping it running—all the people they had lost through illnesses and untreatable health conditions.

Then there were the ones who were taken, who would've still been helping to keep the fire going and keep the vineyard safe had Admiral's people never come calling. Cooper. Fergie. Hamsa. Sam. Doc. Lyndon. Not to mention Mikey, Jen, Steph, and Rich, who were still in France. He was currently unable to contact them. He felt his anger beginning to surface, shutting it down before it brought on the inevitable anxiety vomits.

*Go and see Teddy, then get some fucking sleep, man.*

He said a quick goodnight to everyone before he left, making sure they had the extra winter duvets, blankets, and candles, then took a torch and stepped down into the basement. He heard Teddy around the corner, mixing the corn oil with paint thinner and acetone, but Ryan's eyes felt as if they were glued to the cage door further inside. He walked over, finding young Callum sitting in the watch chair, surrounded by candles.

"Ryan." Callum looked up in surprise, shifting his glasses. "I didn't know you were coming down."

"It's cool. You're not in trouble," Ryan said and chuckled. He hadn't spent much time around the lad, who generally worked out in the crops but had recently volunteered to help Dominic with various security details. He'd been trained with a pistol but was yet to see combat. He wasn't much older than Lyndon. "Can you give us five minutes? Go get yourself some rice."

"Okay. Sure. No problem." He stood, marching off like he'd just been given an order by his commanding officer.

Ryan sat carefully in the chair, head lowered, and his hands crossed between his knees, contemplating why he was breaking a promise to himself. He lifted his eyes to the prisoner in the cell. The bitch that killed his nephew. Admiral's daughter. Hannah Caven.

Her tall frame lay on the single mattress of the cold floor, wrapped under two blankets as she tried to read a book by two dying candles.

Her dark red hair swept behind her shoulders, and her hazel eyes squinted at the pages as she flicked through.

Behind the open pages of the book, a shadow of a smirk emerged on her face. "What's so urgent that you needed to see me for the first time in weeks?" she asked, placing the book down. Ryan didn't answer. Instead, he leaned forward, holding his hands between his knees. "Go on." She sat up, wrapping the blanket over her. "What's so important?"

He stayed quiet, not giving anything away. "Have your sanitary requirements been met?" he deflected.

Her smirk returned this time. "Somewhat. Your pretty little fiancée did provide me with sanitary towels... though washing them in a bowl of cold water and reusing them isn't my idea of a good time. If I could leave a review for your hospitality, I'd give you three stars. The care is great, but the room is too cold, and the food is shit."

"I'll get you another blanket, and I'll tell the chef to stop putting shit in your food," Ryan replied dryly.

"Funny. Almost as funny as the bullet I put in your nephew." She let her gaze slowly drift down Ryan's body as she pronounced every word of her statement.

Ryan felt pain and the urge to rip the door off and kill her, but she wasn't going to have this moment, no matter how much she was trying to get under his skin.

"No reaction?" She pouted sarcastically, taunting. "Did you know you have the same 'fuck me' eyes your girlfriend has? You're looking at me like she does. Undressing..." She let the right shoulder of her blanket fall, nearly exposing her breast. "I'll keep it a secret if you want to. Maybe we can ask her to join in? I've never had a woman before, but I'll let you both take me. You both look like you need a good fu—"

"It's not going to work, no matter how much you try," Ryan interrupted bluntly, sitting back in the chair and sparking a cigarette. "Unless I knew I didn't need you as a bargaining chip anymore."

"What are you talking about?"

"This... all this shit you're doing. Trying to get us to kill you, giving your dad carte blanche to attack here. Smart. I didn't take you for a fucking martyr."

"You can take me any way you want," she moaned teasingly.

"Or a whore," he added, pulling his Glock out from the back of his waistband and resting it on his knee, barrel aimed directly at her head. "Oh, this?" he said, looking at the gun. "This isn't for you... just yet."

"Just yet? Is this your idea of foreplay?"

"No, it's not. This is me telling you that maybe, or maybe not, your dad's supply ship from Venezuela has been found." He watched the smirk disappear from her face. "And maybe, or maybe not, your dad's location has been found, and he won't have the chance to come here and save you."

"So that gives you no reason to keep me alive?" Hannah realised. "I've been goading you all into killing me already. Why would I care?"

"You'd care because no one knows you're here, so I'm not compelled to report your death... no matter how it was carried out," he said coldly. "There will be no record of your execution, and I won't face a jury for any war crimes."

"Everyone here will know."

"They'll know I killed you," Ryan heard the stairwell door shut, signalling for him to wrap up the conversation, "but they won't know how I killed you." He tucked the Glock back in his trousers. "Stop talking to everyone like shit. Stop threatening Cassy with your ideas and fucking behave for the remainder of your stay. If you behave, I promise I'll only use the gun. If you keep pushing buttons, however... what I'll do to you will make The Bully Killer look like a fucking amateur."

# 11

*No signal.*

Ryan huffed and tossed the smart radio on the table. It had been five days since he'd spoken to Mikey, and he was still waiting on an update from Harper.

He had yet to tell everyone about the possibility of the fight being over, and he wasn't sure if he could bring himself to do it. It was the false hope. A broken promise, like the many he hadn't been able to keep. He could've used talking to Mikey right now, and he was at his wit's end of what to do, the silence killing him.

*At least Steph is in good hands, with Mikey watching out for her.*

The bottom of his stomach dropped like an anchor, and he felt disgusted with his moment of self-pity. He wasn't the only person who had lost family. Everyone here had.

*Everyone deserves to know.*

He took the handheld radio and said, "Drinker. Can you call everyone for a meeting in half an hour?"

"Aye. Anything serious?"

"No. Just something I need to share."

He replaced the handheld with the smart radio and tried dialling again.

*No signal.*

Ryan took to the cafeteria's podium, wondering how everyone would react to him withholding the truth and how much trust he would lose. His phantom fingers ached, though he quickly dismissed it.

"Hi, everyone. Thank you for being here on short notice," he started. "I've heard it's been productive in the rice rooms?"

Teddy proceeded to tell Ryan about the amount they had threshed and the newer batches being sown. The news was looking good on that front, as they could provide food for at least another hundred people for six months. Dominic then explained that the fridge and freezer motors had been checked, and due to the weather, they weren't using as much corn oil to sustain their workability.

"Well, we're looking good on all these fronts, and with the corn oil we retrieved, we have a good foundation taking us into the new year," Ryan said, clearing his throat. "But I do have something I need to tell you." He leaned on the podium. "I still haven't heard from Mikey or Harper, but there is something I didn't forward to you all last time I spoke to the lieutenant." An awkward pause filled the room. "I didn't know how to tell you. I, er, didn't want to give us a glimmer of hope just for it to be snatched away."

"Hope?" someone asked from in front, but Ryan didn't catch who. All he felt was the weight of the world on his shoulders.

"Yes. Hope," he continued. "The reason the other groups of survivors are being delayed is because they're being relocated to the strongholds in Sheffield, Cardiff, and Bournemouth, where they will be looked after by staff over winter. The military is being recalled. All military."

Dominic asked the question that was on everyone's lips. "Why?"

"About a week ago, one of the European Alliance's supply ships intercepted a Venezuelan cargo transport off the coast of Portugal. It's the cargo vessel that's been supplying Admiral. On a search and interrogation of the crew, they have Admiral's location in Liberia, plus the rest of his forces up in the Scottish Isles. They're organising two missions to capture or eliminate... every single one of them. They're going to try and end this."

The cafeteria was still and stone-cold silent, with only the clucking of chickens within the medical corridor to be heard. Ryan let the news sit, waiting for some form of backlash. Every face looked back at him. Confused. Stunned.

"I didn't tell you because I couldn't bear the thought of giving false hope. It was selfish and cowardly of me, and I'm sorry it took me this long to pass it on," Ryan said in an apology.

"You don't..." Teddy paused, then said, "...have to apologise."

"I do. I'm supposed to lead by example."

"You already do," Dominic added. "And no, you're not perfect, but you never pretended to be... boss." He said the last part with a grin.

"Well, thank you." Ryan chuckled, looking over everyone. "Until we get the news that the European Alliance was successful, we're on our toes every day, and we stay self-sufficient." He felt his confidence seeping slowly back into his veins. "You all did brilliantly during the few days we had to reduce the power, and I can't thank you enough. When the other groups of survivors get here, they'll be lucky to have you all by their sides. If anyone needs me, I'll be upstairs for the remainder of the day and night. I've got another long-ass shift."

———

Another quiet, cold night on the top floor was counteracted by Ryan putting his brain to good use, though he felt he was going back on his word and getting ahead of himself. On a map of Maidville, he'd marked down all the main roads and ways into the town, along with the structures that were either most degraded or destroyed.

Cassy's gentle footsteps were loud enough for Ryan to notice. He looked up from the table and rubbed his eyes. She slowly stepped across the restaurant floor, cradling an asleep Alfie while holding Maisie's hand.

Ryan glanced at his smart radio. "It's five in the morning! What are you doing up?"

"Maisie wanted to see you." Cassy smiled, sitting on the chair next to him.

"Really?" he picked up Maisie and sat her on his lap. "At this hour?"

"She's not been sleeping well when you are on your night shifts."

"Sorry. I've been playing around with some ideas for the future."

"Like what?" Cassy asked, looking at one of the maps that Ryan had been altering.

"How we can extend our grounds," he said, turning the map around so she could see his notes. "The land outside our southern wall is just a muddy wasteland. We could put solar panels out there and not have to be so reliant on the corn oil." He moved his pencil, pointing to the northern side of their grounds. "We've never utilised the river outside. Some kind of mill, maybe? Are mills used for flour production? I don't actually know, but there must be something we can use with it?" He looked up to see Cassy was gleaming. "What?"

"You're actually moving forward."

"I'm preparing. There's a difference. I'm aware that until it's over, we're still at war."

"You could've planned all this at any other time, though, considering we've always been at war," she pointed out. "It's like you can see a light at the end of a tunnel."

"Maybe, but I'm not taking my eyes away from the world we live in." He pointed out the window. The towering hill behind the sewage plant on the opposite side of the dual carriageway.

"Maidhill?" She looked out the window. Ryan followed her gaze and stared into the darkness.

"The trees. We'll take them down. We need timber, and it'll take away any hiding spots for outsiders." He knew what he was saying was logical and a huge task, but the reality was it was personal. The tree-covered western slope was where Hannah had fired the shot that killed Lyndon. "It'll take a while, but it'll serve us in the long run."

"I understand, baby." She held his hand. "What else do you think we could do?"

His heart warmed. This was the love and encouragement that made him who he was now. "Well, before all of this," he pointed to the notes, "and when everything is over, the first thing we're going to do is get married."

"Even in the snow?" she asked, laughing at the idea.

"I wouldn't care if it was raining beer or hailing rabbit shit. I'd still marry you."

"Language!" Cassy Scowled, nodding to Maisie.

"Oh, yeah." Ryan bit his lip. "Probably the only benefit I have with you not talking at the moment, isn't it?" He kissed Maisie on the cheek.

"We'll go back to bed now and leave you with your planning." She leaned over for a kiss and took Maisie's hand. "I'll see you in a few—"

A low, mechanical roar broke through the silent sky, gradually getting louder.

"A helicopter?" Ryan looked out the window, trying to see where it was coming from. "Take the kids back, then wake Drinker and Dominic." He kissed Cassy and sent them on their way before asking into the radio. "Callum? Everything okay in the basement?"

"Yes, Ryan."

"There's a chopper on the way. I'm going out to investigate."

"Okay. I, mean, understood."

Ryan grabbed his SIG716 and ran down the stairs and out the front entrance. The helicopter was in view, approaching from the south, and followed by a whole unit of airborne vehicles. Chinooks, attack choppers, Little-Birds. They pounded through the sky, with one breaking off from the formation and descending slowly. Ryan lit a flare and threw it towards the open space in the car park, which the Chinook followed and landed just to the right of it.

The back ramp slowly opened, letting Ryan see inside and raise his rifle to fire as the man walked down.

"Who the fuck are you?" Ryan demanded, ready to fire. Ready to kill.

# PART II

## FULL CIRCLE

# 12

The warm, dark red liquid oozed against the cold stainless steel, swirling with the warm water before disappearing down the sink. Lieutenant Adam Harper carefully rinsed out the wine glass and placed it on the drying rack, trying to avoid accidentally dropping it as his hands shook. He turned his attention back to the open bottle—a gift from Ryan, and in that moment, he was awash with yet more guilt for failing to keep Steph protected while under his care.

He glanced at his watch, screwed the bottle cap back on and placed it in the cupboard above the sink. Now wasn't the time to finish it, nor take it to his family's new temporary accommodation.

The late-night activity would surely be noticed by the other residents within the apartment block, but he didn't care. If someone was coming directly for the vineyard residents, it meant that there was every chance his family could be targeted based purely on nothing but association. The safety of his family came first, and he didn't hesitate when the option to move them to a secure location was offered. It might have been counterintuitive to leave his family in the same apartment block as Mikey, Jen, and Steph, but the newer and buffed-up security detail had been provided by someone he'd trusted for over twenty years and had the bonus that Rook was now stationed there for twenty-four-hour overwatch of the floor they occupied.

His commanding officer and close friend, General Stephen Woodburn, had arranged the move once the attack at the hospital had been officially declared over. There were no words for Harper's appreciation of the arrangement, considering he knew that in the immediate future, he would be leaving his family for Liberia. He didn't like it, but after the tally of eighty-four deaths had been confirmed from the previous day's shooting, the operation to bring in Admiral had been given the green light by the higher-ups within the governing board.

This was the final act. The last battle that remained in the twisted fallout of the war. A fight against someone he had once served with.

"Dad?" Harper's son, Troy, asked softly, confused as to why he and everyone else was awake at this hour. The seven-year-old's eyes were barely open, and his star-covered pyjamas were just as scuffed as his wavy, red hair. He couldn't have looked more like his father if he'd tried, minus the beard.

"You okay, buddy?" Harper replied, crouching with his arms out.

Troy shuffled across the tiled kitchen floor and into his father's embrace. Harper walked out of the kitchen and through the hallway into the open lounge area. Suitcases and boxes had been organised at the far end near the main door, ready to be shipped to their new home.

His eldest daughter, Katie, sat in the armchair, turning pages in whatever sci-fi book she was into that week. "Can I take my bed to this new place?" she asked without looking up.

"The new place is already furnished," Harper answered, now aware that Troy had already fallen asleep against his shoulder.

"I like my bed," Katie stated, her tone sharp and moody like the young teenager she was soon becoming.

"You're only going to be in the new apartment until I get back." He had previously stated this clearly enough, though now wasn't the time to get into it. "You can wait till then."

"Why do we have to go, anyway?"

Her question, though poorly timed, was valid. She hadn't been told about the terror attack at the hospital or that someone could be out to hurt their family. Harper couldn't bear the thought of putting that fear into his daughter, which would eat him alive while he was gone. Yet, she deserved to know and have a chance of being prepared should anyone be stupid enough to attempt an assault.

"I'll tell you once we've moved our stuff over to the new place," Harper said calmly, reaching over one box and picking up his smart radio. There was a message from Rook.

*Your apartment is ready, sir.*
    *Sending two vans your way to pick everything up.*
    *Message me when you're en route. I'll let the guards know.*
    *What did you want to talk to me about?*

Harper idled over his response before eventually typing back one-handed.

*Thank you. We'll be over soon.*
    *I'll knock on your door later.*

"Are you ready?" he asked Katie while slipping the smart radio into his pocket.

She nodded silently, closing the book and placing it in her rucksack. Harper walked back through the hallway to the main bedroom, finding his wife packing the last duffel bags with their family photos.

"Are you going to tell her why we're moving?" Carol asked as she zipped the bag and placed it on her lap. She used the wheelchair's control stick to turn towards her husband. Under her dark black fringe, her eyes gave away that she'd been crying.

"When we get there, I will," Harper said as he approached, carefully sitting on the bed without waking Troy. He held her hand. "Getting you to safety is the priority."

"I know," Carol whimpered, then fell into a full sob. She held her mouth and bit her lip, not wanting their children to hear. "I'm sorry."

"You have nothing to be sorry for. You're allowed to be upset with everything that has happened."

He gave her a moment, passing a tissue so she could wipe the tears and blow her nose. Katie came to the doorway. Her steps had been silent as she walked down the hallway.

"Two vans just pulled up out front," she announced, shouldering her rucksack.

"Thank you." Harper smiled as he stood. "The quicker we get this done, the quicker we can get some sleep."

In less than an hour, all boxes and suitcases had been successfully moved into their new home. Troy had been put to bed on arrival, with his favourite teddy placed next to him. Harper thanked both drivers who had assisted throughout the whole journey and the maintenance staff who had assured the elevator was functional for his wife's needs— another of the many favours Harper would owe Woodburn.

The whole apartment block had been inspected by his own men, and the electric and water supplies were upgraded to accommodate the family during their stay. Most of the work had kept Mikey and Jen up as walls were ripped open and plastered over, but the twelve-hour renovation was worth the minor noise disturbance compared to the thought of insufficient or poorly maintained utilities.

After settling down, Harper insisted Carol and Katie go to bed before they even attempted to unpack, saving their energy for the morning. Carol remarked they were missing a family photo as Harper helped her into bed, swearing it had been in the duffel bag when she packed. He told her he'd find it in the morning or ask the drivers if it had fallen out in their van. His reassurance helped, and she was out within minutes of taking her painkillers, giving him enough time to sit with Katie in her 'new' bedroom, explain what happened at the hospital, and why that meant they had to be relocated indefinitely. For a borderline teenager, she took it pretty well, just like she had with every other horror she'd been told about over the last seven years.

After leaving Katie with her new book, Harper thought it was a good time for a quick inspection of the kitchen and to see whether he'd been given the standard coffee or the officer grade. He opened the pot and held the can to his nose. Smoke roasted.

"Woodburn, you son of a bitch." He chuckled softly to himself. "I don't know how I'll ever repay you for this." He screwed the lid back on and started to check the food supply. The fridge was stocked with orange juice, bacon, and eggs, ready for when they got up.

The new flat was more spacious, but it felt cold, like it was too big. The apartment they'd just left behind felt cosier, even with the wooden and tiled floors. The lower ceilings created a comfort that the new twelve-foot-high rooms didn't have. It was a grand apartment, but even with the stacks of luggage in the living room, it felt empty.

*It's only temporary,* Harper reminded himself. *And they're safe here.*

He gazed over the new lounge, wondering just how everything would look when it was unpacked. At least there would be enough room for Troy to get his energy out and a choice of sofas for Carol to relax on while rewatching her favourite sitcoms on DVD. The thought made him smile. Even if Katie spent most of her time in her room, she would have enough reading space to keep herself entertained.

Harper opened the main door and stepped into the public hallway. The white ceilings and walls came down halfway, where they met the oak panelling, which matched the floor. There were fresh plaster marks running the length of the corridor, as well as signs of the maintenance work that had taken place during the morning and afternoon. He wasn't sure if he preferred his family being at the far end and near a fire escape, but it was the nearest three-bedroom-apartment to the elevator. He knew the floor well after his previous visits.

At the opposite end was the main staircase, which stopped at each floor. The apartment to the immediate right of the staircase was Mikey and Jen's. Opposite them was a small one-bed apartment where Steph was now being treated. Harper walked the corridor, stopping before he reached either of their apartments and knocked on the door to the left. It opened almost instantly.

Rook gestured for him to enter. Harper obliged and was welcomed by the roar of a fireplace. He hadn't realised how much he missed the one back in his old home in America.

"How was the move?" Rook asked as he shut the door and stepped into his open-plan kitchen. "Coffee?"

"Not at this hour. Thank you, though. And it was tiring," Harper admitted as he approached, sitting in an empty spot opposite a sofa and coffee table. "Woodburn's guys took care of all the heavy lifting."

"Hungarians are damn hard workers."

"That I'll say. I hope the maintenance crew didn't disturb you too much."

"They were the least of our worries." Rook shrugged, handing over a glass of orange juice. "They were done in no time. All the walls have been patched up."

"Woodburn's trying to make it easy for us. He is pissed at the French for letting it happen and beyond guilty for putting us in harm's way." Harper took a sip, mulling over everything. "You know he regrets what happened to you?"

"Not now, Lieutenant," Rook said in a dismissive tone. Saying it was hard for him was an overstatement, but even the best of the best-made mistakes. At the end of the day, Woodburn couldn't have known that arresting Rook and having him on temporary suspension at the vineyard almost got him killed. Admiral had played that card and almost succeeded. "It's behind us, and now I have a job to do." He leaned forward and looked around his new home. "And this is better than my previous quarters."

"You don't miss being out in the field?"

"You know I do, but I have more purpose here. You know any asshole coming after your family has to get through me first."

"And I'm happy to know they won't," Harper said and nodded thankfully. "Do you interact with the guards much?"

"Occasionally. Woodburn's men. The best kind of first line any defence could need." Rook held his coffee cup, taking a moment to savour the smell before drinking a mouthful. "What did you want to talk about?"

Harper cleared his throat, placing his glass on the coffee table. "The man who approached Mikey outside the hospital a few days before the attack has been identified as Lukas Gregorzk. We've located his family's quarters in the refugee area at Combourg. Upon searching their tent, we found surveillance-style photos. Of Mikey, Jen, Steph, and the hospital. Mrs Gregorzk confirmed these were dropped off to him two weeks ago by someone she only identifies as *officer man*."

"*Officer man?*" Rook asked, folding his arms and sitting back.

"Her English isn't great. It's just what she refers to as anyone in any kind of uniform," Harper explained cautiously before carrying on. "When we questioned Lukas after this, he confirmed who this *officer man* is." He held his hands together. "Tech Supervisor Fabian Monreal."

Rook's eyes widened as if a ghost had come to sit in the room with them. "That..." He shook his head. "That doesn't make any sense."

"I know," Harper agreed, knowing the ramifications of this news.

Tech Supervisor Fabian Monreal, the very mole working on the inside against the European Alliance, was assumed to have escaped to Liberia with the group of Admiral's men during the prison breakout. That was two months prior, and it was not possible for him to have supplied the perpetrators of the recent hospital attack.

Monreal himself was the same man who had attempted to frame Rook while helping the twins infiltrate the vineyard, take control of Rennes' defence systems, and even bring down a chopper of six soldiers. Whatever software he'd used had been undetectable, leaving zero trace or evidence that he'd ever been in their system.

"You think that weasel prick could still be here?" Rook asked, his lips thinning and his jaw tightening. He'd abandoned his personal grudge against Monreal once he'd survived the attempt on his life, but all the other innocent lives caught in the mix were what got to him. If there was a chance that the rogue tech supervisor had stayed under their noses this whole time, then Rook would personally set the cheese to bait the rat out.

"Woodburn pointed out earlier that we never had any confirmation that Monreal was actually on that flight when the prisoners escaped, and he already has the technological capabilities to hide his every movement. What better way to keep on doing your work if no one is looking for you?"

"Fucking asshole could still be here," Rook growled, looking out the window into the morning darkness.

"Which leads me onto the next reason to believe he's here," Harper continued. "The signal issue with Ryan isn't related to the system reboot. It's only affecting the satellites that relay signals to Southern England. It's a direct communication blackout against Penbrook."

"How's that possible? The reboot should've cleaned the system out of any hostile malware," Rook stated.

"And you're right. So that could only mean..."

"That Monreal has gotten back into the network since the reboot?"

"Yes. Woodburn has ordered that photos of Monreal are posted everywhere," Harper said, "but if the situation arises, you need to bring him in alive."

"What if he resists?" Rook asked.

"Use whatever force necessary, but any information we can obtain from him could aid our operation when going after Admiral."

"Understood," Rook replied. "When do you leave for Liberia?"

"We have our briefing tomorrow afternoon," Harper said. "All details will be acquired, and then we can get the son of a bitch."

## 13

Not a single creature stirred as Rook performed his hourly sweeps of the top three floors. The silence was welcomed, giving him time to process the information Harper had thrown on him a couple of hours before.

Through all his years of training and service with the Marine Corps, Rook had stood out as a poster child for discipline and keeping his cool. For a couple of years, it was highly recognised that taking back the Polish city of Gdansk was owed to Rook's leadership of a ragtag group of soldiers. Soldiers that he'd been forced to take charge of as the battle raged, wiping out entire units of R.I.C. insurgents. He'd kept a level head with whatever was thrown at him, even the wrongful arrest that derailed his deployment in Gdansk. For him, the chaos had come second nature to brush off and move on.

He didn't feel calm at that second. The ten or so minutes walking through the apartment block served more as a way to try and burn off his bubbling anger. Discipline was no longer on the cards, and breaking the rules became increasingly likely.

The idea that Monreal was still close by and recruiting new followers for Admiral, all the while hiding in the shadows, was excruciating to Rook. The treacherous rodent proudly attempted to kill him and members of Penbrook before the successful slaughter of eighty-four civilians just two days ago.

*The piece of shit thinks he's invincible.* Rook hoped Monreal was too proud not to notice leaving one breadcrumb on his trail.

The morning light crept through the top-floor window, and he shook off the urge to have a cigarette—a habit he'd picked up from a secret love interest who occasionally visited. Rook opted for a coffee instead of nicotine and headed back to his apartment. As he stuck his key in the lock, a clattering echoed out of one of the rooms before a loud thump of a body landing on cushioned furniture. Not taking any chances, he reached behind his back and gripped his pistol while his one working ear followed the noise. It was coming from Harper's apartment. He held close to the wall and pushed forward until it became clear that Harper's wife was trying to calm their son down. Troy was just as energetic as Harper had explained, and Rook internally smiled at the innocence of Harper's son—a beautiful ignorance of how dark the world was on the outside.

Rook pushed himself away from the wall, zipping up his puffer coat before adjusting his beanie. Even after three years, he couldn't get used to any headwear not getting caught on where his left ear should've been. He didn't hold any grudges for the insurgent who'd thrown the grenade. It was war, after all, and Rook had taken the man's life with his combat knife just to even the score. Nothing personal.

The door next to his apartment creaked open, with a sheepish-looking Mikey stepping out, overwhelmed with emotion. It was Steph's apartment he'd just left. "She's bathed," he muttered, wiping his nose, "and back in restraints."

Rook nodded, trying to avoid glancing into the room. He couldn't bear it. He had very little engagement with Steph before she'd been shot, and it wasn't until Rook was keeping her alive while waiting for her emergency evacuation that Ryan broke down, spilling what his sister had been through over the years.

She'd had two people she loved taken from her in four months. To add to that, she'd recently been injected with the weapon that Admiral was using to control people, taking away whatever free will she had to fight back with. It wasn't fair, and that was just one of the many things that ate away at Rook throughout the night.

There was one question about her infection that spear-tipped his hatred for Monreal. Had he ordered them to infect her to drag her further into hell, or was it just to punish Ryan?

Rook dismissed the question. Neither answer was better than the other. "When's the nurse coming to change her drip feed?" he asked.

"About noonish," Mikey huffed. "Why?"

"I'm going to try and find more answers about how this happened."

"How?" Mikey inched closer to Rook.

"You know that prick who approached you outside the hospital a few days before the shooting? Well, I know where his family is, and his wife knows how he was approached."

"What are you going to do?"

"Ask questions, that's all," Rook promised, looking at his watch, then passed Mikey his pistol. "I'll be back well before the nurse arrives."

"Why are you giving me your gun?"

"One: protection for you while I'm gone. Two: metal detectors have been fitted at every major checkpoint. I haven't got clearance to carry in the civilian areas."

"I see," Mikey said, opening the door to his apartment. "What if someone asks where you are?"

"Tell them I'm using my thirty-minute leisure allowance, and I've gone to get bread," Rook answered, turning towards the stairwell and descending, focused on his objective. His answers would be waiting in the refugee camps. And whether Lukas Gregorzk's wife knew it or not, she'd tell him what he wanted to know.

He opened the fire exit and stepped out into the snow-covered back alley where his squad car was waiting, away from prying eyes. Rook never considered himself paranoid but knew when to trust his instinct. The fact that he had been cleared of smuggling Kurustovia but the French were intent on treating him like suspect number one told him two things: they were delusional as to just how deep the problem was within their own system, and also, they were likely waiting for him to slip up in any way just so they could witch-hunt him.

He unlocked the driver's door manually and sat in the seat, taking a moment to reflect on the task at hand. *Get as much information from Lukas Gregorzk's wife as possible, and don't get spotted by the French.*

He counted his blessings that the road and gated patrol of the refugee camps were predominantly Polish, and many of their surviving citizens held Rook in high regard after his defence of Gdansk. Well, most of them had until they started shooting at the hospital where he was formerly stationed. Now, there was no indication of just how many had turned on the very people who were trying to rebuild what had been taken from them.

He twisted the key in the ignition and cleared his throat as the squad car moved slowly forward. He had half an hour to think of the right questions to ask Mrs Gregorzk.

Ten minutes into his ice-road journey, his smart radio vibrated. A message from his on/off love interest, Eliza Fultz. As Chief Technical Supervisor in Rennes Airport, she had been instrumental in helping Rook gain confidential information without Harper or Woodburn knowing. The way he saw it, his commanding officers had plausible deniability should he get caught. It was Eliza's deep digging that let Rook know exactly which tent complex he'd find Lukas's wife in.

He gently lifted his foot off the accelerator while keeping one eye on the road, reading the message carefully.

*Eliza: Just spoke to the medical examiner about the body that was brought in last week. Cause of death has been confirmed.*

*A few bullet fragments found in collar bone and C2 vertebrae. A single shot. Execution-style.*

Rook wondered if Monreal had executed this person himself and dumped the body or had one of the newly recruited refugees take care of it. Between blocking all communications to Ryan, erasing the M.I.A records, and organising a mass shooting, the asshole was clearly busy. What was worse was that Monreal had been one step ahead and was insanely brilliant at covering his tracks.

Rook sped up and gripped the steering wheel, pushing down the frustration and anger inside him.

# 14

Harper had left his family's apartment just after breakfast, making sure to cook Troy a heavy breakfast that would help slow him down after his energetic wake-up. The unpacking had begun, with Katie taking Troy off her parents' hands and helping to unpack his stuff in his room.

Harper made sure to thank her for that and spent an hour with Carol before he left. He wanted to get as much time in with her before the debrief later that morning. He'd take every opportunity to do whatever he could to take his mind off the meeting and just enjoy the moment.

Woodburn's driver met Harper outside the apartments, handing him a folder while he drove him to the airport. It was reassuring to know that his friend had been chosen to oversee the joint operations to bring in Admiral and his people. Of all the senior officers on camp, Woodburn was a more driven and better leader than most combined, but what worked in his favour was his previous knowledge and experience with the target.

Danish Health Minister Eriksen saw Woodburn as the main man to execute the task at hand and to lead the Joint European Army on its very first mission. There would be no anti-American rhetoric within the ranks. This wasn't about neighbouring countries forced to collate. It was about Europe uniting together and fighting as a whole.

After arriving at the airport, Harper signed in at the security checkpoint and headed out the back of the terminal, zipping up his parka jacket. He had been escorted by two French civil volunteers as he made his way to the southern tip of the runway and into Hangar 5, the location for the operations debrief. After helping himself to a pan-au-chocolat and coffee from the temporary refreshment station, he found a quiet corner of the large space and flicked through the folder in his hands, containing the members of each individual team for the whole operation. He held the cup in his right hand and perched himself on top of an empty ammo crate, giving his legs a rest. His left thigh couldn't stop shaking—not from caffeine or the cold. It was fear.

Going back out into the unsecured world wasn't the cause of the dread. He'd seen everything that any scholar of hell couldn't even begin to comprehend and all the different ways blood could be spilt or used as currency. What was causing his stomach to perform gymnastics was the thought of leaving his family behind. It slowly chipped away at his normally calm persona.

He opened the folder and took in the information within. The list of squads and who would be assigned what callsigns. This format was different from what he was accustomed to in the U.S. Marines Corps.

Seven squads of twelve men and interestingly broken up into certain specialities.

Harper looked down the list:


*Team Alpha- First Contact.*
   *Team Bravo- Contact Support.*
   *Team Charlie- Communications and Recon.*
   *Team Delta- Demolitions.*
   *Team Echo- Medical and Tech Support.*
   *Team Fox- Contact and Patrol Guard.*
   *Team Gundam- Bomb Disposal.*

. . .

Harper read over the last squad again. "Bomb disposal?" he asked quietly. "What the fuck is waiting for us out there?" A soft groan left his lips, and a feeling they were walking into something much bigger invaded his moment of privacy. He reopened the folder and continued to read.

To his shock, he'd been designated leader of Team Alpha. He ran down the squad he'd been given command of, thankful that he'd served with every member of his unit at least once. They were all top of their field, and it was a huge reassurance that they were the ones who would follow Harper's command into whatever battle was waiting on the equator.

He closed the folder and sat it on his lap. Though the instructions were clear, this new squad system was going to take getting used to. "All in good time," Harper reminded himself. "It's not the biggest of your worries."

"I've seen that face before," Woodburn claimed as he approached, boots clipping off the concrete as he marched over with his hands behind his back, shoulders straight. His buttoned sheepskin jacket was dusted with snow, yet his brown, side-swept hair remained untouched by the winter conditions. "I know it's not the mission that's got you worked up. What's on your mind, son?" he asked while sitting on the ammo crate opposite.

"There's no point in lying to you, is there?" Harper scoffed, looking up. "If you know it's not the mission, then you can guess what it is, sir."

"Leaving your family here doesn't feel as safe as it used to?"

"We knew Admiral had reach within us, but having the infrastructure to supply weapons to civilians and coordinate an attack... how much further will he go?"

"He'll keep going if we don't go out there and stop him," Woodburn answered, taking the coffee cup from his friend and smelling it. "Since when did you drink iced coffee?"

"I don't." Harper frowned, looking around the hangar. "I didn't realise how long I was sitting here."

Woodburn emptied the contents of the cup on the ground, then turned back to his friend. "Do you trust the security that your family is under?"

"Rook? You know I do. Thank you for organising that."

"The fucking Frenchies have given him a hard enough time as it is, but after their blatant lack of security regarding the hospital and the vineyard people's lives, I won't let them try and besmirch his name anymore."

Woodburn had put his foot down on the governing board and used both his influence and ranking to pull the French resistance in line. All the contempt for Americans had subsided through autumn and winter as Woodburn and his men tightened up the frayed remains of the collective European armies.

The contempt for Rook remained in the lower ranks of the French Security Division, but now the public opinion of them had started to turn after the poorly handled hospital shooting.

The names and faces of the victims had been released, and the outcry demanded justice. It was only fair and expected. There was only one person who didn't know what had happened and that his own people had been hurt.

Ryan.

"What do we tell Ryan when this is all over?" Harper asked sincerely.

Woodburn clicked his tongue, stroking his clean-shaven chin. "That's an issue we'll have to face later. Heck, that could be a war of its own. Right now, we've got a war criminal to bring in." He stood, straightening his jacket. "Briefing is in five minutes. Your seat is waiting for you."


At the back exit of Hangar 5, a newly fitted special operations room was alive with activity as everyone tried to find their seat. Harper recognised many faces among the high-ranking officials of multiple nationalities. It was the remains of what the continent's armed forces had been whittled down to.

Harper found his seat, front row and just left of the centre. He lifted the name tag and sat, eyeing the room. Every face wore a concoction of anticipation and stern professionalism. He wiped his palm sweat on his thighs and sat against the back support, shocked as a fresh cup of coffee was wafted in front of his face.

"General Woodburn said you could use a fresh one," a Scandinavian accent explained.

Harper recognised the wide grin of Major Alexi Forssel and accepted the hot beverage. "Thank you."

Alexi had the honour of becoming a major by nothing other than default, as his homeland of Finland took a heavy hit during the outland invasion from over the Russian border. Less than five per cent of the Finnish armed forces remained, and even less of the population. The title of major was awarded to him by his countrymen, and he wore it with a reserved pride. Not because he thought he'd earned it but because those were the people he would die for.

In appearance, he reminded Harper of Ryan. Long blond hair, though not dreadlocked, very pale skin, intense eyes, though blue and not green. When not on duty, Alexi often wore a vest and baggy trousers, whatever the weather. If you didn't know he was a demolition expert, you could've easily mistaken him for the lead guitarist of a death metal band. Underneath his scruffy demeanour was a driven and focused patriot, determined to win back his country and rid the continent of the infestation that had burned it. His men had watched him in battle and listened to his orders, and he also proved vital when working with other infantry units—such as Harpers. Without Alexi's help, Harper and his team could've easily failed when it came to the defence of Rennes.

"Good to see you, Major," Harper said, standing and saluting.

"Don't salute me, sir." Alexi waved his hand. "You earned your title. I only have mine because of the fallen I now represent."

"It's still your title. Don't undermine it... sir."

"You're just as stubborn as Woodburn says."

"A trait I got from him," Harper pointed out, taking a sip of fresh coffee.

"I don't doubt," Alexi agreed, looking around the room and letting out a subtle but noticeable heavy breath.

"You okay, sir?" Harper asked.

"This is my first time leading a whole mission. Mixed nationalities, different platoons and ideals... and in a country I've never been to." Alexi huffed, then grinned. "After what those dickless fucks did to the hospital and good people here, I'm looking forward to blowing their associates' fucking faces off."

Harper stood motionless. Not in shock or offence but by the sheer steel balls the thirty-year-old had. He wouldn't be surprised if Alexi ran for president once the war was over.

They took their seats and held their notepads.

"Officer on site!" the staff sergeant called out, and everyone rose to attention.

"As you were." Woodburn motioned for everyone to sit and waited for everyone to settle before he sat against the desk and held the switch for the projector. "Ladies and gentlemen. This is the final chapter of our war. The last stain to wipe away before we can even begin to consider rebuilding what is left of Europe. I may be American, but our peers and governing board have placed me in command of both these operations. I expect full cooperation, not just with me, but with every leader of every different army fighting this battle. We are not separated by borders or ideals here. We are one, fighting a common enemy that has spread its influence from the United Kingdom to within our strongholds in the European Alliance and to our international allies of Brazil and Venezuela."

Woodburn clicked the button, and the first image appeared on the screen behind him. Harper felt his skin tighten around his muscles as the dead eyes on the screen stared back. The face of the man behind it all. Someone he'd served with before the war started.

Admiral George Caven. Hannah's dad.

Clean-shaven, dark grey buzz cut, dull brown eyes, and the noticeable crooked nose from the boxing tournaments he'd won in his late teens. Harper tried to block the good memories he had from serving with Admiral Caven. He couldn't fathom how this once-decent man transformed into the hostile, genocidal demon he'd become. Someone who took pleasure in killing his own countrymen if they didn't follow his newfound beliefs.

"Admiral Caven," Woodburn confirmed loudly for the conference, and a faint whisper of pencils scratching against paper whistled through the air. "Head of this new frontier for 'English Future'. This man is responsible for the capture and weaponisation of Kurustovia45 and its use for the 'Termite' army he's using to overpower pockets of survivors."

Woodburn clicked the projector button again. Another face pierced into Harper.

Connor.

Clean-shaven, rounded head. Dark blue eyes that burned like an exploding neutron star. Thin lips that looked like a sneer, no matter the facial expression. Harper had a small comfort that the photo was old, and now the left side of Connor's face was a twisted mesh of melted and reformed skin, with the left eye being completely sealed shut. A small gift from an encounter with Ryan.

"Admiral's next in command. Sergeant Connor Lovell. Make no mistake about it. This man will kill you just for seeing him. He's responsible for rounding up any survivors, and I mean any survivors— young and old. You've all heard the rumours, and they're all true. This man is the butcher of the human meat cattle."

A wave of flashbacks hit Harper in the heart, overloading his senses. He'd seen Connor's 'handiwork' with his own eyes and the lengths he would go to torment people with his actions. He rubbed the bridge of his nose and tried to focus, but the outright depravity hit back harder as the images were forever forged into his brain. The stench of barbecued flesh and bone and the smoke that overwhelmed from the fire. Ryan's unconscious body on the floor, bound to an armchair, and he had been forced to watch two of his friends be eaten in front of him.

At that time, Harper had stayed true to his training, managing to keep his feelings in check when bringing Connor in, but now it was truly digging his way into him. Not just for Connor's actions, but the fact he'd been extracted from their custody by someone from the inside... and that man's face was next to take up the screen.

Woodburn clicked the switch, and Monreal's face mocked them all. Straight blond hair cut with a fringe above the eyes, thick glasses, and a thin smile.

"Fucking Jeffrey Dahmer-looking motherfucker," Alexi whispered to himself.

"Tech Supervisor Fabian Monreal," Woodburn announced, looking over the room. "He's been working us from the inside on behalf of Admiral. He's been using unidentified, encrypted software to turn our own systems against us, manipulating security protocols to remain undetected. Monreal is the man responsible for the release of Sergeant Lovell and the rest of Admiral's team, bringing down a chopper with six of our own on board and supplying the attack on the hospital. We currently can't confirm his whereabouts due to the technology he has. If we find him in Liberia, he is to be brought in for trial and answer for his crimes." He paused. "All other targets are shoot to kill."

"How many men did Monreal help to escape?" a male voice called from somewhere to Harper's right.

"Ten, including Connor," Woodburn answered, continuing onto the next slide, showing the remaining mugshots of the men Monreal helped escape. "The other nine escapees are members of a splinter group that consists of former British military. S.A.S. Royal Marines. Navy. Their loyalty is to Admiral under the codename 'Project Zodiac', and their objectives have yet to have been identified."

He moved to another slide, an aerial view of the west coast of Africa.

"Our offensive on the Liberian jungle will be led by me. Our goal is to get in and get out with all targets either detained, or neutralised. Force is only used to incapacitate them, but if the situation calls for it, you have absolute authority to put these pieces of shit out of commission permanently. You have all seen your squads and team listings." Woodburn stood at the front with his arms behind his back. "This mission goes under the codename 'Operation Catfish'."

Leaders of the respective units were heard scribbling on their notepads. Woodburn continued, listing the leaving dates and points of interest. He reminded everyone not to even try to speculate on Admiral's reason for heading to Liberia in the first place and that Chinese whispers would do more harm than good.

Harper knew some of the absurd conspiracies regarding Admiral's pilgrimage to Africa, ranging from identity-altering plastic surgery to raising an army from within the Liberian jungle. Admiral wouldn't stay at the equator forever, and his detest for third-world countries had been highlighted many times.

"I'm now going to pass over to newly promoted Major Forssel," Woodburn announced, nodding for Alexi to join him. "He'll be leading the second offensive in the Hebrides."

Alexi stood, stepping slowly up to the podium. "Thank you, General." He appeared whiter than normal. Harper thought it could've been the lighting, but underneath Alexi's cool veneer, he seemed nervous for his first led mission. "I'll be leading the second operation, codenamed 'Wolf Pack'. Our target area is an island in the Outer Hebrides, West Scotland. This is the holding site for Admiral's followers and their captives... ready for slaughter." He looked across the room. "Our teams and units consist of all remaining Scandinavian and Baltic infantry. We travel by air, refuelling in our stronghold in Sheffield, North England. Once we land at the Isle of Skye, we travel by boat, docking on the shores of North Uist."

More pencils scribbling on paper.

"We leave two days after Operation Catfish, only embarking on North Uist once we have confirmation from Woodburn that stage one of Catfish has been successful." Alexi nodded to Woodburn. "Wolfpack's invasion comes as a surprise, and we know the hills that Admiral's followers have themselves hidden under."

The slideshow changed, showing a cluster of excavators and diggers on a coastline. "This collection of heavy-duty construction equipment was found off the western coast of Southern Uist. The Outer Hebrides' most southern island. It seems that when they abandoned their first subbase in Milton Keynes, they took their equipment to dig themselves a new home. This is how they avoided our thermal drone scans for the past year," Alexi announced while his eyes darkened. "As you all have heard, they have an army of sub-servants. These 'Termites' have no regard for their own safety. They don't need guns—they will take you down in other ways without thinking of their own lives. We are outnumbered but not outgunned. When it comes to the Termites, our orders are shoot to kill. We don't know how many captives or hostages we're going to have to extract, so this is both an eliminate and rescue mission."

"Timing is key on this, folks," Woodburn said, approaching the front. "None of this goes ahead until Catfish has landed on the Liberian beach. The callsign will be *Omaha*. You all have your files. I suggest you study them with what time we have left. Catfish leaves in two days. Happy hunting."

## 15

R ook snuck back through the fire exit and into the apartment block, hastily making his way upstairs and unlocking the door to his apartment. His brief questioning of Mrs Gregorzk had revealed something of relevance to the situation but also a glimmer into just how far Admiral's claws went into the European Alliance.

He left the door open as he ruffled through the drawer by his desk, looking for the list of perpetrators of the hospital attack—another valuable piece of intel Eliza had acquired for him. He scanned the names of all who had been either killed or detained at the end of it all.

"Steaming Jesus," he whispered, folding the paper and placing it inside his jacket pocket. Mrs Gregorzk hadn't been lying, and every name on the list had come out of her mouth. They all had one thing in common—they all worked at the docks, where shipments were sent or received from the other ports along the coasts of northern and western Europe. With Monreal's untraceable tech, they could move anything within the European Alliance without detection. There could be more uncounted or phantom weapons moving between ports at this very second, ready to supply the next attack.

This information had to be kept under the radar, but there were two people who had to be aware of this. Rook drank what was left of his now cold coffee and left his apartment, knocking on Mikey and Jen's door. The door creaked as Jen peeked through the opening, then she removed the chain and let him in. Mikey pulled himself up from his sleeping position and carefully rested his injured foot on the coffee table.

"So," Rook started, sliding the piece of paper over to the couple, "Mrs Gregorzk doesn't exactly talk the best English. She did confirm that her husband and his friends were approached during their shifts on the docks. The names she gave match the ones on this list."

Mikey gave the list a puzzling glance. "What's this list?"

"That's the list of men who pulled off the hospital shooting," Rook confirmed. "All ten of them are dock workers and her husband's friends."

"So, you think they were recruited down at the docks?" Jen added.

"Unfortunately, it makes too much sense... and that's not even the worst of it." Rook paused, knowing what he would say might send Mikey off the rails. "Besides the fact they could be transporting undocumented weapons in or out, the docking station they work at is where the medical or chemical supplies come in from Brugge... which also happens to be where the serum for Kurustovia is being produced. They've had undocumented access to the shit."

"How would Monreal convince these guys to steal it?"

"The same way he convinced them to shoot up a hospital and come after you. He's either got something they want or has promised them something." Rook sat forward and said, "Also worth mentioning, when I showed Mrs Gregorzk the photo and called him Monreal, she referred to him as *officer man*."

"Officer? I thought Monreal was a tech supervisor?"

"He is."

"So he's pretending to be someone higher up?" Jen asked. "Gives them a sense of security that someone with authority will help them."

"Could be the case." Rook stroked his chin, then rubbed his eyes.

"What's the next step?"

"Other than Lukas in the cell, the only other leads we have to any of Monreal's movements is maybe the body we found last week. It's a long shot, but if we can identify who it is, something might come up that gets us closer to bringing the fucker in."

"What are you going to do if you do find him?" Mikey asked, handing over the pistol.

"Well, I'd love to turn his face into waffles," Rook said, taking the weapon, "but we don't know if he's the only person Admiral has got to. If he does have more on the inside, I can't risk them getting spooked and going into hiding. As for Monreal, I'll bleed every bit of information from him until there's nothing left."

———

A thundering vibration woke Rook in an instant, and he shot up from the bed and snatched the smart radio as it hummed against the empty mug on his bedside table, answering the call.

"You know my sleeping hours are three till seven," he huffed, pulling his socks on.

"Good evening to you, too," the female voice replied in a strong Bavarian accent. Eliza knew all too well when his daily personal time was, but her tone was clear that this was a professional call. "I was just calling to let you know that Monreal's workstation, including his terminal, was searched again."

"Any sign of the software he was using?"

"No. Everything was clean."

"Dammit." Rook sighed and asked, "Anything else?"

"Your friends Woodburn and Harper were here to oversee it," Eliza reported and hesitated before adding more. "They just had the briefing for the upcoming operations. Harper looked shaken up. He's coming to see you on his way back. He said he'd be an hour."

"I'll get the coffee on then. Thank you for the heads up. See you tomorrow?"

"Only if you've tidied the place." She hung up.

Rook switched the lamp on and looked around his bedroom. Clothes sprawled everywhere, and unwashed bowls of wheat flakes and banana skins cluttered his chest of drawers. "Even at the world's end, women can still moan," he joked to himself, pulling on his boxer shorts.

He had fifteen minutes before his alarm would've gone off, so he used the extra time to tidy and hoover, though leaving the crockery in the sink until he had a few spare minutes the next morning. Once he was happy with the minor tidying, he finished getting dressed and armed himself, locking his apartment door as he left.

His early evening ritual consisted of checking in with the guards at the front desk and then inspecting every door, window, exit, and entrance. Once he'd gone through his checklist, his next duty was to make sure the three apartments he was responsible for were okay. Harper's family and Mikey and Jen were fine for supplies, making Rook's life easier with not having to place an order with the asshole that was once his designated handler. The same guy who delayed the response time during the hospital attack.

Rook spent more time than usual in Steph's room. She was unrecognisable from how he first met her. The weight she'd lost from being bedbound was scary, even to someone like him, who'd found captives throughout the war and had no other alternative than to eat the dead. Her hair was as pale as her skin, and even the green glint in her eyes had somewhat faded.

This condition would remain permanent unless she began to eat properly or find a reason to live again. Her stare was void of any such drive, as if she was begging the ceiling to fall on her at that very instant. She wanted death.

Rook checked her room before leaving, making sure her restraints were tight—a job he hated more than he could've ever thought. Steph was, as described by Ryan, someone who had taught him the ways to keep pushing forward no matter what life threw at you, now spending every waking minute wishing it would end.

There were very few things that managed to get under his skin, but every time Rook had to close and lock the door on Steph, there was a gnawing feeling that he was helping pound her into her own hell every time. He shut his eyes as the lock clicked, only imagining how Ryan would react when he was finally told about everything that had happened.

The main man at Penbrook Vineyard wasn't the most physically impos-
ing. Even Rook knew he could take him down if an altercation happened
between the pair, but Ryan had that one thing about him that bought
unpredictability and wrath. A one-on-one fight with Ryan, fine. Hurting
those close to him? You better hide in the darkest corner of the planet.

Harper's voice echoed from the reception as he greeted the guards,
followed by his boots treading up the stairs. The lieutenant rounded
the corner to the hallway, eyes tired but narrow. "How is everyone?" he
asked, brushing the snow off his coat.

"Your son burns through energy at a rate that would've made the
Chinese blush," Rook replied honestly. "Think your wife is considering
getting him a cage for the daytime."

Harper smirked, knowing what a terror Troy could be. "His sister
used to be the same. I never had to do morning workouts with her
running around the place." He unzipped his coat and folded it in his
arms. "Have you got a few minutes later? We've been given the brief."

"Yes, sir."

Rook offered Harper a chair in his living room and poured them both a
coffee, sitting on the armchair opposite the coffee table. "When do
you ship out?" he asked.

"Morning after tomorrow," Harper answered, pulling the cup to his
mouth. "We're taking a chopper to the last of our aircraft carriers."

"The U.S.S Gavato?"

"She's currently anchored in the Bay of Biscay. It'll be two days
until we reach Liberian seas, then two days until we launch the operation. Once we've landed ashore, the operation in Scotland will be initi-
ated, which is being led by Alexi."

"The Finnish kid?"

"He's thirty now."

"And when the war started, he was only twenty-three," Rook
pointed out, visibly confused by the decision to place someone so
young in charge.

"Woodburn went through the process thoroughly," Harper
explained. "Alexi has more credentials and awards for bravery than any

of the Scandinavian officers. When his seniors were killed in battle, Alexi took charge and guided his men to safety and, in the case of Brugges, victory. Have you seen those men around him when the shit hits the fan? He pretty much turns them into Vikings. Even I witnessed it."

"And even you know he's not major material yet? Granted, one day, maybe, but not now."

"No, he's not," Harper admitted, "and Alexi didn't want that title. It was given to him by those men he saved. When the European Army is finalised after these operations, then he'll be designated a more suitable title."

Rook sat back and rubbed his forehead. Though he felt bound to protect these people in the apartment block, this was one operation he really wanted to be part of. "Woodburn signed off on Alexi?" he asked.

"Ever since the French's fuck up for blaming you with Monreal's doings, he's really put his foot down, and shit is actually getting done. You should see the governing board. French, Polish, and Danish ministers are practically bowing to him."

"The man is efficient," Rook agreed, though visibly at a disagreement with the idea of putting a thirty-year-old in charge of a wide-scale operation. "Who's staying behind for this one? We still have refugees and survivors we need to maintain order over."

"You'll have Woodburn's Hungarian sector providing security and order. You know them, they don't fuck around, especially if Monreal tries to get another attack to kick off again."

Rook felt a bit more relaxed with that news. The Hungarian armed forces were monsters in the field and took whatever commands they had seriously. They were the only security unit he trusted after seeing them on duty in the reception.

Harper finished his coffee and placed it on the table, eyeing the small satellite-dish-looking piece of equipment on Rook's window ledge. "What's that?"

"Something I got from a friend in a secret place." Rook winked, pulling a laptop from under the stack of magazines and opening it. The screen displayed four separate live feeds, covering the front, rear, rooftop, and fire escape of the apartment block. "They record in forty-eight-hour feeds. Just another layer for security."

"Did Eliza sneak you that?"

"That obvious?"

"Well, I know it definitely wasn't the French," Harper remarked, sitting back in the chair and keeping his eyes on the screen. He rubbed his chin like he was thinking out loud. "Could she get any more of those devices?"

"Possibly." Rook shrugged, closing the laptop. "What for?"

"Ryan. He's going to be on edge when all of this is going on. If he can have some security, it might help him keep his shit together."

"How will you get it to him?"

"I've asked Alexi to stop over on his way to Sheffield just to update Ryan. He can make the transfer then."

Rook felt his heart skip a beat. "What happens when Ryan asks how everything is?"

Harper huffed, rubbing his hands nervously. "For everyone's sake, I'm going to ask Alexi to lie."

# 16

---

Harper kissed his family goodbye while they slept on the pull-out sofa bed, not wanting to wake them up for a teary farewell before he left. He switched off the DVD player, which had been playing the main menu's fifteen-second loop for hours.

He'd made the most of his last day with them, refusing to let the usual nerves and anxious chatter get in the way of their family time in front of the fireplace while playing board games. He'd already ventured into the unknown enough times and for longer periods. Granted, this was against soldiers he'd once served with, but with Woodburn at the helm of Operation Catfish, there was only one outcome from all this. This was the end of this war, and no one would get in his way.

Harper left an envelope-enclosed letter on the side table and quietly left the apartment, making it to the car waiting out front for him.

"Mind telling me why you requested my ass pick you up at this God-forsaken hour of the morning when we already have a contingent of drivers on standby?" Alexi asked loudly from the front seat, turning round and showing his near maniacal eyes.

"Morning, Major," Harper said with a grin. "There was a reason I wanted you." He pulled out a small case and lifted it into the passenger front seat.

"What's that?"

"It's a small surveillance device I want you to drop off to Ryan."

"Will he know how to use it?"

"Drinker is with him. He knows how to use it."

"Drinker? Well, fuck me in a vodka bottle. I'm looking forward to seeing that fuckwit." Alexi started driving to the airport. "How did he handle adapting back to civilian life?"

"Last time I saw him, he'd settled in well with his new community. Though he did say that under the surface, it was like he was still at war. There's no escaping it."

"Ain't that the truth, sir." Alexi nodded, pulling up to the airport's front entrance. "Well, this is where we part ways. Try not to get too sunburnt in Africa. I'll see you on the other side, sir!" Alexi said and saluted.

"Will do, Major." Harper playfully mocked and saluted back, closing the passenger door.


During the two-hour wait before take-off, Operation Catfish was organised into its respective squads, with Harper leading Team Alpha. His uniform had his callsign, *Alpha One,* stitched onto both the left breast pocket and right arm.

Harper used the time to get familiar with his squad, identifying everyone by their own callsigns. During the weapons check, they exchanged their own stories of fighting and survival during the war. Amongst all seven teams, eighty-four would be heading on foot into Liberia.

There was no clear indicator that Admiral had recruited any of the Liberian populace into his ranks or if the war between druglords still raged across the oceanside capital, Monrovia. All Operation Catfish had to go on was the intel they found aboard the Venezuelan cargo ship, which pointed to two compounds in the jungle off the port of Cape Palmas, Southern Liberia.

Cape Palmas. The last official mission Harper had with the US

Marines Corps before the collapse. Three years before the war started, Liberia was considered to be the fourth poorest country in the world before a huge economic boom from an unknown source.

In every tabloid photo, a young Islamic Russian named Aslan was seen shaking hands with the country's political leaders while opening hospitals and drug rehabilitation centres for a high percentage of the population that were jobless addicts. He didn't come across with malicious intent with the work he was doing in the country, but that would all change in no time.

The release of a video that set the war into motion was traced back to an IP address in Cape Palmas. The video showed the inside job that would lead to 9/11, and the very reveal of that act would turn America on itself, sparking the flame that would burn the country.

Harper and Woodburn were assigned to SAS Task Force 205, which included Admiral and Connor, to bring Aslan in and disprove the video's credit. After attempting an assault on Aslan's mansion, the chase led Harper north to Gibraltar, where he lost contact with Admiral, and then the bombs started exploding on April 24th of that year. Everything after that was its own hell, and now Admiral had gone back to where it all started.

"Full circle," Harper said to himself, keeping his eyes on the map of Liberia.

The first Chinook powered up on the runway, and both blades thumped cold air into the hangar.

"Alpha and Bravo teams, you're up!" Woodburn shouted, clapping his hands together. Both squads got into formation and jogged cautiously onto the snow-covered tarmac. Harper zipped up his overalls and pulled on his heavy jacket, following the teams out towards the boarding ramp. One of the corporals saved him a seat on the right side, and Woodburn took the one opposite. He pulled on the headset piece and switched on the comms unit. Once everyone was on board, the ramp closed slowly, and the cargo space was dimly lit under a red light.

*"Alright, gentlemen of Operation Catfish,"* the pilot said over the comms. *"I'll be your captain for the day. It's about three hours until we reach the U.S.S Gavato. Please make sure your chairs are in the upright position and*

*your baggage is under your chair. If you have any complaints about my flying, feel free to leave a complaint at idontfuckingcare@suckmyballs.com."*

The Chinook rose and banked slowly to the right. Harper pictured the city below as they ascended, picking up speed once they reached cruising altitude. He shared one final moment of thinking about his family and the day they spent together, then shook it from his mind. They would be in good hands with Rook, and now wasn't the time to worry. It was about the mission now.

"I hear you've already been to Liberia, sir?" the corporal next to Harper asked.

"Only briefly," he answered. "Our target moved out quickly once he heard we were on his trail."

"Also heard some of the guys you went with are the same guys we're going after now?"

"That's affirmative, Corporal," Harper confirmed, glancing back at Woodburn. "I can tell you now, though, they're not the same men we once shared bread with."

"I don't think anyone's the same since all this, sir," the corporal added before pulling his helmet down over his eyes and leaning back, trying to catch a few hours' sleep before they embarked on the aircraft carrier.

Woodburn raised his eyebrows and smirked at the brief conversation before signalling that all the other men had taken it on themselves to get some extra sleep. "We used to do the same," he reminisced.

"Iraq and Afghanistan were totally different," Harper reminded him.

"You're right," Woodburn agreed. "This is much worse."

# 17

"What do you mean the cooling unit has malfunctioned?" Rook anxiously repeated the information he'd just been told over the smart radio. The sudden call from the medical examiner had brought the worst news possible with it. The morgue's chill units had malfunctioned during the early hours of the morning, and the only body that remained after the mass burial of the hospital shooting victims had decomposed. The body of the unidentified murder victim who had washed up at Mont St Michael was useless.

"I wish there was more I could tell you. One of the cooling units could've burned out after Health Minister Eriksen oversaw the transport of the hospital victims," the examiner said softly. "I have to deal with this mess now."

"Shit!" Rook said under a heavy breath. "Sorry, Doc, didn't mean to take it out on you." He hung up and dropped the device onto his sofa, treading softly back into his bedroom and sat on the end of the bed.

"You know, most men aren't this tense after a two-hour session of lovemaking," Eliza said as she sat up, running her hand down his bare chest from behind.

"Well, that's an upgrade," he said, kissing her hand. "Last week, you said we were only *fucking*."

"Don't mix my words," she demanded coldly. "What was the call about?"

"The freezers in the morgue have gone down. The body is pretty much decomposed soup on the floor now."

"Gross."

"Yeah. Poor bastard has to mop it up." He sighed, pulling his combat pants on. "And now I can't find out who was on Monreal's case."

"Maybe not from the corpse itself," Eliza said, hinting at more information. She pulled the duvet up to cover herself and added, "But there are other ways to find out who it is."

"How? Monreal has played around with the M.I.A list. I can't find out who's missing and who isn't."

"Not from our database, no, but you can use other sources to find out who this person could be."

"I'm listening," Rook said, pulling his long-sleeved T-shirt on and tying his hair back into a ponytail.

"You said that Monreal had recruited those Polish men from the docks?" she said, lighting a cigarette.

"Smoking after sex? And I'm cliché?"

"Shut up and listen. One group of people we don't keep in our database is the Navy whenever they're docked. That stays with the captain of the ship and his manifest. I'd say, given that they were transporting a biological weapon in testing, that someone caught onto where the shipments were going and confronted Monreal."

"You think the body could be one of the Navy?"

"It would make sense why no one has been reported missing on our end."

"Wouldn't there be some kind of record with the Navy?"

"Most likely. I can contact the HQ in Brugges tomorrow if you like?"

"Why do I feel like this is a trade?"

"It is a trade. You let me sleep here tonight, and I'll make the call tomorrow. If not, you can wait a couple of days."

He could only admire her negotiation skills, and after everything she'd done for him before, he was at a conversational disadvantage. "Okay, deal." He pulled his boots on. "Just don't use all my hot water allowance." Rook left the apartment and immediately heard the shower start running from inside. "For fuck's sake," he said aloud, then laughed internally.

His usual checks on the three rooms were uneventful and standard, though he opted to spend a bit more time than usual with Harper's family, considering it was their first night alone since he'd deployed for Operation Catfish.

It wasn't until midnight that the reception guard shift swapped out, and Rook performed his checks on the building, securing all windows and doors. It wasn't until he got to the top floor that he saw the exit wide open, with a stone jammed in the hinge to keep it from closing.

Rook drew his pistol and checked around, with no snowy footprints leading inside. He gazed outside and saw a set of smaller footprints pressed into the snow, leading out onto the open rooftop. To his surprise, Harper's daughter was the small person standing in the middle of the open space, gazing upwards.

"Katie?" he asked, putting his pistol away. "Are you okay?"

She turned to face him, her eyes teary. "Sorry. I know I shouldn't be here," she said and sobbed. "It's just what I do when Dad goes away."

"Hey, hey. It's okay." He approached, hands out in defence. "I know it must be hard."

"He always says that while he's gone, we'll still be under the same stars."

"He's right, you know?"

"And he's always gone," Katie said, wiping her eyes. "I'm always looking at the stars."

"Explains your fascination with sci-fi novels," Rook thought out loud, then realised it was loud enough for Katie to hear. His eyes nearly bulged out of his face in embarrassment, and he felt himself turning red. "I'm sorry. I didn't mean anything bad by it."

"It's okay," she said with a slight cackle. "They're shit books anyway."

He didn't know how to respond to her swearing and mentally

cursed himself for being more awkward around a twelve-year-old girl than he was around gunfire. "I won't tell your dad you said that," he said. "Listen, Katie. I can't have you up here—"

"I was just leaving," Katie said, cutting him off. "Please, don't tell Mom I was up here."

"No, not that. Stop," Rook enforced, empathising with her situation. "Look, I'll make you a deal. You can come up here every night until your father gets back, but only for five minutes a time and while I'm guarding you." He offered his hand. "Deal?"

Katie hesitated, then reached out and agreed. "Deal."

Rook guided her back inside and locked the rooftop exit, mocking himself for having to make two deals with women inside the space of five hours. After helping Katie sneak back inside, he checked in on Eliza, who was now asleep, and made himself a coffee.

He spent the next couple of hours with the laptop open, observing the screens that displayed the outside of the building. His quiet shift broke with the ringing of Eliza's alarm, and a few short minutes later, she was fully dressed and ready to leave.

"Don't forget your end of the deal!" he called out, sipping from his cup as she left. He took himself back to the open kitchen and started cooking himself some eggs and bacon, keeping an eye on the screen and the guards who were caught off by the unexpected female leaving the property. He cut himself a thick wedge of bread and added it to the plate, then sat at the coffee table, his eyes drawn to the camera overlooking the back exit. A hooded figure stood in plain view, waving at the camera.

Rook leaned in, trying to make out who the person was. He left his breakfast, grabbed his gun and hastily made his way down to the exit, opening quickly and aiming the weapon at the stranger.

"That how you treat majors in America?" Alexi asked cockily, removing his hood.

"Alexi? Fuck man, what are you doing sneaking around? And don't call yourself a major. I know you don't even like that title."

"Well, I agree with you on that."

"How did you know about the camera?"

"Harper told me. After all, it was you who got the other device that

I've been asked to sneak to someone in England." Alexi shrugged dismissively and asked, "May I come in?"

Rook frowned, not happy that someone else knew what surveillance he was running, but relented and replied, "Sure."

The two entered his apartment, and Alexi poured himself a cup of coffee without adding sugar or milk.

"What can I do for you, *Major?*" Rook snorted, offering him a seat.

"I leave tonight," Alexi said, getting straight to the point. "As you know, I'm making a quick stop at this vineyard place. I've heard a bit about it and of the main man, Ryan. How can I know he's not going to open fire on us when we land?"

"To be fair, you don't. He threatened to kill me if I hurt his family the first time I met him. You should hope that Drinker is there to help identify you."

"And if he's not? Can't I contact him before?"

"The internet signal has been jammed over their coordinates." Rook shook his head, then clicked his fingers. "But they do have a set of short-wave radios. Fifty-mile range. You can let him know you're coming beforehand. There is always someone on watch, so even if Ryan isn't on duty, they can let him know."

"Okay," Alexi huffed nervously. "I don't fancy being killed by a civilian before my first operation even starts. Even if I deserve the responsibility or not."

"You'll be fine, man. I've heard a lot about how your men look up to you, and even if you aren't officially a major right now, you will be one day."

"Thanks. I have Danish Minister Eriksen to thank for throwing that title on me, at the request of Woodburn, of course."

"Don't involve me in any of that politics shit," Rook said as he stood. "That's not my game. Just stick to your training and everything you know. You've got a full squad behind you that believe in you. Get the mission done and get back."

"I will, and thank you, Rook." Alexi saluted, which was returned. "Any idea which channel Ryan's radio might be on before I attempt contacting him?"

"Not a clue. I'd go through them all before he blows you out of the sky."

Alexi laughed and left, giving Rook enough time to finish his breakfast before performing his early morning security checks. Another day of security and another day of watching the screens.

———

Inside the roaring Chinook, Alexi stood as the chopper began its descent onto what had been identified as Penbrook Vineyard. The pilot confirmed a flare had been dispatched to signal where to land. Alexi considered that a good sign, as he hadn't been able to establish contact with anyone on the ground.

The landing gear touched the ground, and the ramp slowly opened. Alexi told his men not to even think about raising their weapons unless fired upon. It was counterintuitive to everything he was trained in, but after everything Harper had done for him in the past, this was a favour that he needed to repay.

In front of Alexi stood a man, weapon by his side. Blond dreadlocks tied back, green eyes that appeared to glow in the dark. Those same eyes narrowed in, and the man raised his gun, pointing it straight at Alexi.

"Who the fuck are you?" Ryan demanded.

# 18

nother figure ran out from the winery's front entrance, weapon raised as they joined Ryan by the side. Alexi held his arms out and slowly stepped down the ramp.

"Alexi?" the Scottish voice asked, and Drinker removed his hood.

Alexi heaved a heavy breath and smiled. "Yeah. It's me, old friend."

"You know this guy?" Ryan asked, not taking his aim away.

"Me and Harper fought with him," Drinker explained before turning back to Alexi. "What's all this?"

"Lieutenant Harper asked me to stop over on the way and drop this off to you," he said, keeping calm and taking the bag off his shoulder, then holding it in front of himself.

"What is it?" Ryan asked forcefully, slowly stepping forward.

"It's an AnCam Surveillance system," Alexi explained, then switched back to Drinker, "like the ones we used to hold Rotterdam's ports."

"What's it for?" Ryan asked, leading the conversation.

"Harper wanted to help ease your nerves while the operations were underway. We still can't establish an internet signal for your area, so he wanted to offer this to give you more security until it's all over."

"What's all over?"

Alexi smirked, unsure if Ryan was just stubborn or truly untrusted everything. Either way, it was clear he was going to have to be told outright. "You see the direction all these choppers are headed?" He pointed to the sky. "We're going to the Hebrides. We're going to finish off Admiral's men."

What appeared to be a small flicker of hope ran across Ryan's stare before it hardened again. "Do you trust this man, Drinker?"

"I do."

"Do you trust what's in the bag?"

Drinker approached, taking it from Alexi and examining the contents. A laptop, four small cameras, and a portable satellite radar. "It's exactly what he says it is."

Ryan stood still for several seconds, then slowly lowered his rifle. "Your friends with Harper?"

"I consider myself to be." Alexi smiled and hoped he looked sincere.

"Do you know how my sister and friends are?"

Alexi was expecting the question and managed to keep the same friendly look on his face. "They're fine," he lied. "You can see them all once this is over."

Ryan's eyes softened, and a small smile appeared. "Thank you." He laughed, looking at his gun. "Sorry for all that."

"You can apologise by giving me some of that wine when this is done," Alexi replied, holding his confidence, even though he'd just lied to someone who thirty seconds ago was ready to kill him. He clicked the receiver on his comms unit. "*Eagle One*, we're ready to proceed to Sheffield."

"*Copy that, Atom One,*" the pilot replied, and the blades started up almost instantly.

"Good to see you, my friend!" Alexi saluted to Drinker.

"Aye! Good luck," Drinker shouted above the roar.

"Thank you!" Ryan added as the ramp door closed.

Alexi held onto the railing as the chopper ascended, feeling his shoulders relax as they continued their voyage north. He turned back to his squad, most of whom had resumed catching up on sleep, apart from his lieutenant, who caught Alexi's eye.

"That's the guy, isn't it?" Lieutenant Iversen asked. "The guy who saw two of his friends eaten in front of him?"

"What gave that away, Lieutenant?"

"The look in those eyes. That's a look of someone close to cracking."

"I saw that too," Alexi agreed, wondering just what Ryan might do if he found out Alexi lied and Harper wasn't there to explain why. *Harper, I think you fucking owe me one now.*

## 19

"Okay. Get this," Eliza announced, pushing past Rook and into his apartment. She waved a bit of paper around and placed it on the coffee table. "I spoke to the captain of the Brugges transport ship, and when I bought up their shipments of Kurustovia, he wasn't aware of any shipments before two months ago. Which means it was being smuggled in before that."

"When did they start working on a cure?"

Eliza first lit a cigarette and then said, "Five months ago, after Connor was bought in. And the first successful testing wasn't confirmed until two months ago in Brugge's laboratory, by the order of Danish Health Minister Eriksen."

"So, the first documented Kurustovia antidote was officially shipped here two months ago?" Rook said out loud. "But how did Monreal know all the smuggled prototypes prior to that would be effective in contamination?"

"He didn't until they had human test subjects. Someone who volunteered to show their devotion to Admiral."

"The twins."

"Precisely," she carried on. "After it was proved effective, they shipped more under the radar to infect the people at the vineyard."

"Is it possible that someone on board the captain's ship discovered this and tried to uncover it? Monreal had them killed?"

"The captain hasn't had any missing men or accidents for two years. Our mystery body isn't one of his."

"Goddammit!"

"But there is some good news, followed by bad news."

"Let's hear it."

"There was a report of a container of yarn that went missing five months ago. The same time Monreal is suspected to have got his hands on the Kurustovia prototype. The captain believes that this missing yarn is most likely what the prototype was hidden in. The bad news about this is, the size of that crate could hold tenfold more Kurustovia than we recovered after the twins gave up their stash."

"So, there's more out there?"

"A lot more, but when I checked the inventory for that delivery, there was one unexpected name who signed off on it."

"Who?"

"Danish Health Minister Eriksen."

"You gotta be fucking kidding me?" Rook almost gasped, taking the shipment invoice. "Looks like I need to pay our health minister a visit then."

"Hold on there, cowboy," Eliza warned. "You're already jumping to conclusions on this. That particular cargo trade consisted of medical supplies, and it would only make sense that she showed face and signed off on it."

"Or maybe Monreal got to her and made sure she got the package in safe and undetected."

"Well, even if that is the case, you go poking around Health Minister Eriksen, Monreal would know you're getting closer. Start listening to your brain instead of your heart."

Rook let Eliza sleep while he occasionally glanced at the laptop monitor, jotting notes down on the pad in between them. His thoughts raced as he tried to compile all the events over the previous months into one picture.

1.  First untracked shipment of Kurustovia, signed off by Eriksen. Five months ago.
2.  Monreal declared M.IA/goes rogue. Three months ago.
3.  Twins manage to infect Rich and Mikey with Kurustovia prototype.
4.  Mikey is brought over to Rennes, and Eriksen signed off on the first approved batch of Kurustovia. Two months ago.
5.  Monreal helps Connor and Project Zodiac escape. His location is still unknown.
6.  A body with a military uniform is discovered. Two or three months submerged decomp. Definite murder and attempt to hide identity. Still unknown.
7.  Hospital attack. Polish dock workers having access to weapons and Kurustovia. Monreal identified as *officer man.*

Hours faded through the night, and Rook couldn't piece anything together that would give away Monreal's hiding spot. The thought that the prime suspect had actually vanished with Project Zodiac was very much a possibility, but that wouldn't explain how he'd managed to cut all communications with the vineyard over the last two weeks or pulled the strings for the hospital attack.

*Is he still here? Or does he have a helping hand?*

The mystery body was now a dead end, and the attempt to follow the untracked Kurustovia prototype was moot. Rook's thoughts darted back to the communication block on the vineyard. For Monreal to achieve this, he had to have access to an electrical port and be close enough to the Rennes wireless signal, narrowing down the field that he had to operate in.

Monreal's private quarters were in the airport, like all the other tech supervisors in the comms room, but it had already been cleared, swept for bugs, and turned over by the security after the breach to the prisoner corridor had happened. There had been no sign of Monreal for months. It was like the man had just vanished whenever he needed to.

Rook reread the list of events again, and only one other name stood out to him. Someone who was nearby, with authority, and had been on sight when the prototype went under the radar.

Danish Health Minister Naomi Eriksen. *No one can be trusted.*

## 20

After a long two days at sea, the time had come for Operation Catfish to deploy.

With the U.S.S. Gavato anchored two miles off-shore, Team Charlie had used hypersonic remote-control drones to scan the thick forest behind Cape Palmas, identifying the two compounds hidden at five and twelve miles into the jungle. Even with the low resolution, Team Charlie clearly made out the men wearing grey T-shirts and black pants. It was the trademarked uniform of Admiral's men.

There was a heavy knock on Harper's chamber door. "Two minutes, Lieutenant," the first officer shouted from the other side.

Harper loaded the magazine into his standard-issue M4 assault rifle. He lay the weapon in his bunk, tightened his tactical vest and helmet, and lastly, pulled his backpack on his shoulders. He knew he had everything required for this mission after checking at least six times over the last hour. He left his room and marched through the thin, low-ceilinged corridors of the ship, focused and in the zone. He stepped onto the deck where the soldiers of Operation Catfish were waiting and stood next to his squad. The Atlantic winds hit hard with a deceiving chill, and the full moon lit up everyone.

Teams Alpha, Bravo, Charlie, and Delta were to head in by foot to the first compound, with teams Echo, Fox, and Gundam to be called in for assistance should they encounter heavy resistance fire. It wasn't a tactic Harper was used to, but then again, everything was new to him as systems and protocols were reconfigured to suit the new world.

Harper led Alpha and climbed down the netting into their raft first, then switched on his body camera and braced as the engine pushed the boat against the waves. The bumpy journey took ten minutes, giving the salty air and standard pre-operation nerves enough time to dry his throat out as they bounced towards the shore.

As the dingy approached, the signal was given to disembark. With their rifles raised and night vision goggles down, they pushed through the waist-high water and onto the sand. Teams Bravo, Charlie, and Delta followed sharply, and all forty-eight men scanned along the treeline.

"Catfish Actual, this is Alpha One," Harper said into his shoulder-mounted radio.

"*Go ahead, Alpha One,*" Woodburn replied.

"We're on the shore. Send word to Wolfpack to wait for our signal."

"*Copy that.*"

The jungle teemed with all kinds of life as they silently pushed through the thickness. Harper focused on the laser attachment of his rifle while maintaining their steady pace, trying to establish any voices beyond the blanket of animal, bird, and insect callouts that polluted the night-time silence.

"*Alpha One, this is Bravo One.*"

"Go ahead, Bravo One," Harper answered soft and clear into his mouthpiece.

"*We've reached the perimeter of the first target. No tangos at the watchtower.*"

"Copy that," Harper confirmed, signalling for his team to continue.

Two minutes later, they reached a clearing. Harper held his fist in the air, and his team came to an immediate stop. Two empty watch towers looked over three separate buildings, all of which looked like the lovechild of a warehouse and industrial factory. Corrugated walls, tin roofs and a large, dry-stone chimney each.

"Alpha in position," Harper reported.

*"Bravo in position."*

*"Delta in position."*

*"Charlie in position."*

"Move in," Harper ordered, and they shifted steadily along the thick grass.

Team Alpha infiltrated the first building, breaching through the back double doors and into a flimsily built corridor of dry walls.

"Clear," Harper called as he swept the room to his immediate left. He felt a hand carefully squeeze his right shoulder, the silent signal for, *'I'm moving past you now'*, as Alpha pushed further inside.

"Clear!" Alpha Two called after sweeping the next room. The process repeated all the way through the school-like building until they reached a huge storage space, not too dissimilar from the hangars at Rennes. Harper secured the bottom floor as the rest of Alpha climbed the stairs and checked the metal walkways that encircled the above open space.

Harper waited for confirmation from his team before talking into his mouthpiece. "Bravo, Charlie, Delta, this is Alpha One. Our building is tango free."

The other squads replied with the same results. It was like no one had been here or had been tipped off.

"Goddammit," Harper cursed. "Catfish Actual, this is Alpha One. The place is deserted."

*"Say again, Alpha One,"* Woodburn replied, clearly frustrated.

"I repeat, it's deserted. They're gone," he said, scanning the walls and locating the power source. "Bravo, Charlie, Delta. We've located a generator, powering on. Eyes up." He waited for confirmation and lifted his night vision, pulling the lever. A few lights cracked and burst as the machine rumbled before lighting up. The compound's perimeter spotlights flickered on, illuminating the space between the buildings. Smoke arose from the middle of the compound's grounds, coming out from the earth.

"All teams, we have a potential fire hazard coming from the

compound's central point," Harper said into his radio. "Looks like they've tried to burn evidence before they left."

"It's not just there, sir," Alpha Two responded from behind, a queasy expression on his face as he pointed at the back of the warehouse.

Harper blinked hard at where his sergeant pointed, his stomach turning as he was hit with flashbacks from when he'd first met Ryan. At the back end of their building was another huge hole dug into the dirt, with a mesh fence hung over the top. Behind that were empty oil barrels, all filled with bones, the skulls giving away that they were clearly human.

"What the fuck is that?" Alpha Three asked, wide-eyed.

"That's..." Harper paused, staring back into a nightmare, "...that's their barbecue." He turned back to the pit outside, still smouldering. Among the ash and what remained, there were a few evidential pieces of clothing and shoes. He took in the piles of bones, deducing how many people it could've been. Thousands. "How the fuck did fifteen men do this?" he whispered to himself.

"*Alpha One. This is Bravo One. We've found something.*"

"Go ahead," Harper replied.

"*You're going to want to see this for yourself.*"

"On my way. Alpha, secure our building. Don't touch anything until Woodburn gets here."

"Yes, sir!" Team Alpha replied in unison.

Harper jogged to the opening of the second building, where Team Bravo waited for him. "What have you found?" he asked, seeing a similar barbecue scene at the back of their room. "The barbecue? Yeah, we had one at ours, too."

"It's not that, sir." Bravo One shook his head, then pointed to the wall behind Harper.

He turned, following the stains of dried blood above the opening he'd just walked under. It was there, looking down on him in vain, just like all the other horrors he'd been forced to see throughout the war.

A flag made of human skin. Though the colours didn't match, it was clearly an imitation of the stripes and stars of America. He shuddered and turned so hard that he nearly fell over. He bit his lip and let out a slow, heavy exhale.

He'd seen one of those before and had months of night terrors trying to expel from his mind. This was just a way to mock Harper.

*Has Monreal passed my personal file over to Admiral?*

"There's more, sir." Bravo One handed him a photo. "We found this attached to... that." He motioned to the skin flag. "There's a note on the back."

Harper took the photo and read the note.

*You know I'm here. Now you can find out why.*

Turning the photo over, he studied it for only a few seconds before he recognised one of the men in the image shaking hands with someone else he vaguely recognised. He read the surveillance time stamp in the bottom right corner. 12$^{th}$ December 1991.

That's when he clicked at exactly who and what he was looking at.

"Oh my God." He almost fell out of his skin. "Woodburn. You need to come see this now."

# 21

The chirping wildlife was silenced as the choppers ripped through the air and smothered the early morning songs. Tropical birds scattered from the treetops and vanished towards the sunrise.

A secure perimeter had been established around the small complex, with all teams on point to repel any potential ambush. Harper didn't suspect an impending attack, though. In fact, he knew they wouldn't be disturbed while they searched the area. Admiral had left everything intact just so they could see what he was doing.

Woodburn jumped out of the Blackbird chopper, marching over to his friend. "Where is it?"

"In this one." Harper nodded to the structure behind him. The two strode across the open area, and Woodburn got a glance of the fire pit with the clothes.

"Have you got an estimate for how many locals have been... burned?" Woodburn asked.

"Negative, sir. This pit was clearly for burning clothes and personal artefacts. The pits in these two buildings have the physical remains... You can't forget that smell. We haven't begun counting the bones yet. A wild guess would be thousands."

"What benefit would Admiral have from killing thousands of the local populace? And how did he manage it?"

"I think you'll get your motive inside, sir." Harper opened the side door to an empty room with a table and two chairs. The discovered photo sat in the table's middle. "You'll need a seat for this."

Woodburn obliged and pulled the chair out, picking up the photo once he'd sat. He examined the front, eyes widening as he took in the three figures in the photo. "Is this genuine?"

"According to the timestamp, that's when Black Ops would've been in the area," Harper confirmed.

Woodburn placed the photo down and held his hands together, contemplating. The image held insurmountable consequences. The photo was of two men, one with a young boy by his side, shaking hands in the centre of the very compound where Operation Catfish was currently situated.

On the right side stood a tall, well-built Caucasian man. A man who would become recognisable around the world in early 2024. Terry McPherson, a former CIA operative, who had recorded and released to the Russian media a video of him and a team rigging the structures of the Twin Towers with explosives just after the 1993 World Trade Centre attack. Those charges would be detonated on the morning of September 11, 2001. The inside job that would cause America to invade the Middle East in a war that would last nearly two decades. A war that would cost millions of innocent civilian lives and later be revealed as started by one of America's own in a hate-fuelled ambition to wipe out the core of Islam.

Terry McPherson's reveal was the spark that turned the nation on itself in a civil uprising so fast that it didn't even have time to be named. With the crumbling of America, Russia and China took full advantage to invade in an attempt to 'restore order'.

The man was hated universally.

The other man and the young child in the photo were what rang the alarm bells in this exchange of pleasantries. The small boy, in particular, would grow up to become the key to The Fast War and Inland Invasion starting. The child's name was Aslan, and thirty-three years after this photo was taken, he would broadcast a video across

Europe announcing the beginning of the end. A Russian and Islamic uprising and retaliation for the war in the Middle East.

The very war Terry McPherson started. The very man Aslan's father was shaking hands with.

"Aslan's father was in cahoots with McPherson?" Woodburn asked out loud. "That doesn't make any goddamn sense."

"I know," Harper agreed, standing while removing his helmet. "Permission to begin searching for intel?"

"After Teams Echo, Fox, and Gundam arrive." Woodburn stood and looked down at the photo. "I'll call it in now."


Team Echo touched down and began examining all three fire pits. Teams Charlie and Delta combed through the first building while Alpha and Bravo searched the building where the photo was found. Fox and Gundam filed through the last and smaller of the structures, which had more of a laboratory feel to them.

Harper watched over as Echo carefully examined the few pieces of intact clothing on the edge of the fire pit. The early morning sun seared at his skin, and the mosquitos were already beginning to find their breakfast. He slapped one on the back of his neck and wiped his hand on his thigh.

During the long afternoon in the West African sun, more clues started to unravel regarding Admiral's reasoning for being there and what he'd done to the locals. The laboratory held research on inflictions such as endometriosis, Stephen Johnston syndrome, and lastly, Kuru. Decades of notes compiled into turning these conditions into biomechanical weapons.

"This country has a torn history," Woodburn announced. "Most of the population has either become addicted to drugs, been involved in sexual violence, or..." he paused, giving Harper a chance to absorb the next part, "...eaten human meat."

"Cannibalism is a thing here?" Harper asked, somewhat ironically around the cooked remains of thousands of people.

"It was during the civil conflict of the late eighties and early nineties. That leaves a whole country to test on."

"Test what on?"

"The first production of Kurustovia. Twenty years ago," Woodburn said, handing Harper some checklists from the laboratory. "The child soldiers from the Liberian civil war had begun to show the first stages of slow-burning Kuru. This was the ideal place to test the weapon—on people who already had it."

"That was fourteen years before The Fast War and the release of the McPherson tapes."

"Exactly, my friend. The Russian/Islamic coalition already had a weapon up their sleeves before the war had even begun."

Not sure if it was the sun or the overbearing feeling that the world had been preparing for his country's destruction longer than had been foreseen, Harper's head swirled, and he found himself having to run off to the side to vomit. What stung the most was that Admiral had been the one to uncover this intel and was now playing a murder mystery with the very operation that had been deployed to take him down.

# 22

"Who are these bad people my dad's going after?" Katie asked as she stared up into the dull red sky. The heavy clouds hung low, reflecting the city centre's lights back down, giving a fake warmth in the winter chill.

"I didn't know any of them," Rook admitted by the open fire escape, enjoying a rare cigarette. He wouldn't have indulged if Eliza hadn't left them out in the open. "All I can tell you is that they used to be good. That's all I know."

"Are they the same people that hurt that vineyard in England?"

"They are."

"How could people who were once good do such things?" Katie asked innocently. A gentle snowfall began as she held her arms out.

"Things can happen that change people," Rook answered as truthfully and diplomatically as he could.

"Like the woman who's tied to the bed all day?"

Rook's eyes shot open, aware of the fact that Katie was clearly referring to Steph. "She has had a lot of bad things happen, but she won't become anything like those people," he deflected while looking at a fake watch, then stubbed the cigarette out on the ground. "That's enough questions for now. Five minutes is up."

Katie huffed but agreed, keeping her silent contract with Rook intact and headed back inside without causing a stir. Rook watched her enter the family's apartment quietly and made sure the door was locked behind once she was in.

It haunted him that a twelve-year-old was aware enough to ask questions such as she had. On a positive note, being aware in this world was what could keep you alive. He entered his apartment and sat in the chair, opening the laptop. He sipped at his orange juice and watched the screens with intent, nearly dozing off twice. Knowing he was better than that, he started working out with the small set of dumbbells by the sofa. Eliza's lust had started to take up more of his resting time than he cared to admit.

He continued his workout until the first show of sunlight, and a roar from next door caused him to jolt forward from his sit-ups. Instinctively, he swung his door open and burst into Steph's apartment.

She was thrashing wildly on the bed, nearly tearing the restraints off. "They took my blood!" she screamed.

Rook ripped the medical cupboard open, then unzipped the wallet of syringes and reached for the vial of sedatives. Fabric tore behind him, and bare feet hit the floor. He slowly turned, seeing the frail yet on-guard Steph metres away from him. Drool dripped onto her feet, and her eyes locked on to him as she tried to speak through her clenched jaw.

"You need to know." She heaved uncontrollably, arms twitching. "They took my blood."

"I know." Rook held his hands out in front in a calming gesture. "I know they did. Harper's going to get the people who took Lyndon from you."

"No!" Steph roared, charging towards Rook and picking him up under the shoulders, then thrusting him through the glass cabinet. "They took my blood!"

Mikey burst in one-footed, hopping over and pulling Steph away. She kept repeating the same sentence.

"Rook, now!" Mikey yelled, trying to restrain her on the floor.

Rook pulled himself from the wreckage and knelt, plunging the needle into her arm.

"They took my blood," Steph cried softer, her body weakening and the wheezing calming. "They took..." She fell limp.

Rook carefully removed the syringe, rolling it away from them and sat, letting the adrenaline burn off. "Thank you," he wheezed to Mikey, rubbing the back of his neck.

"Sure." Mikey nodded, pulling himself from underneath Steph, cushioning her head under his knee. "How the fuck did that happen? She isn't due her shot for another two days."

Steph's body radiated an unbelievable amount of heat, so much so that Rook carefully made his way over to the window and opened it. "She's burning up. She was screaming like she had a night terror or something. All she said was, 'They took my blood,' and then pulled herself free of the restraints."

"PTSD and Kurustovia?" Mikey stood on one leg and then collapsed butt-first on her bed. He held the restraints in his hand. "We're going to need some more of these."

"No kidding."

Jen approached the open door. "Is she okay?"

"For now," Rook said, turning to her. "But in future... this is going to be a road of hell for her."

With the three of them, they lifted Steph onto the bed and watched over her as Rook put in a call for more restraints to be delivered.

Rook paced the corridor as he waited for the restraints to arrive, unable to settle or focus as the one-minute event played repeatedly in his mind. Never had he seen such strength or speed on even the toughest of soldiers or fittest athletes. A power fuelled only by an uncontrollable overload of adrenaline, strong enough to give a malnutritional, bedbound woman half his size the ability to rip her restraints off and throw him into a medical cabinet.

What tore his heart out was the fight in her eyes, like she was trying to hold back as she repeated the same sentence. The conveying that they killed her son, and she just needed someone to know.

Someone to hear the love she had snatched from her. Her face was enraged, but her eyes said it killed her.

*She didn't attack until you mentioned her son's name.* He pressed his head against the wall. *You shouldn't have said his name.*

He couldn't take seeing what Monreal had done to everyone anymore. "I know how to get to you," he growled softly, pushing himself off the wall and formulating his plan.

Once the restraints had arrived and been securely fastened in place, Rook left his pistol with Mikey, stormed downstairs and out the back door, entered his patrol car and roared towards the airport.

The road security waved in protest as Rook smashed through the barricade, nearly crashing into another patrol vehicle outside the airport's front entrance. A team of officers were waiting for him as he jumped out of the car and bolted towards the doors. One of the guards tackled him by the waist, pulling him to the ground.

"I have to see inside Monreal's room!" he shouted, grabbing the guard by the shoulders and throwing him off. He was ready to continue for the door before the taser bolt slammed into his thigh, sending thirty thousand volts through his body and rendering his muscles into violent spasms. He toppled sideways, unable to stop the two kicks to the ribs that the overeager guard delivered. After the minor assault was over, he was handcuffed and dragged by the arms through the empty terminal, all the way up two flights of stairs and over to the passenger holding cells, which currently served as the prison block for Rennes. The very same cells Connor had been rescued from.

Without warning, he was tossed onto the singular mattress in one of the cold, dingy cells. The handcuffs had been removed via gunpoint, and then the door slammed shut on him. The guards made their usual redneck jokes as they laughed and closed the main door to the corridor.

Though in pain, Rook cackled on the mattress and carefully pulled himself up, assessing the damage to his side. "Fucking pussies," he laughed. "I'm out cold, and you still can't break a rib?" A sobering thought was that Steph's attack hurt considerably more than theirs did.

He took in his surroundings and the one dim bulb that vaguely lit up the windowless area. The cell was barely three by three metres, with a single mattress, one pillow, one sink, and a seatless toilet.

"Hey, fuckers!" Rook thumped against the door in a fake protest. "Let me the fuck out! Your mum is on my schedule tonight!" He repeated the process, getting no answer from any guards who might have stayed silently in the corridor. Minutes passed, and there was not even a hint of movement or anyone coming to slide his viewing window open. "At least tell me what's for dinner. If it's snails and frog legs, at least they'll taste better than your garlic-stained mum."

"They're not coming in, you know?" a Polish voice replied from the cell next to Rooks. "They only come when it's time to feed."

Rook grinned behind his door, knowing the real bait had worked. "That's good to know... Lukas."

"Do I know you?"

"We've met briefly."

"Ah, the American soldier reduced to hospital security?" Lukas taunted.

"Yeah. That guy," Rook answered, ignoring the remark. "The same soldier that knows exactly where your wife and children are. Your English is clearly better than hers, so you're going to answer some questions for me."

"I know your rules. You'd never harm a woman and her children."

"Harm? No. Inject the same shit into them that you put into Steph? You best believe I will," Rook lied, knowing he'd have to strengthen his bluff. "I just got myself arrested and took a kicking to get here to you. What the fuck makes you think I won't put your family on medication for the rest of their lives?"

Bare feet trod over tiled floors, slow and calm. "It seems the situation has, as you say in America, gotten under your skin."

"Considering everything your 'handler' has done over the last three months, I think most people are starting to get to breaking point."

"You have no idea what our *handler* has done."

"Where is Monreal hiding?"

"If you don't know where he is now, you'll never know," Lukas rasped dryly.

"Really not in the mood for riddles."

"Well, that saves both of us time because I'm not giving you riddles."

"When did you last see Monreal?"

"Three months ago. We helped move him after he went M.I.A."

"That's bullshit. He's been in the camps recruiting you and your dock worker pals. Where is he?"

"I don't know, and that's the truth. You could tie me to one of the lie machine things, and it would show that I'm telling the truth. The only place I know he'd visit is the morgue."

"The morgue?" Rook repeated, thinking to himself. "Did Monreal tamper with the cooling units? Did he sabotage them so we couldn't identify the body?"

A metallic clunk echoed up the corridor, along with the creaking of the door being pulled open. Multiple footsteps approached, but one pair stood out above the others. A pair of high heels clipped across the floor and stopped outside his door. Rook stepped away just before it was pulled open.

To his utmost shock, the female standing before him was none other than Danish Health Minister Naomi Eriksen. "You're lucky Woodburn has a soft spot for you." She looked unimpressed through her thick-framed glasses. "I came as soon as I heard. Come on."

In Lukas's cell, feet shuffled backwards before a body slumped casually on a mattress. Rook didn't quite get the answers he wanted, but at least he had reasonable cause to believe that Monreal had been at the hospital in the last week. He made no attempt to avoid eye contact with the guards as he exited the cell and followed Eriksen towards the exit, but to his surprise, she was leading him into the airport staff quarters.

"Woodburn has you wrapped around his fucking fingers," one of the guards protested, though ignored by Eriksen. They stopped outside a door with red tape across the front, and Rook was handed a key.

"You wanted a look at Monreal's room?" she said. "Here you go."

Though Rook's objective was actually to get closer to Lukas, he had to play along and pretend that searching Monreal's room was his main goal. He knew he wouldn't find anything in there, but this was the façade he had to put on in front of Eriksen. She may have just bailed him out, but he still didn't trust her—not when she had signed off on the first batch of Kurustovia land in Rennes, whether she'd been aware of it or not.

"Thank you." Rook took the key and pulled the red tape down, unlocking the door and stepping inside. It was his first time seeing the place, and it had been just as stripped down as he'd heard. A double bed with no duvet, one single desk and a wardrobe.

"What are you looking for?" Eriksen asked.

"Signs that Monreal has been back here recently," he lied, pretending to examine the area. Monreal may have needed access to Rennes' mainframe to manipulate the cameras, but he wouldn't have been stupid enough to go back to his own room. He feigned a random question to keep up with the charade. "Is this corridor under guarded surveillance now?"

"You'll have to speak to your friend about that," Eriksen said, eyeing Eliza, who stepped into the room, glaring at Rook. "Miss Fultz will escort you back to your apartment. If the rumours are true, she'll know exactly where it is."

Eriksen left, leaving a burning and awkward tension between the secret couple.

"I can explain..." Rook started.

"Don't!" Eliza said, cutting him off.

## 23

"What the fuck were you thinking?" Eliza screamed, slamming the driver's seat of Rook's car with her palms and starting the engine.

"I thought you didn't want me to explain?" Rook replied, slapping the seatbelt on as the car jerked forward.

"There's fucking cameras with microphones in the staff quarters, cowboy." She said that so angrily it almost became a hiss. "You want him to know that you're coming after him?"

"Are there microphones in the prisoner corridor?"

"What. Why?"

"Because that's where I intended to end up," Rook explained forcefully. "I wanted to talk to Lukas. See if he could give me any information on Monreal's whereabouts."

Eliza took the info on board, and she reluctantly stayed quiet while driving. "Did you get any information?" she huffed. "And no, there aren't any microphones in the prisoner corridor."

Rook was silently ecstatic to know that but refrained from displaying it. "Lukas said that it was likely that Monreal would've visited the morgue at some point."

"Why would he do that?"

"Turn the freezers off, destroy the evidence and body," Rook hinted.

"That would make sense, on his part at least," Eliza agreed, turning off the motorway and towards Rennes. "Has the medical examiner said anything about any tampering?"

"Not on our last call, but I'm checking in with her when we get back."

The remaining five minutes of the journey happened in stubborn silence, with Rook not wanting to apologise for taking the fight to the next step and Eliza for her outburst. To his surprise, when she parked out the back of the apartment block, she switched the engine off and got out with him, following inside.

It wasn't until they walked past Steph's door and got into his apartment that Rook felt the need to explain.

"Look," he started, "I know what I did was hot-headed, but the woman in the next apartment is one of many of Monreal's victims. She's infected with that shit, and this morning she had a freak-out based around the loss of her son. Right now, I don't care that the son of a bitch framed me or tried to have me killed. It's other people that he's trying to hurt that I'm going to prevent."

"You don't think I know that?" Eliza turned to face him with teary eyes. Her usual cold and focused demeanour evaporated. "You forget I used to work with him. All those times he sat while under my watch, probably planning and using our system right under my nose?" She laughed angrily at herself and wiped her nose. "You think I don't want that bastard caught for everything he's done?"

Guilt and shame hit Rook in the stomach. Eliza had been key into getting intel over the past couple of weeks, and it wasn't just for sexual favours. For her, it was personal, too.

"I'm sorry," he said, taking the accountability on his shoulders. "It won't happen again. I just lost it with what happened this morning."

"It's fine," Eliza said, sitting down. "Aren't you going to call the medical examiner?"

"Yeah, on it." He pulled the smart radio out and started making the call. "Want some coffee?" he asked, and Eliza accepted. He tried the call twice, both times disconnecting after a minute. "Dammit. I'll try again later."

There was a knock at the door as Rook passed the hot beverage over. He felt naked without his gun as he slowly approached, looking through the spy hole. It was Jen with some kind of casserole dish.

"I thought we'd been quiet when we came in," Rook said as he opened the door.

"You were," Jen replied. "You forget Mikey's hearing is off the charts now." She handed the dish over. "Tomato and chilli pasta. Thought you could use a refuel after today."

"Thanks." Rook smiled, taking it.

Jen caught a glimpse of Eliza and smiled. "Well, I'll leave you to it," she said and left.

"Is she one of the vineyard survivors?" Eliza asked as Rook shut the door.

"Yeah, that's Jen, seven months pregnant," he answered, sitting the dish down, taking the tin foil off and observing the meal.

"Vegetarian," she noted.

"It's how they've lived for years."

"Isn't that bad for the baby?"

"Ryan's boy turned out unharmed," Rook explained, handing her a fork. "Now, shush for the moment. This is probably better than the food in the canteen."


There was no early evening lovemaking for the pair, and Rook let Eliza fall asleep in his bed, pulling the covers over her as he got ready for his night shift. He struggled to pull on his long-sleeved T-shirt but was amused that the pain didn't come from the guards who had a few cheap shots at him.

His first port of call as always was checking the locks, windows and doors, then made sure to return the casserole tray to Mikey and Jen. He asked where they learned to cook like that, and Mikey admitted it came from living with Ryan for so long before the war. It was a small catch-up and collective mourning for what happened with Steph earlier in the day. Rook filled them in with what happened during his afternoon, though he didn't divulge any information that he'd gathered from Lukas. Plausible deniability was how he saw it for the couple. They said they'd watch over Steph for the rest of the evening, knowing Rook would've been tired from his day, and now understanding that it was Eliza who'd been keeping him awake, to which, even he saw the funny side.

After leaving them, he stopped by Harper's family's apartment and made sure everything was okay. They were low on coffee and bread, which Rook said he'd have delivered in the morning. Troy had bumped his head during one of his usual afternoon energy bursts, but other than the small graze on his forehead, everything was okay.

He sneaked back into his apartment to steal another cigarette and Eliza's lighter as she slept. It was his own stress relief for when Katie was ready to make her nightly rooftop visit, which came later than normal that time. At two-thirty, the door to Harper's apartment finally creaked open, and Rook closed the laptop and met her in the corridor.

"Sorry," Katie whispered as they climbed the stairs. "Mom took her medication later than normal. She'd had some wine before."

"No need to explain," Rook dismissed as he unlocked the rooftop door.

"We haven't heard from Dad yet."

"No news is better than bad news."

"What do you mean?" Katie asked, confused.

"If your dad was in trouble, the U.S.S Gavato would've radioed here to let us know," Rook explained, lighting the cigarette. "We would've heard if anything had gone wrong."

"I guess so. From what little we've been told about this, it sounds like he's chasing monsters."

"He's not the only one," Rook whispered to himself as he inhaled.

# 24

The sight of bones and human remains had become a daily reoccurrence in the seven years since the first day of the war. Across the whole of Europe, mass graves had been uncovered in the countryside while bodies were left to rot in cities and towns. Some showed the scars of warfare, others were crushed by mass stampeding during panicked attempts to escape the chaos, and a smaller percentage were the result of suicides. In a comparatively smaller percentage of the nine hundred million people lost since 2024, those were subject to the hands of what remained in the world. Cannibalism wasn't rare anymore, particularly across the Mediterranean, and high numbers of sacrificial killings had been discovered from Italy up to western Scandinavia. Sometimes, the motive was nothing more than the leader of a particular group of survivors who had lost the plot and demanded they purge themselves of whatever demographic they saw as a threat that week.

Murder and rival killings took place on a regular basis between opposing factions, and everything in between established that unless some kind of order was reattained, blood was the new currency.

Harper watched as the final set of bones were carried to the mass grave and gently lowered in. The last set of one thousand, four hundred and seventy-one in this compound alone. All butchered and prepared in ways he'd regretfully seen before.

The unfortunate locals who had been promised shelter by Admiral from the newest civil conflict raging in Liberia were employed to help get this compound up and running efficiently again. Both a workforce at his fingertips and a food source for when they served their purpose.

Smoking pits, meat hangars, and drying racks had been uncovered, pointing towards prolonging the meat's shelf life and preventing them from having to eat over a thousand corpses within a few days. What really disgusted Harper the most was the amount of untouched fruit that grew all around them. They were only interested in the meat.

"We've just heard from Operation Wolfpack," Woodburn stated as he approached. "They've swept the islands of Bernray and North Uist. No contact with Admiral's people. No prints in any snow. No signs of anyone." He saw Harper's bland expression as he watched soldiers cover the bodies with sand. "Alexi has begun a sweep of the next island."

"When do we move out?" Harper asked without looking, referring to the next compound seven miles further into the jungle.

"One hour."

"Copy that," Harper acknowledged and turned away from the mass grave. He had expected the stomach-churning debauchery that they would find in the first twenty-four hours in Liberia, but there was no preparation that the mind could handle when it came to seeing the human body violated in brutal ways. The newest factor in the equation was the puzzle pieces that Admiral had left behind for them and the ramifications that could come from what they had been shown.

Harper wanted to tell himself he didn't care. If there was an answer, then Admiral should've just said it and not played yet another one of his games while taking all the lives that Harper now watched get covered in sand. "What's Admiral's deal with all these fucking games?"

"What do you mean, my friend?" Woodburn asked as he shuffled closer to Harper.

"Connor went through a game with Ryan when he could've just killed him. The twins could've killed Ryan and his people yet gave him a choice to spare them. Admiral could've waited for us here or left us with the answers for that photo."

"I wish I knew. I'll guess we'll find out when we get the bastard."

"Yes, sir."

Operation Catfish prepared for the next stage of the mission and began their five-mile trek through the thick Liberian forest and would come into hostile contact within half an hour—a solo spotter and a local. Their AK47 was only loaded with ten rounds, leaving them all but guaranteed to be put down. A walkie-talkie fell beside their body as they were swiftly dispatched.

Team Alpha secured the sight as Harper approached the body and the radio with a hushed whisper teasing through it, "*You will know what we know.*"

Harper knew the Midlands accents as Admiral's. He resisted the urge to talk back and switched it off, signalling for Catfish to continue forward as the sun went down. Their night vision displayed the jungle in bright, luminous green, and the laser's sights moved with precision through the thick, broken undergrowth.

*We're under the same stars.* Harper's thoughts went to his family, missing them terribly and reminding himself what he was fighting for. At least he would get to see them again, unlike the families Admiral had destroyed or harvested.

Uninterrupted for two hours, the mission moved at a steady and patient pace. They knew that their targets were waiting for them, and one misplaced step could prove disastrous or, worse, fatal.

"Two clicks from target," Charlie One confirmed, bringing everyone to a halt. Harper held his breath and listened. A high-pitched whir activated to his right. The remote-controlled drone moved higher through the canopy and found a clearing above the treeline before whizzing forward in the night sky.

"Eyes on the target area," Charlie One reported. "Thermal imaging indicates multiple bogies. Two watch towers with spotters and three armed patrols circling the grounds."

Alpha Four handed Harper the portable screen that displayed what the drone saw. Another compound with four buildings in total, three of which matched the structures they had just left. The last of the four was taller, with two industrial mining conveyors on either side. The image zoomed out, showing the trees' bases were well above the rooftops of the compound. It was in a quarry.

A thick puff of smoke erupted from the bottom left corner of the screen, and then the image cut out. Three seconds later, an explosion shook the treetops.

"Drone is down," Charlie One confirmed.

"Copy that," Harper answered. "Proceed as planned. They know we're close."

## 25

Harper stood defeated in the centre of the second compound as Delta Team confirmed the fourth and final building was empty. He lowered his head and kicked the dirt in frustration as Catfish began searching for intel.

With the new morning sun searing hotter than the day before, Harper removed his helmet and wiped his brow. "Catfish Actual, this is Alpha One," he reported on his radio. "The second compound is empty."

"*Repeat your last*," Woodburn replied.

"The compound is empty, sir. Alpha and Bravo are securing the perimeter."

"*Roger that. Standby for our arrival.*"

"Yes, sir," Harper confirmed, looking into the thick brush of dense jungle, knowing the Bravo team was performing a fifty-metre-perimeter sweep inside it. He wiped the sweat from his overgrown beard and flung his palm in the air. There was virtually no breeze, and the scorching sun felt clammy in the jungle's dense humidity. His red hair felt like it was going to combust at any second.

Half an hour passed before Harper was called into one of the abandoned buildings by his team, and even though shielded from the sun, it did very little to cool him down, nor did the rise in anger with the new information his team presented. Another 'clue' from Admiral.

In his hands was a detailed blueprint of the Twin Towers' underground car park, marked with parking spots. Other documents compiled extensive lists of different explosives and van rental companies in the Tri-State district, all dates marked mid to late 1992.

Another document listed the individuals who would eventually take part in The World Trade Centre bombing of February 1993. The event that would gain McPherson access to the towers and rig them with the explosive charges.

Woodburn received that information shortly after he landed and held the same dumbfounded and enraged expression as Harper. What was left of their home country was unknown to this day, and though the terror attack was nearly forty years ago, seeing someone' detailed planning into harming American civilians still stabbed them in the heart.

"So, what we've learned so far is," Woodburn said, analysing out loud, "Aslan's father orchestrated the 1993 bombings. From this, McPherson would use the attack to pose as insurance inspectors and plant explosives that would be used on 9/11." He tapped the back of the chair he leant against.

They stood in silence and flicked through the recent evidence, combing through every fine detail within the documents. There was no clear link to why Aslan would have motive for something his father was involved in. None of it made a lick of sense.

"Wait," Woodburn said out loud, standing from the table. "McPherson said he bought the towers down because it would be their fight against Islam."

"We know that, sir."

"Purchasing the explosives from an arms dealer who just happens to be a Muslim was his way of framing them. If he had ties or links with Aslan's family, maybe he had inside links to other terrorist cells. It would've put them at the top of our most wanted list."

Alpha two approached the pair with more documents in his hand, dread painted across his face. "I think you'll get your answers here, sirs," he reported. "I don't think you're going to like this."

Woodburn took the documents first, eyes widening as he scanned down the list, flicking through each sheet of paper before closing his eyes and passing them to Harper. "Son of a bitch!" he growled, placing his hands on his hips.

"I'm sorry you had to see this," Alpha Two said, eyes heavy.

Harper took the papers and read down the list. Nineteen photocopies of passports. The names that every American patriot had involuntarily tattooed onto their hearts.

The nineteen hijackers of 9/11.

In this small, isolated compound in the middle of Liberia was where the largest terrorist attack on American soil was planned.

"This is how McPherson knew 9/11 was coming," Harper said coldly. "He was here when it was first planned."

"And this is what Admiral wants us to know," Woodburn croaked as he nodded solemnly, looking away. He very rarely displayed grief, but he was clearly repressing it now. "The sole reason for The Fast War and the destruction of our country was manufactured here, in the same place Kurustovia was created." He straightened his shoulders and turned, clearing his throat. "Make sure you round up all intel you find and get us a Sit-Rep on Operation Wolfpack."

"Copy that, sir," Alpha Two confirmed and left.

Harper sat silent and confused until a mosquito snapped him out of his thoughts. He slapped the insect with the back of his hand. "One goddamn thing doesn't make sense about all this."

"What's that, my friend?" Woodburn asked.

"Why would Aslan start a war in retaliation for the invasion of the Middle East if his family helped fund the very cause for it?"

"I'm sure we're going to find out, and it's going to be from Admiral. He knows what he's doing..."

"Sir." Alpha Two stepped back in. "U.S.S Gavato can't establish communications with Wolfpack or Rennes."

"What do you mean? Is no one answering?"

"It's not that, sir. All communication has been... terminated."

# 26

Rook burst into the operations room, having taken less than five minutes to drive well above the speed limit to the airport. He left Mikey with his pistol and hauled ass the second he got the call from Eliza. That time, the airport security staff were ordered not to touch him.

"Which terminal was Monreal's?" he asked loudly, looking at the computer screens across the room. Eliza pointed him to the flickering screen at the far end. "Are you sure he hasn't been here?"

"My shift started two hours ago." Eliza shook her head, sweating and nervous. "I would've killed him if I saw him."

Rook knew that to be true, so he turned his attention to the rest of the team who'd been working before Eliza's shift. "Did you see him?" he asked one by one. "Are you working with him?" getting more aggressive with each question, and everyone became more terrified.

Eliza pulled him back and told him to calm down. The workers were just as clueless and mortified as to what had happened.

Rook reluctantly reeled back and steadied himself. "When did communications cut out?" he asked.

"Twenty minutes ago," Eliza explained. "General Woodburn was preparing to land at the next compound."

"Were they under attack?"

"No. Just as with the first site, it had been abandoned. It's like Admiral had a warning that they were coming both times."

Rook sat in the chair, frustrated and defeated, while glaring back into the security cameras. There was no point in checking the footage; Monreal would've easily altered it. "And his screen flickered to life just as the communications shut down?"

"To the very second," Eliza said, folding her arms over her chest, distraught. "He wasn't here. I promise you."

Rook knew she wasn't lying, so he turned to the other tech advisers and saw the same gaunt expressions. They had all worked with Monreal, too, and had all been betrayed by him. The flickering screen at Monreal's terminal was laughing at him. "When did that last get turned on?"

"During the check after the hospital attack. Both Harper and Woodburn oversaw it."

"Who was the technician who performed the check?"

"Alfonso Gondalo," Eliza said. "I've already called him in. He doesn't know that you're going to be questioning him, and neither does security. It's only us here that know." She pointed around the room. "We want Monreal dealt with just as much as you."


Alfonso Gondalo had barely got in the room before Rook had cornered him and locked the door.

"You're the last person to have checked Monreal's workstation, correct?" Rook asked sternly.

"Yes... yes," Alfonso stammered, confused and looking around the room for support, but all the faces he met were judging him. "What's going on?"

Eliza stepped in. "Forty minutes ago, we lost communication with both Operation Catfish and the U.S.S Gavato, just as Monreal's terminal miraculously switched itself on and began doing that." She pointed to the screen. "You were the last person to use it, Alfonso."

Alfonso glanced at the monitor. "Has Monreal been here?" he asked nervously, to which he was met with a nonverbal answer.

"You're the last confirmed person to have been on his terminal. So, I need to know exactly what you found the last time you were on it or what you did to it," Rook said, laying down the law.

"Nothing!" Alfonso protested. "I found nothing! I was supervised the whole time, told to leave it on and report my findings." He waved some paper in the air. "This is the diagnostics!"

Eliza snatched the papers and read through them as Rook guided Alfonso to the terminal. He sat the Spaniard down and asked what the hell that flickering was. Before Alfonso answered, Eliza walked over and sighed.

"The Nat type is safe, and the core processor was functioning normally. No irregular data went in or out from this terminal. It was clean."

Alfonso tried to access the terminal, but he was locked out. He ran his hands around the back of the screen and shot Rook a terrified look. "You have to believe me. This wasn't me," he pleaded.

"What wasn't you?" Rook demanded.

Alfonso slowly moved his hand away, and the screen went blank while holding something in his palm. A thumb drive. Everyone stopped working and stared. "This wasn't here before. He must've been here."

"What the fuck is that?" Rook growled. "What did you do?"

"Please." He tried to hand it off to Eliza. "Monreal must've been here."

"Fuck!" Rook flipped the table over, then stormed back to Alfonso. "What time did you finish your check of this terminal?"

"It's in the transcript." He pointed to the papers. "Around seven in the evening. Six nights ago?"

"So, you're saying in between then and now, Monreal had access in here with no one spotting it?"

"Well, no. That's not actually possible either."

"What do you mean that's not possible? Because if not, that only points to you."

"I mean, it's not possible because metal detectors were fitted after the hospital attack."

"What does that have to do with anything?"

"Monreal would've set them off. He has a metal arm and bullet shrapnel in his neck."

"He has...?" Rook stood back, nearly falling over. "He has what?" he asked and steadied himself against the flipped table.

"From the battle of Rennes. Two injuries that were repaired."

Eliza approached, unsettled by Rook's reaction. "What's wrong?"

Rook stood straight and breathed hard, rubbing his face in anger. "Are these metal detectors connected to the system?"

"No, they're manual. Why?"

"Fucking shit!" Rook roared. "How long ago did Monreal go M.I.A?"

"Around three months ago."

The taunts of Lukas's words echoed through his mind. *We moved him when he went M.I.A. The only place he'd visit is the morgue.*

"The fucking body in the morgue had a metal arm, bullet fragments, and had been put in the water three months ago." He ripped his beanie off. "I've been chasing a ghost. Monreal has been dead this whole fucking time."

"If Monreal is dead..." Eliza stammered, "...who's been behind everything?"

## 27

Harper was flung forward as the rocket exploded metres behind him. He landed face first in the dry dirt, unintentionally inhaling a sharp mouthful as the impact shocked through his chest. His back screamed, and he felt warm blood trickle around to his stomach.

Behind the ringing in his ears, another rocket fizzed overhead and crashed into the first structure, ripping open the back wall. Harper's eyes followed the rocket's trajectory back to the source, staring down a face he hadn't seen since he had personally arrested them.

A top of the quarry's farthest edge, there he stood. Connor. In the flesh. The twisted skin on the left side of his face, down through his shoulder and arm. He was badly sunburnt, and that added a devilish glow to the sinister smile he wore while holding one-eyed contact with Harper. He shouldered his RPG and disappeared as gunfire was returned from Team Echo.

A strong arm picked up Harper and dragged him to cover in the second hangar. Woodburn sat his friend down and checked him over.

"Are you hit?" Woodburn asked, panic on his face as he removed Harper's tactical vest and examined his back. "I said, are you hit?"

Harper had to lip-read behind the high-pitched trilling in his ears before shaking his head. He attempted to get to his feet before Woodburn pulled him back and sat him down, directing orders to Teams Alpha, Bravo, Charlie, and Delta while handing Harper some water.

Harper rinsed the dirt out of his mouth and spat it on the ground as he tried to stand, failing to hide the pain that tore down his shoulders and the back of his legs.

"Sit down, Lieutenant!" Woodburn ordered sternly, pulling rank over his friend as he waved over the medic from Team Echo. "Attend to him and keep him with Team Echo." He switched to his radio. "Fox, Gundam. This is Catfish Actual. We have come under heavy fire. We need your assistance."

*"Roger that. On our way."*

For the first time in their friendship and service together, Harper saw something on his friend's face that he had never shown before. It wasn't fear. It wasn't regret. It was nervousness. "Bad time to get the jitters, sir!" Harper wheezed.

"You can give me that shit when we get home," Woodburn said, forcing the words out somewhat anxiously. He nodded to Harper and the medic before taking off into the open and reuniting with Team Alpha in the next building.

Time seemed to stand still as the medic removed pieces of shrapnel from the top of Harper's back and calves. Each removal stung, and the disinfectant hurt more as the young corpsman dressed the larger wounds first.

On the floor, Harper's shoulder-mounted radio relayed the details of the team's situation as they pushed after Connor and the discovery of mineshafts atop the western tip of the compound.

*"Team Alpha moving in."*

*"Roger. Team Bravo right behind you."*

Harper gripped the chair's top tightly, trying to shake his vision back to clear. Every fibre within him wanted to help with this next step of the mission. They were so close to them now.

The medic finished and knelt in front of Harper, zipping up his field kit. "You're all patched up, sir." He took out a thin eye torch and checked both eyes. "It looks like you have a minor concussion. Under General Woodburn's orders, I can't let you go back in the field."

"Where's my weapon?" Harper demanded, looking around.

"General Woodburn has it. He's ordered me to keep you behind. I can't let you go back out." The medic repeated.

"Woodburn's orders?"

"Yes, sir."

"Goddammit." Harper winced.

The treetops swayed violently as the reserve team's chopper began to close in. Harper groaned and reached for his tactical vest, holding it in his right hand as he leaned forward against the chair support. The choppers emerged over the treeline and hovered downwards, creating their own little tornados of Liberian dirt as they touched down. Teams Fox and Gundam filtered out and formed a small perimeter around the compound's central area.

He stared at where he'd been standing a few minutes before and the mark left by the rocket that had just missed him. What struck Harper was that no one else had been hurt from the blast, even though Connor had the surprise factor and a clean line of sight. Something was wrong. Something was off. He knew Connor should've made that shot on them.

"Alpha One?" A soldier from Team Fox approached. "Where's the base of operations here?"

"Base of operations is in that warehouse. We need to secure all the intel. It's highly classified until further notice. Make sure we're ready for immediate evac. Our targets are close."

"Roger that, sir." The soldier took to the warehouse and started giving orders to his team.

Harper swallowed his pride and accepted he couldn't continue with the next part of the mission, whether it was an order or just his friend looking out for him. He rubbed his temples angrily as the screeching stopped and had been replaced by a piercing headache. His eyes caught one of the medics searching through one of the cooler boxes, a look of confusion on their face. "What's wrong, Corporal?" he asked while wincing.

"Must be a mix-up in our inventory, sir," the medic answered as he sorted through the supplies. "We're supposed to have ten packs of A-positive blood, but I can only see nine, sir."

"Has anyone been in need?"

"No, sir. But if the shit is about to hit the fan, we're going to need every backup available to us." The medic stood and asked the team leader of Echo, who was positioning more supply crates around the warehouse.

Over the radio, the order was given for Teams Alpha, Bravo, Charlie, and Delta to continue on foot and proceed into the mines.

This was it. Admiral's last stand.

*"Alpha Three is down!"* came the first alarm of the radio. *"Multiple Tangos."*

*"Delta Four is down!"*

*"Laying suppressive fire!"*

*"Grenade!"*

Harper jolted to his feet, the wounds to his back numb under the adrenaline while he rushed to the screens of body cam footage. Two were motionless on the ground as gunfire flashed across the images. The IDs confirmed it was Charlie Three and Delta Four.

Even in night vision mode, the back and forth made it nearly impossible to gain any situational information in the barely lit tunnels. Despite a couple of casualties, the teams seemed to be gaining an advantage as they pushed forward.

Harper's eyes darted to the top right. The body cam for Catfish Actual. Woodburn. His hands clamped around the chair as an enemy sprung out, but Woodburn put them down with a sharply executed shot to the chest. Harper's heart thumped, and his nose began to bleed.

*"Delta Two is down!"* another cry came.

*"I'm hit!"*

More men were dropping. Harper had to take action.

"Team Echo. Those are our men in there. I want four members to come with me and four members of Gundam."

"Roger." Echo One sorted between his team, as did the leader of Gundam.

The medic who'd treated Harper earlier handed him his own M4 while helping to put and fasten his tactical vest back on.

After rounding his makeshift team, Harper limped from the warehouse as another callout hit him in the heart. The one he was dreading.

"*Catfish Actual is down.*"

## 28

R ook paced across the control room, silently trying to piece together every detail of what had happened over the previous three months. The motive for Monreal's murder was obvious and, unfortunately, brilliant. For whoever was responsible, it gained them access to his quarters, a mere two-minute walk from the prison corridor and a direct line into the control room's interface. Access to everything. Security, cameras, controlled locking systems, all the while systematically making everyone look for Monreal while he had been slowly decomposing off the North French coastline.

With all eyes looking for the wrong person, they could blend in. Unnoticed. No suspecting eyes looking for the technology they were using to disable Rennes from the inside.

Rook held the thumb drive in his palm. A simple, clean device with no distinct features. How was it possible this was the very thing that the user had used to frame Rook before? Instigate the jail breakout? Or organise the hospital attack?

Without waiting any longer, Rook stomped over to Monreal's desk and pushed the drive back into the USB port. The screen flickered back on, flashing like static before a small window popped up in the middle. A warning.

. . .

*Havkat Programme installation into same device detected.*
   *Shutting down exterior drive.*


"What the fuck does that mean?" Rook growled just as the screen blinked rapidly before cutting to black. The back of the monitor sparked, with the smallest puff of smoke emerging. He peered behind to see the red-hot thumb drive, which had melted its plastic casing into the port. "Can any of you computer folks tell me what the fuck a Havkat Programme is?" he asked loudly, almost like a command.

No one had heard of such software, never mind used it before. Eliza took to her computer, searching the database to see if any malware under the same name had passed through Rennes' network since it was installed.

"Okay." Rook clapped his hands together. "I need a list of everyone who has been in the command centre since Alfonso checked Monreal's computer. It has to be someone who works within the airport. I want all technicians and supervisors, security staff, even the fucking lunch ladies." He grabbed his coat and pulled it over his shoulders. "You have one hour. Let's get to work people."

"Where are you going?" Eliza asked, standing from her chair.

"I'm going to get a description of whoever the fuck this is from Lukas's wife," he said, storming for the exit while ripping one of Monreal's security photos off the wall. "The fucking bitch lied to me about Monreal being this *officer man.*"


Rook didn't leave fourth gear as he hammered it to the refugee camps, zig-zagging hard as he skidded outside the entrance into a full 180 degrees. He exited the rover, slamming the door shut behind him and barging his way through the checkpoint.

The young guard raised his rifle at him, begging in rough English that they at least check him for a weapon before letting him through. The boy's hands shook, and Rook knew that any sudden movements could result in a finger slipping on a trigger. He eased slightly, letting the guards perform a quick patting down before letting him through.

He recognised the thick tent and lifted the flap open, finding a shocked Mrs Gregorzk. Rook signalled for her to move her children out of sight, but his facial expressions alone would've convinced her to do that. She came back out from the children's enclosure, shaking, her head low.

Rook held up the picture of Monreal. "Is this *officer man?*"

She nodded slowly, and the temperature in the tent began to rise with instant effect.

"No, it's not," Rook said forcefully. "He's dead." He pointed at the picture. "Who is *officer man?*"

Mrs Gregorzk began to cry, shaking her head while jabbering in Polish.

"You're not going to tell me? Maybe Lukas will then." He turned to leave.

"No!" She grabbed his arm. "No!" The sobbing continued, but she was trying to compose herself. "Big man." She motioned with her hands. "Tall man. Clean clothes. Nice clothes."

"Nice clothes?"

"Officer clothes. Important man."

Rook didn't want to believe an officer was responsible for this, but rather, it was someone posing as an officer. His smart radio vibrated. "Eliza? Have you got the names of everyone?"

"I don't think we need to," she answered, scared. "I know what Havkat is."

"What? What is it?"

"It's not a programme. It's a Danish noun. It means Catfish."

"Catfish?" Rook repeated, knowing he'd only heard that name used once around here. "Like the operation in Liberia right now?"

"That's right. The same operation that was greenlit by Minister Eriksen."

## 29

G unpowder and freshly disturbed dust filled the mineshaft like a thick smog, and the screams of injured soldiers echoed off the walls and into Harper's ears. He followed the laser on his rifle, pushing slowly forward with extreme caution. A hand softly grabbed his shoulder, Gundam One, letting him know he'd be taking point with his night goggles to lead the way.

More cries called through the tunnels, and more oddly, a metallic rattling. The daylight behind faded as they pushed further into the unknown horrors waiting for them.

Harper pulled his own night vision down. "Going dark," he whispered through his headset, signalling for the rest of the rescue team to follow suit. A few small rocks dropped from the ceiling ahead, causing them to pause as they followed the wails of anguish into the winding darkness.

The first body appeared at their feet.

"Not ours, a local," Gundam One confirmed. "Fuck 'em."

Harper kept eyes on the body as they crept past, picking up the pace. The air was thick and already stank of blood.

The metallic rattling grew louder, and the screams became muffled, like they had been gagged. The tunnel gently bent right into a large opening. A twenty-foot-high cave.

Harper gently tapped the shoulder of the man in front and took point, motioning for everyone to hold. Footsteps ran off into another tunnel, just out of his vision on the other end of the opening.

Harper pushed around the corner, almost blinded as his night vision was bombarded by daylight shining in from the cave opening to the left. He lifted the goggles and returned his hand to the grip of his rifle. Bullet casings and grenade damage clattered all over the ground, with tunnels winding off in different directions. The cave opening led to another quarry, at least fifty feet high.

On the opposite side of the cave, chains rattled, and men cried out from behind their gags. Harper adjusted his eyes, seeing what was waiting for them. Teams Alpha, Bravo, Charlie, and Delta had been chained to the wall and nail-gunned in place, both dead and alive. Duct tape covered their mouths, distorting their screams as they hung suspended off the cave floor.

Harper quickly searched for Woodburn, who wasn't with these men. "Secure this area," he commanded, keeping to the cave opening and the quarry ridge. They were like fish in a barrel at that point. A medic attempted to remove the tape from one of the wounded, but the man started shaking his head violently, begging not to. After Team Gundam secured the cave entrance, Harper walked over to examine the situation and the men.

There was a wire running behind all their ears, cleverly hidden beneath the tape as it ran past their lips and across the other cheek. Harper followed the wire to the last man, where it moved down the wall and into the ground.

"Are you rigged to something?" Harper asked the survivor who had protested. They nodded. "Fuck. Catfish base, this is Alpha One. We need the Burrowclaw in here." He requested that the unmanned digitech-bomb disposal unit be deployed to them. With the machine's millisecond readout, they could at least figure out how to disarm whatever device the men were attached to.

*"Roger that, Alpha One. Preparing Burrowclaw now."*

Harper followed the wires into four fresh dirt piles in the ground and two more in the cave walls. If the explosives were powerful enough, they would bring the top of the cave down on them.

"You need to see this, sir." Gundam One approached with a photo. "It was on one of the bodies."

Harper took it, and his face dropped just as quickly as his heart sank. It was a photo of his family. The photo his wife said they lost during the move. In the back garden of their home, a summer barbeque, celebrating Troy's first birthday. Something new had been added to it. A message on the back.

*We all lost this.*

He choked hard, both the sorrow and anger curdled through his veins, then realised there had only been one copy of this photo. Whoever took this had access to his family. Been close to his family.

This was just another game to Admiral, and he'd been ballsy enough to get his inside man to go through Harper's family's belongings just to taunt him over here.

"What the fuck do you want with me?" Harper hissed, wiping a tear. "Why are you doing all this?" Everything felt like a humiliation. His lips curled, and his eyes burned. "How the fuck did you get this here?"

The Burrowclaw wheeled slowly into the cave's opening as the caterpillar tracks crunched across the ground, avoiding the freshly dug areas. The smallest of its extended arms elevated, and its subsonic shutter clicked rapidly over a five-second period. It repeated the process over the four dirt piles, then retracted as the information was relayed back to the team in the compound. Everyone held their breath, and some prayed until they found out how dire their situation was.

*"Alpha One. The wires on our men are decoys, but the bombs in the walls and grounds are armed."*

"Can we start evacuating our men?"

*"Yes, sir. It won't affect the trigger mechanism, but there is a trip wire that leads north of your location."*

Harper checked his watch compass and turned to face north out of the wide cave entrance. "I guess we're not going that way then," he said out loud and turned back. All eyes remained glued to him. "You heard the man." He nodded to the troops. "Let's get our boys out of here." He switched back to the headset. "We're going to need assistance. Send what you can inside and help us get our men out."

*"Copy that, sir."*

Harper marched to the survivor nearest him, fingers cramping as he reached for the mouth tape, trying to ignore the heavy nose breathing on his hand. Everyone held their breath. One quick tear and it was removed. No explosion. Just the sounds of the soldiers' unbearable pain.

"Alright, let's move," he ordered as Team Echo began to try and remove the embedded nails.

He wiped his forehead with the back of his hand, looking at his family photo again. A setup. A message for him. All planned out.

*They wanted me to see this.* He shot a look across the cave. *The chains were already here. The nail guns.*

He looked back at the photo. "How did they know I wouldn't be here for the first assault?" he whispered while his hands reached behind to his freshly bandaged wounds. Then it hit, unlike the rocket that had missed him. Connor wasn't aiming for him or Woodburn. *It was an attempt to put them out of action while the first team went in. Just so they could do...* he looked at the impaled soldiers... *this.*

"They're keeping me and Woodburn alive," he blurted, pressing over to one of the injured men. It was Alpha Two. "Where did they take Woodburn?"

"The tunnel!" they cried as Echo One administered morphine. "The fucking tunnel."

The support team arrived as Harper pulled himself up and began to limp into the opening at the far end.

"Where are you going, sir?" Echo One asked.

"I'm going to get my friend. You get our boys out, and we'll meet back at base." With that, he raised his rifle, lowered his night vision goggles and disappeared into the opening.

Harper focused ahead of him, following the laser dot as the passageway slowly ascended and veered left.

*You want me? I'm fucking coming.*

Admiral had his attention. Taking Woodburn and displaying Harper's family was personal, and the fire had been lit inside him. Just for good measure, he promised himself that he would bring the snake's head back and show it to the surviving soldiers once it was all over.

*The game ends now.*

Harper's left hand tightened around the foregrip, and he begged someone to jump in front of him so he could satisfy his rapidly growing bloodlust. *Cool it!* he admonished himself, keeping his focus in the zone. A faint dripping started to grow louder as he pushed higher inside the tunnel system.

Daylight crept in through the end of the tunnel, and the passageway began to widen as he approached. Harper lifted the night vision goggles and pushed forward, the dripping getting louder. Carefully checking both flanks as he stepped out, he saw what was causing the noise.

A human body hung from the tree to his left. Freshly skinned and torn of most of its flesh. A pile of clothes lay strewn behind it. One of Catfish's uniforms. The helmet. Tactical vest. Harper's original M4.

"Mine?" he stuttered, squinting and not wanting to believe his eyes. They weren't lying; it was the M4 he'd been issued. The same one Woodburn had taken from him. "No. No. No," Harper cried, staggering to the body and spotting the nametag on the overalls.

*Catfish Actual.*

In his anguish and panic, his foot caught the trip wire.

Explosions thundered from back inside the tunnel, one at a time and headed further inside. To Harper's left, the quarry filled with smoke and screams as the cave imploded in on itself, crushing anyone who hadn't been killed in the initial explosions. A plume of dust, rocks, and wooden shrapnel blasted out of the tunnel and hit Harper, knocking him backwards and landing under the body.

"Fuck. Fuck," Harper spat as he cried, rolling away and punching the dirt he lay on. His hands shook while removing his helmet, and he wiped the blood away. "Why kill him? Why kill him?" he hyperventilated, not wanting to look back at his friend's mutilated corpse, and then it became a scream. "Why kill him?" He slumped against the nearest tree, trying to keep his gun up.

His heart thumped against his ribs, and his diaphragm felt like it would tear if his lungs tried to take any more air in. Rocks continued to fall, and the dust was yet to settle. Tears and snot streamed down, getting stuck in his moustache and beard. He spat, crawling over to the pile of clothes, keeping his eyes away from the body as he searched the pockets. He tore the name patch off the sleeve, carefully placing it next to the photo in his chest pocket.

*Get back to operations. Evac immediately,* he ordered himself. *Are you just going to leave your friend there?*

He grabbed his thick, red hair in frustration. For the first time in his military career, he didn't know what to do. A heart-wrenching scream left his lungs and ripped through the valley, which bounced right back and hit him. The verification of loss, trauma, and the devastation that he hadn't caught the people responsible for it all.

Thumping blades roared across the sky, and dust whipped around, smothering the devasted quarry's ridge. The recognisable sound of a Chinook grew as it began its approach to Harper. He waved his hands in the air, both for attention and a signal of his own defeat. Instead of slowing and descending, it continued past, its back ramp down. The passengers were in full view. Grey T-shirt. Black pants. Admiral's men.

Harper gapped in horror as they waved with a victorious sneer, and the ramp closed as the Chinook carried on further into the jungle.

"Catfish Base, this is Alpha One. Do you copy?" Harper radioed.

No reply.

"Catfish Base. Do you copy?"

"I wouldn't worry about them." A voice laughed to the right, and Connor stood at the top of what remained of the ridge.

Harper turned sharply, and the one-eyed monster grinned back. He was at least fifty metres away. He raised his gun, but Connor had already taken off, disappearing over the top and out of sight.

"I'm gonna kill you!" Harper roared, pulling himself to his feet, picking up the second M4 and strapping it over his shoulder. This was his chance for something he never entertained. Revenge.

He scrambled forward, fingers gripping into the dirt and his boots slipping as he crawled up. Jagged rocks cut into his screaming palms, and his feet gave away with each push. He bore through it and pulled himself up to the top, ready to fire.

The first attack came. A hysterical man, blood-covered clothes, black skin, and that hyena laugh. Harper fired twice, connecting with the stomach and chest. They landed at his feet. A local who had become a Termite.

No time to question as the second attacker charged, well in full view. Two more shots. Three more bursts from the left, all brandishing machetes. Harper's firing was precise, dropping them alongside the others. *Revenge...*

He surged forward, never lowering his weapon. More attacks followed, and more Termites fell. A quick reload, and he continued, moving across the top of the quarry back to operations. He didn't know what was waiting, and he didn't care. Blood was going to be paid.

Another pounced from the front, taking Harper's attention as he dealt with the attacker. A Termite used the distraction and delivered a slash to the back, not cutting through Harper's tac-vest, but his exposed arms took a hit. They tried to deliver another swipe to his gut, but Harper dodged, ramming the back of his gun to their head and firing four shots into them after they crashed to the floor.

He forced himself through the pain and continued with everything he had, firing indiscriminately at anyone who dared approach, armed or not. One Termite couldn't have been older than thirteen and had been dropped just as cold-bloodedly as any other would've been. Harper emptied another magazine, reloaded, and kept going.

Then the spear came straight for his legs. He dove, but the tip ripped through the bottom of his calf, just missing his Achilles. Quickly returning to a crouch, Harper fired back to where it had come from, then launched a grenade into the area. A cry followed the explosion, to which Harper threw another grenade for good measure.

He reached the end of the open, dry mineral and limped into the foliage, following the slope down to the left and back towards the compound. He stopped at a fallen tree, catching his bearings. Blood rushed through his ears, and his pulse was deafening.

Above the internal pounding of his eardrums, a wave of bare feet stampeded through the brush, going in all directions. Leaves and bushes swayed all around as the Termites swarmed back to the top of the quarry. The laughing mixed with snarling like some new kind of forest apex predator, on the hunt like a pack for their next meal.

Harper stayed motionless, holding his breath.

The swarm passed by, pounding up the slope towards where Harper was expected to have made his last stand. He slowly stood, moving his finger back to the trigger and silently limped through the carved pathway until the back of one of the warehouses came into view just beyond the trees.

He held tight to the building's exterior, slowly creeping around the side. He'd never taken steps so calculated before. Then the urge to rush came.

Admiral's voice.

Just as he picked up the pace, the pistol whip came from behind, knocking him clean out. His face clattered into the dry ground.

Connor stood over Harper's limp body.

## 30

H arper refused to open his eyes until he'd figured out where he was. His back was supported, and his feet were firmly on the ground. Wooden. A chair, but he wasn't bound. The back of his head throbbed, sending irritating pulses through to his eyes and temples. He needed water, and his skin burned under the sun.

*How long have they had me here?*

His right calf burned, and the dry, crusted blood had collected in his boot. The back of his left arm was exposed, and the slash felt like it would reopen with any minor movement. His chest and shoulders felt lighter, and a quick glance showed that his tac-vest had been removed. He carefully lifted his head to get a glance out further in front.

Roughly ten metres ahead, Connor spoke to someone in the back of the helicopter, "Project Zodiac has just touched down at site C. They'll start work on the sister's blood within the hour," he informed whoever he was talking to, closing the passenger door shut on them and turning to Harper with a curious gaze. "Looks like our man of the hour is waking up. That was a hell of a fight he put up there."

"A damn hell of a fight," Admiral remarked, walking from behind and standing next to the helicopter. He handed one of the M4s to

Connor before grabbing a bucket of water and throwing it over Harper.

It was warm, shooting up his nose and making him choke. He rubbed his face, confirming that he hadn't been bound to the chair at all. He scanned through the gaps in his fingers to see if he could make a break for it.

No. Connor was armed and faster than him.

"It's been a while, Lieutenant," Admiral said first, crouching in front of Harper. "You're not bound to that chair because I have no intention of killing you, and neither does Connor."

"Is that what you said to Woodburn?" Harper spat scathingly, shaking the image from his head. "Is that what you fucking said to my friend?"

"I strongly recommend you control your emotions," Connor interjected. "The last person I had in a chair was Ryan. I know you know how that ended for him."

"He's right about you holding your emotions," Admiral added. "Now is the time for you to listen and nothing else. Please read between the lines on that. For old times' sake, I don't want you to do something stupid." He dropped some papers on the ground. "Pick them up when you're ready."

Harper glanced at Connor, who held the gun tightly enough to show that he would shoot if he tried anything. He leaned forward, picking up the papers, which turned out to be photos—ones that he'd seen already. The Twin Towers. The blueprints. The boarding passes.

"Have you not wondered why I left all that for you?" Admiral asked. "And done everything possible to keep you alive through all this?"

"Left me alive?" Harper said while wincing. "You killed good men today."

"Don't worry about the chorizo and pasta lovers," Connor taunted. "They're just as dispensable as the skinny's here," he said, referring to the locals.

"Stay on track, Harper," Admiral continued. "Don't let your emotions get in the way. Look at the photos again and tell me why you're here."

"I don't know, you piece of shit!"

Admiral shook his head sternly and paced, preparing himself for what he was about to reveal. "The photos here are the foundation of what bought your country down. It must be confusing because, from both aspects, it looks like 9/11 was both a terrorist attack and an inside job."

"Which was it then?"

"Both. It was a terrorist attack that was meant to look like an inside job," Admiral explained harshly.

"That doesn't make any goddamn sense."

"Actually, it does," Connor said, biting his lip.

"Think about it," Admiral continued. "What's the best way to take down the West? You don't go to war with the West. That'll be suicide. No. What you do is you make the West turn on itself."

Harper stared blankly, trying to understand what was being said.

"You frame America for a false flag operation that killed over three thousand of its own people and intentionally put the blame on someone else," Admiral carried on. "Nobody would know that McPherson had been supplied by the very people who flew the planes into the towers. All done to convince you to go to war against an inferior enemy, then frame you for false pretences."

"I don't... I don't..." Harper squinted, trying to make sense of it all.

"Oh, for fuck's sake," Connor groaned. "They made 9/11 look like an inside job, and when your invasion of Iraq and Afghanistan was exposed to be instigated by an event that involved you murdering your own citizens, America would turn on itself. And that's what happened, isn't it? It fucking worked."

Harper sat still, burning, head screaming. "You mean to tell me the fall of my country and the war across Europe was started by a hoax?"

"The biggest one in human history," Admiral confirmed softly. "Not done out of love, or revenge, or religion, but... nothing but a hatred for the West. The match that has burned nearly a billion lives to date. The fire that annihilated your home country."

Memories flooded Harper of his family's home. Every good moment before that video of McPherson came out to the public. Then the mass rioting and looting, which rapidly turned into lynching, then became a full-blown civil war. The first report of a tank crew being overthrown and the dead soldiers hanging from street signs. The mask of every American dropped, and within days, it had become a fight for yourself or a fight against those who don't follow your views. Every minor disagreement, cancelling or social media feud became street warfare.

The last phone call Harper received was from his mother just before the lines were cut. That was the last he heard of her in Santa Monica, just as Christian militants rolled in and battered the progressive town into the ground, targeting anyone who had attended a pride festival the previous summer.

He was called on to be evacuated with his family and put on a new duty. Locate the source of the video leak, where he and Woodburn would be paired up with SAS Task Force 205. The specialist unit led by the very man in front of him.

Admiral clicked his fingers in front of Harper's face. "Stay with me, buddy. I know that's a lot to take in. It gets worse."

"Worse?" Harper cackled, somewhat hysterically and sorrowful. "How can that be any worse?"

"This kind of worse." Connor pulled out a vial of clear liquid. "You know what this is, don't you?"

Harper nodded, wiping his tears away. "Kurustovia45."

"The engineered version of Kuru, designed by a lab here back in 1995," Admiral said, taking the vial from Connor. "You see, it was their plan to release this onto the survivors of the war and just watch us tear each other apart. When they realised they couldn't make it airborne, they kept it on the back burner to use on prisoners, like what they did with Connor and me. But it wasn't the only infliction they tried to weaponise. Endometriosis for infertility. Stephen Johnson syndrome to make our immune systems turn on ourselves." He placed the vial in his pocket and held out Harper's family photo. "We all lost something because of that hoax, and these people tried to wipe us all off the face of the planet, including your family."

"How did you get that?" Harper snarled.

"You're going to find out in the next two minutes." Admiral dropped his head, sensing it was time. "Listen very carefully. Here's what's going to happen." He took the M4 from Connor and approached. "Connor and I will be unarmed when I place this on the ground. We will stand by that helicopter, and you will have more than enough time to reach and grab it. It's loaded." He fired a shot into the sand to prove his claim. "But here's the question. Will you join us and help take down the people who destroyed your country and started a conflict that has taken over nine hundred million lives, or will you try to shoot us? It's your call."

"Join you?" Harper almost gasped. "In what? Genocide. Enslavement? Cannibalism?"

"Join us in nullifying every western-hating scum that was involved in taking this from you and three hundred million other Americans. A fight back against the systematic attempt to wipe out the West. A modern-day holocaust. Jesus Christ and you people call us fucking Nazis?" Admiral shot back, holding Harper's family photo out and sticking it to the M4. The weapon had been placed on the ground, and just as promised, Connor and Admiral walked slowly backwards, standing in front of the pilot's door.

*Is this a ploy? I know they're infected. They can run faster than me.* Harper tried to weigh the situation. *Maybe I can fake joining them? Just get out of here alive and back to your family.*

Woodburn's hanging corpse brought a wave of hate.

*They could do that to anyone. Anyone. Your family. They still did it to your friend. He's your fucking friend!*

"Time's almost up," Admiral warned. "Think about it. You won't be just helping us get rid of the vermin, but with you at our side, you can help me negotiate Hannah's release safely. We won't have to kill the vineyard people."

"Hannah's release?" Harper said out loud. "You know she's alive?" Only three people outside the vineyard knew that. "How do you know she's alive?"

"From the same person who got me that photo of your family," Admiral admitted. "It's time to make your call."

*They're everywhere. They've been near my family. They've been near Woodburn's family.*

The thought of Admiral or Connor touching his wife or children did it, and he leapt forward, pulling the rifle into position and locking the sight on them.

The passenger door of the helicopter flung open, and a muzzle flashed in the darkness, followed by a gunshot.

A burning sensation ripped through Harper's heart, then the impact of ribs cracking inwards and muscle being torn into thousands of pieces. Oxygen failed him as he tried to breathe, but it was like he was being drowned from the inside.

Harper dropped to his knees, falling backwards, and the cloudless midday faded from bright blue to black.

# 31

The patrol car nearly slammed through the front gate as Rook finally broke to a stop in the middle of Eriksen's driveway, slamming the car door shut after he jumped out.

"Evening, gentlemen," he said, waving to the two guards at the front door. "Don't mind me. I'm a V.I.P for Mrs Eriksen, remember?" They refused to budge, keeping their cold, condescending stare on him. "Look. I haven't got time for this shit. I'm going to knock on that door, or you're going to let me in. Understand?"

"She is busy now. It's time for her children's injections," one of the guards muttered.

"Injections?" Rook frowned. "What for?" He saw the other guard glance at his colleague, almost telling him to shut up.

Rook had enough, snatching the pistol from the nearest guard's holster and pointing it at the still-armed one. "Fucking drop it, and open the fucking door. Now." They complied, and Rook led them inside by gunpoint into the reception area. He took their radios, made them strip to their underwear, and then locked them in a storage cupboard. He then sifted through the keys and walked to the master apartment on the first floor, letting himself in.

"How many times do I have to tell you to knock, even if it's…"

Eriksen paused as she walked out from the lounge, stopping in her tracks as she saw him. "Sergeant Rook? What are you doing here? What's the meaning of this?"

Rook's eyes lowered to her left hand. A vial he knew all too well. Kurustovia. "What's the meaning of this? I should be asking you, what's the meaning of that?" He pointed to her hand, about to draw the pistol, just as her daughter walked out.

She asked something in Danish, and Rook politely smiled as the daughter skipped back to the living room, but not before making sure he'd spotted the cotton ball taped to her arm.

Eriksen smiled the whole time, then her face dropped when she turned to Rook again.

"It's only for the little one's sake that I'm not pointing the gun at your head right now," he said coolly. "How'd they get infected?"

A tear puddled under her left eye and then ran down her cheek. "I-I can't tell you. He'll kill us if I do."

"Who will? And how did you use the Havkat Programme without anyone seeing you?"

"The what?" she asked, desperate and confused. "I don't know what you're talking about."

"Bullshit!" Rook tried to keep his voice down. "The software used to turn against our systems against us is called the Havkat Programme. That's Danish for Catfish, isn't it? The same name is for the operation happening in Liberia right now. The operation you greenlit and we just so happened to lose contact with an hour ago."

"I only greenlit it. I didn't name it."

"Who did then?"

She looked at the vial. "He did. He organised all of it."

"So help me God, you better give me a name, or your children will grow up sick and in an orphanage."

"He infected my children, blackmailed me with their health to give him more power."

"Who did?"

Eriksen glanced upwards to a small camera above the front door. "I didn't tell him," she said to the device. "Please, I didn't tell him."

Rook followed, her glance. "Is he watching right now?"

"He could be," she whispered. "He'll blow us up. He'll blow your friends up, too."

"What the fuck are you talking about?"

"I'm not telling you who it is, but maybe if you pull your head out of your inbred behind, you could figure it out."

Rook stepped back, trying to unriddle whatever Eriksen was saying. She was scared and trying her best to keep her children alive.

Someone had poisoned her children and used the serum as a way to bribe his way into power. Someone making decisions. Someone who named Catfish. Someone in charge of Catfish.

Woodburn.

"What? No." He refused to believe it. "It can't be."

Then it all hit him.

Woodburn was one of the last people at Monreal's terminal. Woodburn had ordered the system reboot, which disrupted communications. Woodburn was the one who started the theory that Monreal was still alive, making them look for a ghost and not for him. Woodburn was the one who signed off on Rook being transported to the vineyard last year.

Woodburn was *officer man*.

"Who else knows?"

Eriksen shook her head. "Just me and the goons he used to attack the hospital."

"How is he going to blow you up when he's in Liberia?"

She glanced at the camera. "He could be watching now. The buildings are rigged."

"Rigged?" he asked out loud, then remembered the 'heavy-duty' refurb just after the hospital attacks. An order carried out by Woodburn himself. "Bombs are in the walls?"

She nodded, sobbing and heaving.

"Get your family out of here now," he said, turning for the front door and storming out of the building. He started the ignition and pulled his smart radio out. "Mikey. Listen to me very carefully. Get Jen, Steph, Harper's family, and get the fuck out. Now. No time to explain. Just do it."

He hung up and dialled the next number. "Eliza. I need you to do whatever you and your staff can to get me through to Harper now!" He rubbed his forehead, honking the horn as he sped past a delivery truck. "I'm five minutes out. Get any link you can and get us connected to him or the U.S.S Gavato."

Rook hauled up the stairs three at a time before bursting into the control room, catching everyone by surprise. "It's Woodburn," he huffed, leaning over Eliza's desk. "It's fucking Woodburn." Behind his desperation to share the revelation, he hadn't seen the horrified expression on Eliza's face. Tears leaked as she covered her mouth, pointing to the screen before her.

Rook peered around and took in the live feed. Harper's body cam, laying on the dirt-covered ground.

"His is the only body cam still functional." She wept. "We tried to contact him, but the signal off the New Zealand satellite is one way." She rewound the footage, Harper's last moments before he collapsed on his back and rolled to the side. A pair of boots walked by, and then Woodburn's voice echoed through Harper's microphone. Eliza played it over the speaker.

"I didn't want to have to do this," Woodburn said coldly, out of shot, "but we are going to take back what was ours and eliminate everyone involved in the downfall of our country. I thought that's what you'd want, too. I'm sorry I misread you, my friend."

Eliza sped the footage forward until it was now live, and Harper's body was being dragged across the ground, with treetops passing across the screen. It stopped before the camera lifted higher, shifted to the side, and remained a few feet off the ground, as if it were suspended or on a table.

"You put your faith in the wrong people." Connor's voice could be heard behind the sound of metal slowly scraping against metal. "How are you going to deal with the vineyard?" he asked.

"Ryan's been in the dark for months. I can easily bait him without having to fire a shot," Woodburn answered, coming closer. "I'll get Hannah out alive for you."

"Thank you, my friend. It's been good to have you back," Admiral said. "I'm sorry. We gave him a chance to see the light."

"I know you did," Woodburn answered. "But he was weak. It's his family I feel sorry for."

"Excuse me, gentlemen," Connor interrupted, followed by the sound of a blade cracking through bone. "I can't take this body apart while you're near it." Another thud and more bone splitting. "Are you sure you want your first taste to be of your friend?"

Eliza trembled, turning away and covering her eyes. Rook swallowed hard and lowered his head, punching the desk.

"Better him than anyone," Woodburn replied. "Just make—oh shit!"

"What?" Admiral asked.

The bodycam shuffled, ripped from the tac-vest and held in front of Woodburn's guilty face. "The light is green. Someone in Rennes is watching."

"Execute Catfish now, General," Admiral ordered.

The camera dropped, landing in a small brush, with the table and Harper's legless body in full view. His detached limbs were being charred over a fire.

"Is this recorded?" Rook asked, turning Eliza back to the chair. "Can you send this to Ryan?"

"His smart radio isn't equipped for this kind of file, even if he had the signal to receive it," she said hysterically, downloading the file into a jpeg form.

"Can you email it?"

"To who?"

Rook looked around, trying to think. "Can you send it to Alexi?"

"If they're online." She panicked, pulling up the IP and satellite code Wolfpack's base of operations,

*File downloading. 30% Complete.*

"Come on, come on," Rook willed the computer.

An eruption shook the building, blasting the windows out and launching glass through the control room. Above the screams and confusion, Rook staggered to the windows and peered out as another blast ripped through the sky, followed by another. They all came from Rennes city centre.

Right where the accommodation was.

Rook pulled up Mikey's code on his smart radio, putting the call through. No answer. He tried again. No answer. Another explosion, and the panicked screams finally reached the airport windows. The control room's emergency systems activated, and the alarm started blaring.

"Our self-defence systems have come online. All surface-to-air missiles are armed and locked!" Eliza shouted as she climbed back up to her desk.

"What are they targeted on?" Rook asked as he ran back to her station.

*Download 78% Complete.*

"We're locked out of the systems!" one of the technicians cried, frantically typing to try and override.

"Can't access the local server," another called.

*Download 95% Complete.*

"Oh fuck," Eliza gasped, her second monitor bringing up the self-defence target. A tall tower standing above a huge building with one runway. "The target is us."

*Download 99% Complete.*

The first missile screeched from over a mile away, beginning its targeted journey towards the control room.

*Download Complete.*

"Fuck it." Rook hit send on the email before closing his eyes and pulling Eliza below the desk.

# PART III

## THE RAT AND THE CHEESE

## 32

Ryan threw his left forearm up and deflected Drinker's right hook while using his own shoulder to push the Scotsman back. Firmly planting his heels against the snow-covered ground, Ryan jumped into a counter-offensive, throwing two right-hand punches of his own, both of which were blocked. Drinker caught the third punch, pulling Ryan in and using the momentum to throw him over his shoulder, slamming them both hard onto the frozen ground.

Ryan wheezed and opened his eyes just as Drinker's fist came crashing down towards his face.

"I told ya," Drinker huffed with a huge grin on his face, fist dangling inches away from Ryan's nose. "Don't do the same punch three times in a row. You're way too predictable." He unclenched his hand and held it out.

Ryan grabbed it and let Drinker pull him to his feet. A chunk of snow managed to find its way down the neck of his hoodie and slid down his back. "At least these sparring rounds are lasting longer than a minute now." He cringed, trying to reach behind his back and displace the frozen discomfort.

It had been over a week since Alexi had dropped off the AnCam system, and there had been no news regarding the success or even failure of the operation that was taking place. No one had contacted from Rennes. The silence was too much to take for Ryan, so he'd asked Drinker to teach him some kickboxing in their spare time, just to give his mind something to do.

"Aye, you're picking up the basics fast," Drinker noted as he started to warm down, "but if you do come into a hand-to-hand fight with one of these guys, you're still way off the mark."

"Anything else I can do to get better?"

"Not really. It's all down to experience. Admiral's men have it. You don't. That doesn't mean you should quit before you start, though, and hopefully the situation won't even arise where you have to start using your new skills."

"Hmm," Ryan subtly agreed, rubbing his left shoulder from where it had impacted the ground. He reached into his bag and pulled out a cigarette.

"What the fuck do you think you're doing?" Drinker asked, almost bemused and offended.

"I've just had my ass handed to me, in the snow, for the fourth time this week," Ryan explained. "Think I'm allowed a smoke."

"You ain't earned that yet."

"What the fuck else do you want me to do?"

"You wanna be a better fighter?" Drinker asked rhetorically. "You've gotta get fitter."

"So?" Ryan whined, sensing something was coming that was most likely going to wind him up. He tossed the cigarette back into the bag and stood with his hands on hips, waiting for the bad news.

"Four laps," Drinker said, using his finger to motion around the vineyard grounds.

"You're fucking kidding, right?"

"Nope."

Ryan groaned like a stubborn child and began pacing up the drive-way. "Are you not joining in?" he protested.

"Don't need to," Drinker said with a snort. "Harper did this shit to me for months. It's my turn to pass it on to you."

"Well, whenever Harper gets back, I'm kicking both your slave-driving asses."

As Ryan began his surprise cardio session, he remembered the last time he'd completed the same four-lap jog. It had been a roasting summer day. Alfie was barely three days old, and Doc was the one who had timed him. Only six months had passed since that day. Alfie was nearly sitting up by himself, the scorching weather now replaced with the heaviest snowfall anyone had ever seen, and what was left of Doc was now buried at the back of their grounds with everyone who had been taken from them since the Termite War began.

Six months of false promises, desperate uncertainty, and living on the edge of a blade that wanted to cut their life in two.

*I need you to say it's over, Harper,* Ryan pleaded in his head as he completed the first lap in just over seven minutes. His body found a steady rhythm, but his thoughts were going faster than he could handle. *I need this all to end.*

By the time he'd completed the second lap, endorphins were running riot in his muscles, and the extra weight of the snow on his shoes had all but vanished as he sped up, trying to outrun the confusion that bounced off the inside of his skull. There was no peace to be found in the war against Admiral, and as much as Ryan wanted to take Connor's life, he knew the fate of their enemies would be in the hands of the European Alliance. *I need blood to spill,* Ryan begged internally, wondering just how the operations in both Liberia and the Scottish Isles had fared in their fights. Something told Ryan that the long-lasting silence meant it hadn't been a clean sweep. *What if it's still ongoing?*

He completed the third lap in just under six minutes. The brisk, sharp air warmed the second he inhaled, and sweat drenched his hoodie and jogging bottoms. It could've been summer for all he knew. His feet squelched into his previous lap's footprints, flicking a muddy slush up his back with every step. The only other sounds were his determined breathing and the slapping of his soles against the ground. Everything else was silent.

*What if Harper lost?*

Ryan began to slow, coming to a complete stop as the foreboding thought embedded itself into him. It took control, paralysing and numbing the world around. The light grey clouds appeared to turn dark, the maze walls looming over as they constricted the vineyard, consuming everything they had built and fought for. Ryan's home began to destroy itself around him. Everything they had achieved would all be for nothing if Admiral had won.

"No!" Ryan roared, snapping himself out of it. He clenched his hands a couple of times before rubbing his face. "No." He began to run again. "Not for nothing."

By the time he'd nearly finished the final lap, his muscles began to cramp, sensing the end of the exercise. The lactic acid ripped through his calves and up his thighs.

*Harper did not fail. I will not fail.*

Against his own judgement, he broke into a sprint and rounded the final corner behind the spinach patch, slipping and landing elbow first on his right arm, which his ribs landed heavily on top of. Angrily ignoring it, he pulled himself up and continued, though limping by the end of it as he finally met the driveway and collapsed to his knees.

"Eight-minute final lap," Drinker announced, looking at his stopwatch. "What took so long? And what the fuck was that shout?"

"I slipped over." Ryan pointed to the fresh mud on his clothes, though lying about when it had happened. "Needed a minute to recover."

"Aye, ya wuss!" Drinker smirked. "Thought you were tougher than a grazed knee."

Ryan chuckled nervously, glad that no one had seen his momentary pause. He leaned into his open bag, taking the cigarette and matches. The nicotine felt great, but the quick inhale caused him to cough so hard that he wretched. He spat thick saliva onto the snow and leaned over, trying to regain normal breathing.

"I don't need to tell you smoking's bad for you," Drinker said sarcastically as he picked up their sports bag and threw it over his shoulder.

"Funny," Ryan coughed. "Because being mouthy can get you a smack in the face, but there's no health warning for that."

The pair started their walk back to the winery.

"After those girly punches you threw today, I don't have to worry about that."

"Asshole."

As they reached the gravel car park, the winery's front double doors opened, with Cassy leading out one of the horses by the head collar. The rest of their small herd followed, with all the community's children mounted atop. Ryan saw Maisie on the last of the horses, her favourite. Where all the others were tall and dark, that particular one was much smaller and almost hazel red. He was aware that the classes were taking the animals out for a run-around today and to teach the children how to change the feeds, muck, and water.

"How's school today?" Ryan asked, flicking the cigarette behind him. A mixture of excited voices blurted back at him from the children, which helped warm up his soul. It wasn't just the innocence of it all, but the genuine moments where they weren't screaming or frightened for their lives that helped lift Ryan.

Those moments were what the vineyard had achieved.

*We won't lose. We can't lose,* he forced himself to repeat over and over.

"We're staying close to the building," Cassy said reassuringly as she gently pulled the horse's lead. "We won't be going out to the walls."

"I know you won't." Ryan raised his eyebrows. "Because I'm on lookout when I get upstairs."

"Who's watching Alfie?" she asked. "Sandra needs to make dinner."

"I am." Drinker raised his hand. "I said it was the least I could do after kicking your fiancé's arse for three hours." He turned and winked at Ryan. "Scared I might take your missus away?"

"You take me away from Ryan?" Cassy shot back, unimpressed, before the charade dropped, and a cheeky smile spread across her face. "That would never happen, seeing as you're gay."

"For the love of f..." Drinker moaned before cutting his curse word off in front of the children. Ryan couldn't help but break into hysterics, sending him to fall onto his pained knees as he lost all control.

Drinker stormed inside, leaving Ryan to say goodbye to Cassy and the kids before limping upstairs to the restaurant. Each laugh was met with a pained cry as he hobbled upwards, and then, a few steps short of the top, he stopped. The brief happiness and even the pain in his knees evaporated, and a dark sadness washed over him, numbing him to the spot.

*I don't want to lose this.* He sat on the stairs, his smile dropped, and his eyes filled with tears. *I can't deal with this.*

He held his face in his hands, repressing the urge to let it all out. He wiped his nose and forced himself to stand, making sure all the tears were gone. *What's wrong with you?*

Reluctantly, he finished his ascendence and stepped into the restaurant. Dominic sat with his back turned, eagle-eyed, out the front window. Next to him, a laptop screen displayed feedback from four small, portable cameras hidden at the four main junctions into Maidville.

"Anything come up on the screens?" Ryan asked as he lowered his bag to the nearest table.

"Can't get any porn," Dominic joked, turning round to reveal his white-toothed grin. His black complexion seemed to have turned a touch pale during the severe snow, and his clean-shaven appearance now sported a small afro and patchy beard. "Though I did get to watch Drinker kick your ass again."

"It was a closer sparring session than two days ago," Ryan said defensively.

"Whatever you say, *boss*."

Ryan ignored it and pulled the replacement hoodie out of the bag, changing his mud-covered one. "Who's on laundry today?"

"That'll be me." Dominic stood. "I said I'd swap with your missus because she's doing the teacher shift today."

"Ah, cool." Ryan smiled, nodding to the dirty hoodie in his hand. "Take that with you when you go down then, *boss*."

"Motherfucker." Dominic grinned, and then his bulky frame strode over and snatched the hoodie. "At least it's good to see you joking again. I thought for a while you were going down a dark path."

"What do you mean?"

"You've been quieter than you usually are, and you haven't been out to the graves in a month."

"You been spying on me?"

"Not really, but we both know the Lord sent me here to watch over you," Dominic joked, then bit his lip, "You don't have to worry about your sister or Mikey and Jen. They're in good hands. And as for us... the army is going to deal with our enemies. It's not your issue," he said, attempting to assure Ryan. "Your butt needs to be watching out that window because we have a small classroom having a field trip today."

Ryan wondered if Dominic had seen his moment of paralysation earlier or if the resident vicar/teacher/security overwatch was just naturally gifted at saying the right thing at the right time. Maybe it was true, and he was sent from God. "Thanks," he said weakly before hurrying to the window and checking the small school trip.

"I'll see you in the morning, *boss*," Dominic said as he left down the stairwell.

"For fuck's sake," Ryan whispered to himself, though he knew he was lucky to have these people around him. It was a blessing and rarity in this world, and God only knew what other groups of survivors had witnessed or been forced to do just to get through each day.

He checked over the L96 sniper rifle before sitting it across his lap and focusing on the laptop display. Nothing moved or seemed out of place on the four live feedbacks. Camera three was the furthest away, nestled in a bird box and facing the main road that led out of Maidville towards Gatwick. The line of sight pointed for a couple of hundred metres down the A25, but creeping on the left side of its monitor was a sight that made Ryan want to puke every time he saw it. The hotel entrance where Doc and Sam were murdered in front of him. He quickly moved his eyes away to Camera One, showing the barricade at the northern end of the carriageway.

He added to notes left by Dominic.

*Camera One- Northen Barricade: No activity.*

*Camera Two- Petrol Station: Couple of birds.*

*Camera Three- Southern Barricade: No Activity.*

*Camera Four- Maidhill Peak: No Activity.*

He left the pen by the pad and shouldered the rifle. The soft trotting of the horses crunched against the snow, and some of the children laughed while Cassy tried to talk above them. Ryan watched them come back around the front of the building, pulling the rifle into firing position and aiming towards Maidhill. Though Camera Four was well hidden up there and had yet to pick up any movement, Ryan didn't trust it.

Instinctively, he searched the treeline, just waiting to see someone pointing a rifle back at the vineyard. Anxiety gripped so hard that his fingers spasmed, clamping down against the trigger. Behind the panicked, sharp breaths, he pulled away from the gun, thankful that the safety catch was still on.

*Fucking sort yourself out, man.*

He hated to admit it, but there was no point denying it to himself anymore. Something had broken inside his head, and the switch that used to keep his calmness in check had been turned off, and he was now going manically from high to low.

Chaos consumed every waking thought, and there was only one way it could end.

*I need to know what's going on.*

## 33

The morning sun reflected against the snow with blinding relentlessness, and fortunately, the clear blue sky wasn't radiating the warmth that it suggested. Both factors helped Ryan not to fall into the peaceful sleep that his mind and body begged for. A hard shiver jolted down his spine, making his knee flinch and crack against the table leg.

"Fucking cunt!" he growled, rubbing the sore area. Those were the first words he'd spoken through the long, lifeless night and morning.

"I heard that, *boss,*" Dominic announced as he entered the restaurant, placing a mug of piping hot, black liquid on the same table Ryan had just clashed with.

"What's that?" Ryan asked, untying his dreadlocks.

"Some of the coffee that Harper left for Drinker. Thought you could use it after this shift."

"Oh, thanks."

Ryan sipped carefully, trying not to burn his lips. He hadn't tasted coffee for over a decade, which was by choice and not due to the lack of supply since the war. Whereas most benefited from the caffeine, Ryan would lose focus and scatter between tasks, making his profession as a chef extremely difficult.

Coffee was one of the few things they were yet to try and harvest for themselves, but by now, everyone was used to the grape water, wine, and tea grown within their agricultural process.

Ryan felt the surge within seconds, and his tiredness evaporated behind the buzz that reached all the way through to his fingertips. "Fuck me, that's good," he declared, pushing the mug towards Dominic. "You finish that. If I have any more, I might explode."

"You look like you're ready for a rave." Dominic laughed and said, "Save your dancing for when this is over."

"Harper needs to fucking hurry up then." Ryan stood, drumming his fingers against the table. "It all needs to hurry up. I need to hear from him. Fuck, I need to hear from Steph, Mikey, Jen. I need to know Rich has pulled through. I can't take the fucking silence," he blurted, holding his head. "Why haven't we heard from them?"

"Woah, calm down."

"I can't calm down, Dominic. I can't."

"What's going on?" Dominic approached, holding Ryan by the shoulders. "Where's this come from?"

"Everything," Ryan admitted, looking down at his feet tapping against the stained carpet. One of his locks dangled in front of his eyes. The vibrant blond was beginning to fade to a dull grey.

"How long have you felt like this?"

Ryan didn't want to answer. All he knew was everyone felt safer when he was keeping himself together. He couldn't lose it again. "I don't know," he deflected. It was all true. Until yesterday, he hadn't noticed his intrusive thoughts had begun to take hold of him. "I don't think I should drink coffee again."

"You're gonna blame this on the coffee?" Dominic asked with doubt, letting go.

"Yeah. You know I am."

"Okay, *boss*. I'm gonna be upfront, though: if you keep a hell burning inside you, it will consume you. There's nothing wrong with feeling caution during this time."

"What do you mean?" Ryan asked, pulling a cigarette from his pocket.

"I'm not stupid. None of us are," Dominic said factually, looking out the window. "It's been weeks since we had any contact. It's in our nature to assume the worst, given everything we've faced and the enemy this war is against. I talk to the missus about it every night, and it's possible that something might've gone wrong." He took the L96 rifle from Ryan and sat in the chair. "There's also every chance it's gone right, or still ongoing."

"And Sandra just listens to your optimism?"

"She doesn't have a choice." Dominic shrugged, turning to face Ryan. "You will see Steph again. Mikey and Jen, too. We will get an update about Rich. One way or another, we won't be apart forever." He checked the chamber and turned back to the window. "Now, go for your weekly shower. You smell like shit after your jog yesterday."

"Cunt." Ryan sniggered before placing his hand on Dominic's shoulder. "But thank you."

He left the handheld radio on the table before heading down the stairwell. He turned off on the first floor, following the corridor to the end and turning left towards his family quarters. He opened the door quietly, finding Cassy pulling on a hoodie over a turtleneck sweater.

"What's wrong with your eyes?" she asked, tying her dark hair back into a bun.

"What do you mean?" Ryan replied, frowning.

"You look like you've snorted a can of energy drink."

"Oh. Dominic gave me some of Drinker's coffee stash."

"I've never seen you drink coffee," she remarked, unlocking the desk drawer and taking out her pistol.

Ryan pointed to his eyes, saying, "And this is why." He placed his own pistol in the drawer and shut it. "You watching over Hannah today?"

"Yep. Got a whole day with the bitch. Thankfully, she's quieted down since you spoke to her. What did you say?"

"Honestly... I promised her a quicker death if she left you alone."

"You have a way with words," Cassy said, kissing him on the cheek.

"I should've been a motivational speaker." Ryan shrugged while peering into the cot and playing with Alfie's feet. Their six-month-old was currently occupied with a sparkly mobile dangling above him. "I've gotta have a shower."

"I was going to ask if you were."

"I smell that bad?"

"What gave that away?"

"Charming." Ryan rolled his eyes and said, "Have fun on shift. Dominic and Drinker have the other radios if you need anything."

"What are you up to today?" Cassy asked, opening the door.

"Stock-take today. Checking all and every supply of everything. Should be fun," he said sarcastically.

"You can teach Alfie then. Have fun, baby." She kissed him before leaving for her shift.

Ryan sat on their bed and yawned. The caffeine burned off, and the crash started to kick in. He tapped his legs and reached for the bottle of grape water, downing half a bottle and shaking his head hard. Alfie screeched happily while kicking his legs on his bedding.

"Busy day, little man." Ryan reached in and played with his son's feet. "And Uncle Dominic ain't ever allowed to try and give me coffee again."

———

Cassy stepped into the basement with a tray of soda bread and berry compote. She placed the tray in front of Hannah's cell and relieved young Callum of his duty. He was reluctant to go, and to Cassy's disbelief, Hannah convinced him that his shift was over and that he should get some rest.

After watching him eventually head back up the stairs, Cassy took her seat and stared Hannah down. "What have you been saying to him?"

"General chitchat," Hannah dismissed, adjusting her shirt and reaching for her tray.

Cassy observed her movements around the tiny space of the cell. Nothing seemed out of place other than Callum's mood to leave. "Have you been saying anything to make him want to kill you?"

"The kid isn't armed," Hannah pointed out. "But I can promise you, I haven't said anything that would make him want to harm me. Your partner was very clear about those rules." She took a bit of bread.

"Even if it's clear you're all on edge. I could very easily say something to wind you up into giving me a quicker death."

"Why would we be on edge?"

"I'm not having this conversation with you. Ryan was clear."

For all intents and purposes, whatever message Ryan had implanted in her head seemed to have worked. Still, there was a nonchalant attitude that Cassy couldn't put her finger on, and she really didn't trust it.

"There would never be any point trying to get any truth out of you, would there?"

"My, my, Cassy. Whatever do you mean?"

"The things you do, or why you do them. You're just set in your own preservation."

"Well," Hannah answered, wiping crumbs off her jumper, "when you get threatened with a torturous death instead of a quick one, and the person making the threat is the guy who once set hundreds of men, women, and children on fire... it's best to listen to him." She pushed the tray back through the opening. "And seeing as you have a long shift down here today, are you sure this is the foot you want to start off on?"

Something bugged Cassy about that question. *There's being nice, and then there's this. What is this?* "Fine." She crossed her arms and stared Hannah down, saying nothing.

Now wasn't the time to talk. It was time to observe and see what the true motive behind the prisoner's eyes was. The mood from Callum this morning had alarmed her, and whether she was just being paranoid, she needed to figure out what had happened.

Ryan had truly rubbed off on her, and she was starting to trust her instincts.

# 34

Ryan hid his pain behind a tired smile as he stepped into the cafeteria, though his effort to hide the limp was all in vain. He held a sleeping Alfie in his arms as he greeted everyone. Teddy teased him about Drinker being the reason for the injury, though Ryan tried to claim it was the slip that was the main cause. Everything ached. His back was forced rigid, and neither his neck nor hips would allow him to turn sharply. His calves and thighs weighed heavily after the boggy, five-kilometre run.

The waft of fresh soda bread thankfully pulled him towards the hot counter like a tractor beam, where he helped himself to a loaf and a small bowl of corn and thyme rice.

"I'll promise I'll go easy on ya tomorrow." Drinker winked at him from the other side of the counter.

"The fuck you doing in the kitchen?" Ryan asked, peering through and seeing his own daughter kneading dough on the back counter.

"Cassy told me your daughter is quite the baker, so I wanted to learn."

"Is that so?" Ryan frowned with a grin. "Maisie, whatever Uncle Drinker tells you about our training outside, it's a lie. I kicked his ass."

Maisie giggled softly and turned back to her bread.

"This is actually my batch of bread." Drinker pointed to the small selection from where Ryan had just taken a roll.

Ryan bit into it, screwing his face up. "Doesn't taste as good as Maisie's. Hers tastes like love and care. Yours tastes like haggis and alcoholism."

"You can tell me that when I'm kicking your ass tomorrow," Drinker joked, leaning palm first on the counter and lowering his voice. "Just so you're aware," he whispered, "the walk-in freezer is making some weird sounds."

"Weird how? Is it the motor or the fan?"

"Fucked if I know. Do we have anyone here who could identify it?"

"Yeah, me. I fitted the newer parts a couple of years ago. I didn't think they'd start burning through this quickly."

"Must be the cold. I'll keep an eye on it and give you an update before I go to bed."

"Nice one." Ryan nodded, hobbling over to the nearest table and setting his bowl down. He dipped the bread in the rice and took a huge bite. *His bread isn't that bad, to be fair.*

Alfie stirred in his arms, then let out a tiny yawn and clutched to Ryan's chest.

"You can only wake up when Mummy comes back up," Ryan whispered, softly bouncing him while trying to eat his own dinner. After successfully finishing his meal one-handed and keeping his son asleep, he said good night to everyone and headed out the back side of the cafeteria into the maintenance corridor. Next to the two-story vats of rainwater was a collection of smaller workspaces where the vineyard's soap, toothpaste, and detergent were manufactured.

Ryan ran his fingers across the storage cupboards, whispering to himself what was inside each one. "Chemicals... glassware... kitchen parts." He stopped at the third door and creaked it open. On the highest shelf were the three extra motors for the walk-in fridge, and only one more remained for the freezer. They had never been used, and even though they were the correct parts for their particular units, he didn't know if they would be functional after all this time.

*Rennes would be able to help out. They can surely supply you with new equipment,* Ryan's brain pinged rationally, almost catching himself off guard with the optimism that had been offered.

The weeks of silence had given the impression that they were truly cut off and alone. Ryan had been mentally preparing for when the last of the salvaged food expired. Eight years was the maximum for dried rice, and even though they had started to harvest their own, the feeling of being self-sufficient bore heavily on his thoughts. They were only one bad harvest or crop disease away from starving to death.

Many discussions had taken place about what to do in that scenario, and as silly as it would've sounded to anyone on the outside, they couldn't bring themselves to kill their own animals for food.

It wasn't just Ryan who felt like this—everyone had agreed. Luckily, it had never come to that in the early years of the war, and they had all worked around the clock between every harvest to ensure their survival. They hadn't yet had to kill to eat.

*Will we still feel the same if it actually comes to that? Should we start hunting animals on the outside?*

Ryan had been standing still for minutes, eyeing up the freezer motor. He shook his head and snapped out of his haze, looking down at his sleeping son.

"It'll never come to that," he explained to Alfie. "We've done enough so far, and if it comes to shit, Rennes will have to bail us out. They owe us that much." He reached into his pocket and dug out the smart radio.

The screen flashed, only displaying the time. No missed calls. No messages. No signal.

He let out a heavy breath, closed the storage cupboard and headed back to the cafeteria, ready to pass Alfie off to Cassy and begin his night shift on the top floor.

———

The soft, long exhale that passed out his nose was calculated. It was precise. Ryan felt his nerves calm and his body relaxing. The butt of the L96 no longer pressed into his shoulder, but more, it became an extension of him.

The heavy-duty rifle felt lightweight in that zen-like moment, with his right cheek resting softly against the stock and his whole focus through the scope.

*If only it was daylight, and I had a clear shot at the practice targets,* Ryan thought, moving his eye away. Half a mile away, dotted around Maidhill's southern ridge and western slope, mop buckets stood atop fence posts. The ideal sniper practice. Since the first week of the targets being set up, no actual sniper practice had taken place, with a fear of a waste of ammo. The recent trip to Lewes meant the practice could resume, so Ryan spent the night going over the posture and composure techniques Rook had taught him when he'd been temporarily stationed at the vineyard.

If anything, Ryan credited himself for trying to constantly stay focused and positive during these quiet moments, as there was always something knocking around in his thoughts to bring the guilt and hate back.

The sniper targets themselves were a source of guilt, too. Ryan had set them up with his nephew, Lyndon, only a couple of weeks before Hannah killed him. One bullet. One case of misidentifying Lyndon for Ryan, and he was gone. The blond dreadlocks they both wore had been the cause for this.

Every time Ryan looked in the mirror and saw his hair, he hated it. One of his own features was the sole reason his nephew was buried outside and Ryan was still alive. He'd contemplated cutting them off, shaving his head, but it felt like a cop-out. He'd rather confront it and remind himself why his anger must be aimed at the people causing harm and not himself.

His chest began to tighten as he felt the negativity drowning him again. It was becoming relentless. Every day. Every hour. Every quiet moment. Letting out another long, soothing breath, he moved his head back to the scope and pulled the rifle tight. The calmness didn't come, though, and his instincts went on high alert. Something was wrong. Something was different. Something had changed.

One of the monitor displays flickered in Ryan's peripheral, so he sat the rifle aside and pulled the laptop towards him. Monitor Three was dully lit but with enough moonlight to make out figures moving. They were slow and multiple. He opened Monitor Three to full view and leaned in, but the figures were too blurred under the tree's shadows.

*More animals?* He reached out for the handheld radio. He'd alert Drinker whether it was a threat or not. He flicked between the other monitors, trying to find any movement or disturbances. Nothing. He lit a cigarette and pulled the radio to his mouth.

A sound stopped him. One that would've woken everybody. A sound they hadn't heard for a long time.

It wasn't a gunshot, a bomb, or the haunting cackle of a laughing Termite.

It was the church bell in Maidville town centre.

## 35

The signs around Maidville were to aid any survivors in seeking refuge, and they all read the same. The message was clear: not to approach the vineyard, but to ring the church's bell if they were in need of assistance.

They were messages of hope and a promise they could rebuild. Faint glimmers of hope before the Termite War began. No one had rung the bell in need of assistance for over two years, and the only new visitors within that time had bought nothing but death for Ryan's people.

No longer than ten minutes after the bell's ringing, everyone had woken. Weapons were distributed, and families and children were secured in the cafeteria. Ryan ordered a full lockdown and preparation for an attack on their home. He paced across the top floor, thinking of ways they could deflect any assault on their grounds while keeping his eyes on the monitors.

Cassy joined him not long after, and no effort to try and calm him worked. Everyone was dumbfounded as to why they were yet to send out a search party for any survivors. "If you leave those people out there any longer, they could die," Cassy warned as she watched Ryan pace back and forth across the restaurant floor.

"You're sure everyone is awake and armed?" he asked, deflecting from her initial comment.

"I've told you already that they are."

"Good."

"Look," Cassy huffed, "if you're not going to go out there, Drinker and Dominic said they would do it themselves."

"They don't get to make that call," Ryan snapped.

"Actually, no. It's you who doesn't get to make that call."

"Me? You all nominated me to make the tough decisions that no one else could, but now you're all just going to ignore what I'm saying?"

"In this situation, yes. We nominated you because you were the guy who believed we could rebuild. You were the guy willing to go out of your way to save people and help those who needed it." She looked her fiancé up and down. "This..." she pointed at him. "This is not that person."

"Last month, you were begging me not to go outside our grounds anymore, but now you're eager for me to go out into what could be an ambush?"

"Maybe I'm not that scared of you going out anymore. Maybe I've seen how you can survive, and knowing if you go out there, you won't be stupid enough to walk into a trap. Maybe I know you'll come back, either helping people or killing those who threaten us." She approached him. "I know you haven't been the same since Lyndon died, and I know that it eats you on the inside that you have to keep his murderer alive. I know you feel lost without Mikey's advice and not knowing how Steph is recovering."

"What's that got to do with this so-called mutiny against me?"

"What it's got to do with it is that the choice to save these people wouldn't be to spite you. It would be to remind you of who we are and who you made us to be," she explained. "I need you to remember that because we need that version of you. If you have to kill people out there, fine, do it. But if there are people to save, then give them a chance to keep living."

There was a certain matter-of-factness to Cassy's demeanour. She was still very much the voice of reason in his life, but she had lost that innocence in her large, brown eyes. She wasn't as scared anymore, and right now, she was willing to make the tougher decision, even if it meant going against her fiancé. For all Ryan knew, he was looking in a mirror now. She was beyond fed up with everything they were facing, but she was willing to make the right call. The tougher decision. She was everything he had helped everyone else become.

Now wasn't the time to let anyone else suffer because of his paranoia.

"Only Drinker and me go out," Ryan said. "Dominic watches the top floor. You watch over Hannah. Everyone stays armed until we get back." He zipped up his parka. "I'll be down with the torches and flares. Tell Drinker to get the fold-up stretcher, medical bag, four bottles of grape water, and one of the handheld radios. We leave in five minutes." He kissed the top of her head. "Thank you."


The half-moon shone against the snow-covered buildings of Maidville, radiating a dull purple glow as they pushed towards the church. Ryan had shown Drinker the alternative route, avoiding the main carriageway to the high street altogether and taking the back route through the school's rugby pitch. After that, they climbed down across the railway track and clambered up the opposite bank, vaulting over the mesh fence and coming up behind the high street.

They surveyed the ground for any rogue footprints, finding nothing in the back roads. Once they exited the side road, they reached the high street, shining their torches quickly over the middle of the road.

Multiple footprints and different sizes. Some weren't even adults. Drinker kept his gun aimed at the windows around them while Ryan followed the fresh prints, none of which led astray or off the path. Parts of rooftops creaked around them as they carefully moved over the snow, finally coming into view of the church on their right side. They crouched behind what remained of a bench and looked through the gate towards the open double arches of the main door.

Faint sobs, whimpering, and shivering could be heard with the distinguishable sound of a mother trying to comfort their child.

"You, in the church," Ryan called, bringing an almost instant silence to the commotion inside. "You need to answer two questions, and you have to be honest. If you lie to us, we will either open fire or just leave you here. Do you understand?"

"Yes, we understand," a thick, male, Birmingham accent replied.

"Question one: how many of you are there?"

"Sixteen. Six adults and ten children."

"Okay, question two: are you armed?"

Ryan knew this answer always took longer, and if it wasn't an instant 'no', it meant that they were in possession of a weapon.

"We have two pistols," the answer finally came.

"Okay, I need you to slide them out the front door and leave them on the path. Once you do that, we'll enter. Keep your hands where I can see them and stand side by side."

Two Glocks eventually slid out, stopping a few inches into the snow. Ryan nodded to Drinker, and they both moved cautiously towards the door, picking up the pistols as they went. They held their torches under the barrel of their guns and flicked the lights on as they entered.

Ryan did a quick head count as he kept his distance from the survivors. *Six adults. Ten children.* "Drinker, sweep the rest of the building, just in case anyone is hiding."

"Aye. Got it."

Ryan kept his torch on the group. The children and women were terrified and freezing. "Are any of you seriously injured or need medical help right this second?"

None of them answered, but the man stepped forward, hands still in front of his chest. "We're so cold. We need to get them to your vineyard."

"Once my man has done a sweep of the building, and we see you're telling the truth, we can leave. How did you know how to find us?"

"We were told to find this town during our escape."

"Escape from where?"

"Sheffield. The stronghold. It was attacked by some outsiders, and then a group of security staff turned their weapons on us."

"Who told you to come here?"

"Our driver. He was given orders by the team coming back from Scotland."

"The team from Scotland? Why had they come back to Sheffield? Did they complete their objective?" Drinker asked, shining his torch in the man's face.

"We don't know. Everything happened so fast. All we know is that the orders were to find Maidville and someone called Ryan. We saw your signs a few towns back. We followed the instructions and rang the bell."

"Where's the driver who bought you down?"

"He had to drop us a couple of towns away. One of the other transports came under attack, and he needed to provide assistance."

"There's more coming?"

"A lot more. The driver said to tune in to channel seventy-two. They'll let you know when they're within a fifty-mile radius."

"Drinker. Tune into channel seventy-two," Ryan ordered, wondering if there was already a barrage of messages waiting for them. He turned back to the families, lowering his weapon and motioning for the survivors to exit the church. "In about fifteen minutes, we'll have you in a warm place and safe. Walk single file, and no sharp movement."

"Nothing on channel seventy-two so far," Drinker reported.

"Okay. Tune back into our frequency. Let them know to start a fire in the cafeteria. Get sixteen of the sleeping bags and pillows out of storage, and get some food ready. We're coming home."

## 36

Ryan stood by the stairwell, smoking a cigarette inside the cafeteria for the second time in six weeks. He felt compelled to watch over the newest additions to the vineyard, who were now all washed and fed as they sat around the indoor fire. All had been given fresh clothes and sleeping bags, but they wouldn't be assigned their own private rooms just yet nor getting their weapons back. Everything had happened all too quickly, and not enough was known about them yet.

The women and children hadn't said any words other than thank you and please. The man, who identified himself as Craig, was an odd one. Given the circumstances of what this group had just been through, he was cheery and admittedly charismatic. Ryan assured him that all the charm in the world wouldn't make him return the pistols so quickly, which was met with an understanding laugh.

One thing Ryan noted above all else was that each woman was holding an infant, all under a year old at least, yet there was no mention of the fathers so far. Though they could possibly be on another convoy heading south, Ryan decided to leave questioning the women for another time.

"Let them get comfortable and safe before you start pushing for answers," he muttered to himself, stubbing the cigarette out against the wall. A waft of horse and cow dung penetrated his nose as the reception doors opened.

"That's that area mucked out for now," Cassy said as she untied and removed her dung apron. "We'll sort the deer out once we've had breakfast." She looked at the group in the middle. "How have they settled?"

"They can't sleep. Terrified," Ryan replied. "But at least they're fed and washed."

"That's good." She held his hand. "You did the right thing."

"I know. Thank you for making me see it."

"I'm always here to help you. That's why I fell in love with you."

"To help me?"

"No, you idiot. Because somewhere deep down inside that messed up psyche of yours is a person who will eventually see that they need to do the right thing."

"It's getting harder every day," he admitted. "Every time I look in the mirror."

"Why? You should be proud of what you see."

"That's what you all see. All I see is my dreadlocks. The reason Lyndon is dead."

"That's not why Lyndon is dead. That bitch downstairs is," she forcefully reminded him. "Now, while I'm busy shoving animal shit, what's your plan for our new members?"

"Let them rest for now and wait to see if Drinker hears anything on channel seventy-two."

"That's a start." She kissed him. "Alfie needs feeding once he's woken up. There's a bottle of breastmilk in the kitchen."

"Okay. Love you."

"Love you too."

A couple of hours passed before Alfie's cries echoed from the kitchen. Ryan waved to Sandra behind the counter and met her in the kitchen, pulling his son from the cot.

"Thank you for watching him again," Ryan said with a smile, then placed a bottle in a softly boiling pan on the induction hob.

"Always my treat to watch your little ones," Sandra replied, tucking her curly, red hair behind her ears. "Your eldest is joining me in the kitchen again today. We may have to start putting her on the payroll." She winked.

"Maisie does love being in here. She making more bread?"

"She wants to make sweetcorn bread. We have enough corn reserve in the freezer, so I thought it would be fun for her and a treat for everyone."

"Good stuff," Ryan said, testing the breastmilk on his wrist while rocking Alfie. "How's the freezer holding up?"

"Still making the racket sound but hasn't strained too much. I had a look inside today, and everything is fine, though our cat food rations are starting to run low."

"How much have we got?"

"About twenty kilos. Should see us through the winter, but after that, we might have to look at alternatives. Any of our animals showing signs of old age?"

"Nope. All last checks proved them healthy, which is a miracle considering. Hopefully after winter, we can get some meat in from Rennes."

"Do you think everyone would start eating meat if they didn't have to butcher it?"

"That's a question we'll ask later. We have to see how many more survivors are coming our way first."

"And if they bring any more infants with them?"

"What do you mean?"

"Nappies. We haven't done a nappy supply run since Alfie was born. All we have left now are enough to see him till he's maybe a year and a half old."

"Ah fuck. I never thought of that." Ryan turned and looked through the hot counter to the family. Five more infants. "Shit."

"We'll think of something, and as you said, if we need Rennes to supply us for a bit, we'll do that."

"We've got a meeting later for inventory. Can you make sure to bring up the cat food and diapers later?"

"Sure thing, darling."

———

Ryan offered Craig a seat at the table nearest to where the mothers and children slept, not wanting to panic them should they wake before the little meeting was over. Craig was just shorter than he was, with a patchy beard and part stocky, part chunky figure.

"Sorry that we've had to keep you in full view. Everything has happened so fast," Ryan explained, pouring them both a cup of tea.

"We're beyond words for your kindness so far. You don't need to explain about being cautious," Craig said, taking the cup and savouring the warmth. "Everyone has to be this way in these times."

*If only he knew I nearly let them freeze to death.* "I will be asking some questions about you and your group. You know, where you were, how you survived, and so on, but before that, I need all the information you have about this attack and any other people that could be coming our way."

"I'll tell you what I can." Craig shuddered and said, "We had just been served lunch yesterday." He paused and then went on. "The air raid sirens went first, you know, the old school World War Two ones. They were in place as first alarm for the outskirts of the city."

"Sheffield?" Ryan asked.

"Yup. We were kept in the remains of the football stadiums. Not long after the sirens, we heard of a breach, and then the gunfire started. It seemed they held them off, but that was just the initial swarm." He rubbed his hands for warmth, like a chill had come over him. "We were in one of the first transports south. We got as far as Guildford, where we were given directions to you."

"They just left you there?"

"They had to go back and help another group who had been ambushed on their escape. Apparently, it's not just survivors on this next cargo, but something for you, too. Something of serious importance."

"Wait." Ryan paused. "Something for me?"

"Yup."

"What was it?"

"We weren't told. No one was. The soldiers who came back to save us have been fighting the guards who turned on us," Craig explained. "The leader of this group doesn't know who he can trust, so he's sending one of his own men to get it to you safely."

"And it's on his way here now?"

"Hopefully, and with more survivors." Craig lowered his head. "Not everyone made it onto a transport. Some had to flee on foot. They'll still be way up north unless they're found."

"Shit." Ryan dropped his head. "How many other survivors are out there?"

"Thousands," Craig stated sadly, turning to the women and children he'd been looking out for. "We were the only group in the first vehicle. All we were told was to tell you to listen on—"

The reception doors crashed open as Drinker sprinted over, radio in hand. The mothers and children awoke sharply as the Scotsman ran to the table, slamming the radio down.

*"We need Ryan!"* a voice called out.

Ryan grasped the radio and held the receiver button. "This is Ryan. Who is this?"

*"Our vehicles are busted. They have weaponry and a whole army. We're losing momentum."*

"Who are you?"

*"The fact you're on channel seventy-two should bloody well tell you that I'm one of the evacuation crew. We need assistance and were told you would help. Now, is that true, or are me and families of survivors meant to hold these fucking people off ourselves?"*

"How many of you are there?"

*"Christ, are you going to help us or not?"*

"I am, but I need to know how many of you there are so I know what size fucking vehicle to bring."

*"A hundred. Minimum."*

Ryan looked up to Drinker. "Go get the keys for the lorries." He turned his attention to Craig. "Can you drive?"

"Yes."

"Okay, you're coming with us." Ryan pulled the radio back up. "Where are you now?"

"*On the M25, turning off at Leatherhead.*"

"Okay, do you think you can make another three miles downhill?"

"*It'll be a push, but we should make it.*"

"Okay, once you've got to Leatherhead, push east towards the next town, Colton."

"*Why push east, that's away from you?*"

"Listen to me, for fuck's sake." He then relayed the plan to the driver calmly with clear as day instructions. They were to drop the convoy of survivors at Colton Town train station and direct them to the top level of the local library. From what Ryan remembered, the building was still standing and would hold until they were rescued. He then instructed the drivers to park outside the bowling/cinema complex a couple of buildings further along, where they were to take refuge, specifically in Screen Room Three. The infamous Screen Room Three had been securely fortified with steel reinforced doors and walls, once serving as a hideout and ammo dump for the R.I.C. during The Fast War.

The drivers were to bait their pursuers to that building so Ryan could ambush them while Drinker helped get the survivors to safety.

"*Understood, passing on directions to the rest of the convoy,*" the driver confirmed.

"Good. We'll get to you as soon as we can." Ryan dropped the radio and clenched his fists. "Drinker. Get everyone inside here, explain the situation, and arm everyone. Craig. Welcome to Team Penbrook. You're coming with us."

## 37

R yan sat in the passenger seat of the first lorry as Craig drove calmly and efficiently along the battered and treacherous road to Colton. He was in one of the white parkas that Penbrook used for security shifts but without a weapon. Drinker followed in the second lorry about twenty metres behind. The plan to get the evacuation team to the cinema had worked; the survivors had made it to the library roof, and the drivers had secured the doors to Screen Room Three.

That had been thirty minutes before, and now no one was answering the radio.

"Turn here." Ryan pointed at a cross junction, with Craig following the instructions and gently turning left, headed downhill to a small roundabout.

"Where now?" Craig asked.

"Right." Ryan pointed again. "It goes uphill for a little bit, then begins to go down again. Start putting the brakes on and stop before we get to the end of the road."

"Okay." Craig nodded. He followed the instructions and stopped halfway down the road.

"Good." Ryan nodded, rolling his window down and signalling to Drinker to park behind them.

All three men exited and met in the middle of the road. Ryan knew exactly where they were, still well hidden in the middle of the housing street, and the cinema was less than three hundred yards from them. The evacuation convoy would've entered Colton from the opposite side of town, bringing their chasers with them. For all intents, they should've been able to creep into Colton without alerting anyone.

Ryan turned the dial on his radio to the Penbrook setting. "Dominic, we've stopped at Ladbrokes Road. How's everything at home?"

"No one's come looking for trouble yet."

"Introduce them to a bullet if they do."

"No problem with that. Come home safe, *boss*."

"Will do." Ryan turned the channel back to seventy-two and clipped it to his waist. "Drinker, follow me and keep low. Watch all shots. We don't know how many soldiers are in there."

"Aye." Drinker nodded, pulling his G36C into firing position.

"Craig," Ryan turned to the newest member, "keep the lorry's keys on you and hide in that house." He pointed to a door marked number fifty-seven, then handed him a pistol. "Do not engage unless you have to. If you're outnumbered, stay hidden and let them steal or smash the trucks up. We'll find another way back if we have to."

"Shouldn't we leave them running?" Craig asked.

"I don't know how much battery life they have left. I'm not a mechanic. I'm just the guy who's requested to kill demons in the bright of day. Ready?" Drinker and Craig nodded. "Let's do this."

They watched Craig cautiously make his way through the front door of the house and peer back through the shattered bay window, giving them the thumbs up.

"How do you know he won't fuck us over?"

"Because I told him that if that was the case, then Dominic would shoot him on sight if he returned without us."

Drinker looked impressed with the forward-thinking as they moved towards Colton's town centre roundabout. That part of the town was wide open, and after a few more steps, the whole area, including the front of the cinema, came into view. Opposite that, and next to the train station, a multi-storey block of apartments crumbled as the frame structure decayed. Faint rumbling started, then stopped again, causing more of the apartment block to cave in and crash on the empty road.

"No transport vehicles?" Drinker whispered as he scanned the cinema's entrance.

"Hmm," Ryan agreed, keeping low as they circled left against the train station, using the all-too-familiar car skeletons for cover. He picked up the radio. "Are you safe inside?"

No answer.

No transport vehicles.

*Something has happened.*

The tyre marks were visible from well over a hundred metres away, and for all intents and purposes, the evacuation team had followed Ryan's instructions to the tee, stopping outside the cinema.

"There," Drinker quietly pointed out. Following the tyre tracks further backwards was a fork-like pattern off to the side. "It's a three-point turn. They reversed out of here."

"Why the fuck wouldn't they tell us?" Ryan huffed, frustrated, picking up the radio again. "Are you safe inside?" he repeated.

"*They were real,*" a voice whispered. "*I didn't believe they were real. Those monsters were here.*"

The apartment block gave way and thundered down, leaving its bare, metal structure in place as the rubble hit the ground. Ryan and Drinker ducked for cover as dust and snow swarmed the area around the cinema, eventually thinning out as it reached their position.

They moved from car to car, checking every possible hiding spot as they made their way to the front entrance. Hundreds of footprints littered the snow, moving both in and out. Quietly stepping through the shattered front doors, they held their breath and listened.

No maniacal breathing or laughter. No hurried footprints. No Termites to be heard or seen. Ryan signalled towards the defunct escalator, which opened two floors above. The carpet squelched beneath their feet, and as they approached the base of the escalator, something worse invaded their senses.

"What's that smell?" Drinker asked quietly as he ascended, looking back quickly to see Ryan had stopped in his tracks. He stood frozen to the spot and eyes glazed over.

Every kind of roasted meat had its own distinct smell. Years in the kitchen meant Ryan could identify a confit chicken, poached rabbit, or grilled lamb. That wasn't any of those odours.

"That's a person," he muttered, forcing himself up the stairs and keeping his guard up. "That's the smell of barbequed human meat." He clenched his teeth, burying those memories.

At the top of the escalator, smoke hung in the air, pouring out from Screen Room Two.

"They went into the wrong fucking screen room," Ryan cursed quietly. "It's not fortified."

"This could be bait," Drinker shakingly whispered, which was met with a silent agreement.

Ryan turned his head and walked carefully open to the entrance of Screen Room Three, seeing the doors wide open. He felt his hands cramp slightly as he approached, flicking his torch on and looking around the screen and seating area. "Where are you?" he asked quietly into the radio.

*"They were real,"* the trembling voice replied, but not from anywhere inside this screen room.

Ryan looked back out into the main hall, where Drinker was pointing into Screen Room Two, signalling that's where the response had come from.

*They went into the wrong fucking screen room!* Ryan screamed inside, knowing that even if they had barricaded themselves in, the doors would've been forced open if their pursuers wanted them badly enough. He slowly walked back to the where the smoke came from and that damn smell. Drinker followed as they made their way through the entrance, and soft red and yellow light shone against the shredded theatre screen.

A fire crackled, spitting embers in all directions. A faint whimpering could be heard from up the seating section. Still no footsteps or cackling. Ryan had to go on instinct, leading them both inside and ready to fire.

"Oh my fucking God," Drinker gasped softly at the sight of the hell that was waiting for them.

Three spit roasts made from seating frames and the blackened, charred remains of five naked adults. Fat and tissue bubbled under what remained of the crisp, blackened skin, making it impossible to even identify the gender. Residue hissed as it dripped onto the open flames.

"Don't get distracted," Ryan said forcefully, though unsure if the comment was aimed at himself or not.

They searched each row slowly, methodically. The soft, trembling whimpers came from the back row. A soldier, badly beaten and burned. Their hair was completely missing, skin flaking off. Upon seeing Ryan and Drinker, their expression changed to one of incomprehensible fear, more than the pain they were currently in could've matched.

"You can't be here," they cried. "They're coming back, all because of you. Take it and go." The soldier mustered all strength and threw something at Ryan's feet.

"Shh. We're here to get you out."

"The monsters are coming back. They won't take me alive." They drew their pistol and slowly aimed it towards their head. "I didn't think they were real."

Drinker acted quickly, kicking the pistol out of their hand. "What are you doing, man? We've come here to save you."

"You came for that." They pointed at the small, shiny object by Ryan's feet. "Kill me! Please!"

Ryan knelt, picking the object up. A thumb drive. "What's this?"

"Just kill me. I won't go out like my men down there. I won't."

A haunting wave of hysterical laughter flooded the screen room. A stampede of feet boomed from down in the lobby, slamming off walls and funnelling up the escalators.

"Get him up, now!" Ryan pointed, slipping the flash drive into his coat pocket and aiming his weapon in front. The soldier screamed and then fell unconscious as Drinker lifted him onto his shoulders. "We need to get out of this room and to the main hall before they get up here. There's a fire exit behind Screen Room Five. Move!"

Ryan led, and Drinker followed, keeping his footing as they

descended the wide stairs to the corridor. From every wall, the laughter and rumbling thundered into their ears. Ryan peered over the edge of the balcony into the lobby, where shadows and silhouettes danced across the walls. Hundreds of Termites flooded in, pounding up the escalators.

Only one more floor separated them, and Ryan resisted the urge to open fire from his advantageous position. There was only so much ammo and time before he would be swarmed and overpowered. He retreated and followed Drinker, passing the gates to Screen Room Four and heading through Screen Room Five to the back wall. He gently pushed the release bar on the fire exit door and stepped out onto the rickety metal staircase. After letting Drinker out, he carefully closed the door and motioned down the fire escape, which clattered as they hastily made their way down and to the ground.

"They actually set a fucking ambush," Drinker said, adjusting the deadweight body across the top of his muscular frame.

Ryan scanned all around, trying to find any disturbed patches of snow and open doors for an ambush. So far, clear. "They want us to lead them to the survivors," he agreed. Keeping his aim on the fire exit above. "We don't have much time." They pushed behind the back of the supermarket and pro-skater shop, hauling ass into the town centre, while Drinker showed phenomenal endurance to keep up. Ryan led them into the town's central promenade and up a flight of stairs into what remained of the council building, signalling for them to tread softly on the broken glass hidden under the snow. He kept every motion calculated, pulling open the battered, rusty door into a library. The damp carpet squelched under their feet while they moved through the toppled bookcases, reaching the back wall and out the fire exit, coming to a standstill on a rooftop car park.

Ryan stopped short, pointing to the ground. Footprints, everywhere. He raised his gun, aiming over to the arrangement of cars that blocked the entrance ramp.

"Sheffield?" he called from under his breath.

"Vineyard," a soft reply came back. One head rose slowly, then another, and more. So many faces of different ages, races. Ryan couldn't even begin to count.

Termite laughter echoed out from the cinema down the road, and the fire exit doors on all floors crashed open. The staircase structure collapsed under the weight of the barrage, which Ryan watched from the safe distance of the library rooftop. His eyes followed as Termites fell with the structure, the screeching of twisted metal as it slammed into the ground and was met with a nerve-jangling series of crackles. Ryan surveyed the broken mess behind the cinema, realising the structural damage should've hidden their footprints. He raised his SIG, keeping a close eye as the second wave of Termites poured out the safety of the cinema's ground floor exit.

"If they get into the town centre, they'll see our prints," Ryan said out loud, watching them begin to pour through the supermarket and skater shop, fanning out in search of them. "Drinker," he said, "get these people down this ramp and over to the lorries."

"What are you doing?"

"I'm going to keep them inside the town square. I know this place inside out." Ryan pulled his gun up. "Keep the engines running until I get there, and be ready to leave. Got it?"

"Aye, man. Don't be long."

"Go now."

Ryan waited as he watched Drinker round everyone up, telling them to keep their heads low as they descended the winding ramp. Once the final survivors had slowly begun to make their way down and follow the group, Ryan closed the fire exit behind him and quietly stepped through the library until he reached the main entrance. From there, he crawled back to the top of the flight of stairs outside the council building and pulled the scope to his eye.

He aimed in at the top of the shopping centre at the opposite end of the high street and fired two quick, suppressed shots at what remained of the windows, sending glass crashing in all directions. As anticipated, a stampede of Termites swarmed out of the supermarket and scurried across the street to the shopping centre with nothing but pure hatred and bloodlust. Some jumped through holes in walls, others just smashed their way through doors, and within seconds, they were all inside and out of sight.

Focusing on nothing but sound, he kept his mind clear and went into his zen, finger ready to pull the trigger at any stragglers who may spot their footprints. Even at two hundred metres, the destruction inside the shopping centre was clear enough across the desolate town. The Termites were tearing the place apart to try and find them.

A motor grumbled in the distance, followed by more. Ryan moved the scope past the shopping centre to the end of the high street, watching four heavily armoured people carriers slowly approach the shopping centre. One stopped outside the building, whereas another two sped up and turned away from the town, disappearing back the way they had come.

"Where are you going?" Ryan's brain raced, trying to picture where that road led to. His thoughts were cut short as the final vehicle drove straight past the shopping centre and headed towards him, stopping just in front of the library stairs.

*Do not give away your position,* Ryan reaffirmed himself. *They don't know where our lorries are parked.*

Three large, armed men got out, all wearing the same European Alliance uniform that Harper would wear. Grey pants, matching sweaters, and black boots. Their accents were thick, maybe Slavic?

Ryan kept low and still, making sure his misted breath went into the neck of his jacket. The men he watched were pointing in all directions, like they were arguing about where to find something. One of them furiously motioned towards the shopping centre, like they didn't agree with the Termites running over there. The third one called for silence and pointed to the ground.

Using the scope, Ryan focused on what had brought the conversation to a standstill.

Footprints.

The three men followed them up the stairs and then towards the library doors where Ryan was lying down. "Oh shit."

One of the men went to pull up a radio, only to drop to the ground after Ryan fired two shots into his chest. The two others raised their guns and fired roughly in his direction as they tried to take cover behind the vehicle. Ryan managed to wound them both with body shots and was just about to head down and finish them off before he looked up. Gunfire was returned from the convoy outside the shopping centre, and the swarm of Termites began to funnel out in his direction.

"Fuck!" Ryan turned and burst back through the library, the heavy fire slamming through the walls and ceiling, sending plaster and brick splinters ricocheting in all directions. He vaulted over the last broken bookcase and rammed through the fire exit, slamming it shut and sprinting towards the exit ramp. Even with his legs still heavily aching, he controlled his steps and didn't give way to the snow, coming out on the ground floor and thundering across the road. By the time he reached the train station entrance, the library had already been swarmed, with the Termites bursting onto the rooftop he'd just left. He looked right to the end of Ladbroke Road. Two hundred metres.

"Fuck it." Ryan shouldered the SIG716 and bolted across from his position. He was instantly spotted, and the excited laughter of this brazen attempt to flee had amped up. It was a wall of noise that followed his desperate escape. "Drinker! Start fucking driving now!" he yelled.

Both trucks' lights shone and started creeping towards the end of Ladbroke Road. Ryan looked over his shoulder. The Termites were already ground level and closing fast.

"Go! Go!" Ryan waved to Drinker in the first lorry, running straight past and jumping on the passenger side of the second truck. "Craig, follow Drinker and don't slow down," he ordered, climbing to the top of the vehicle and running to the back. He gripped the safety bar and held on as the truck swung right hard, turning away from the town centre and back to the main road that had brought them in an hour earlier.

Ryan crawled to the back and looked out as the Termites gave up the chase, not even attempting to throw spears at the getaway convoy. He pulled the radio up. "Dominic. We're on our way back."

## 38

The two-lorry convoy moved at a steady pace, following the fresh tyre tracks they had left not one hour earlier. Inside the cargo hold of the first truck were two injured soldiers and seventy-eight civilians, a number higher than the total population of Penbrook at any point over the previous two years.

Ryan sat on top of the second lorry, his legs dangling off the back and his SIG716 across his lap. His body felt ablaze, and he was ready to fire on anyone who should be stupid enough to follow them. The choice to act as a gunner from the rear wasn't just for security purposes but also to get as much fresh air as possible. The stench of roasted human meat hadn't only cemented itself in his nose but covered his clothes, too.

Even after the fight he'd just found himself in, and more than grateful to God or whoever out there had been watching over him, his traitorous brain took his thoughts down a road of guilt as the horrors of Screen Room Two hung over like a poisonous cloud.

*Did I get those soldiers killed?* he wondered. *Did I seal their fate?* The questions cycled like some kind of masochistic obsession. Of course, he had suggested they break away from the main pack of survivors as a diversion, but it hadn't been his fault that they had gone into the wrong screen room. It was nothing more than misfortune, and when the cards of bad luck are against you when you're gambling against Termites, the cost wasn't just your life. It was a violation of the human body. There were no bounds of morality they were held by.

*They actually set a trap.* Ryan pulled his left glove off, eyeing over the stumps where his ring and pinkie finger should've been. His daily reminder that even though they were the base level of human savages, they could still use tactics to get to you. His focus narrowed beyond his hand and tightened on the road passing under his dangling legs. His eyes followed a rogue set of heavy tyre prints that veered off to the right and down a housing estate.

*We haven't been down that way,* Ryan said to himself before his eyes widened. *They've been down here!* He got to his feet and ran along the roof, waving his hands to the lorry in front. "Drinker! Ambush!"

A thunderous whoosh of air came from Ryan's left, cutting through his warning and ripping into a deafening screech. The back end of the lorry lifted and swung left, throwing Ryan off and landing him on a chain link fence. A torn piece of mesh sunk through his jacket and dug its way into his left bicep, tearing sideways and breaking off as his body weight caused him to thump on the sidewalk. His heels met the icy concrete first, taking most of the impact until they gave out, and the back of his shoulders completed his journey back to earth.

His eyes clocked the vapour trail coming from the wooded area on the opposite side of the road. The back of the second lorry blasted apart, almost toppling over on the left-hand side. Craig got out the driver's door, holding a bloody gash on his forehead. Apart from their minor injuries, Ryan counted their blessings that all survivors had been kept in the cargo of Drinker's lorry.

From behind, the roar of an engine grew louder, though still well out of sight. Standing above the snow on the opposite embankment, a figure rose and shouldered an RPG towards Ryan. He fired two shots, one of which hit the assailant in the arm and knocked them down.

"Get in the other truck," Ryan ordered to Craig, picking himself up and running over to his wounded driver and taking him under his arm. Drinker had pulled the first lorry to a halt and made his way round the back, providing covering fire as the pair hastily hobbled past him and jumped over the driver's seat into the passenger side.

Once Drinker had gotten in and restarted the engine, Ryan focused on the side mirror and saw two armoured vehicles coming into view. He waited for their lorry to get some traction and continue the journey home before he pulled out the radio.

"Dominic, we have been ambushed on the way home. We are being followed. Two heavy vehicles—they look military. Get ready to open fire."

"Got it. How far out are you?"

"Ten minutes."

"Understood. Get those people and your ass back here safe."

Ryan looked at his blood-soaked parka and ignored it. "You know we will. Out." He then thumped on the cargo partition behind him. "Everyone, hang on tight. This is about to get bumpy. Floor it, Drinker."

The Scotsman hit the accelerator hard, and the twenty-tonne beast showed its full potential as it weighed heavily on the snow, smashing through any debris in its way. The back end swung out, and muffled screams echoed inside the cargo hold as bodies were flung violently to one side. Within minutes, they had joined onto the carriageway that would lead them back to Maidville.

After thirty seconds, the two pursuing vehicles had joined them on the final stretch, closing the gap down to a couple of hundred metres.

"Are we going to leave the barricade open for them?" Drinker asked as the lorry bolted towards the checkpoint.

"Yep," Ryan answered, keeping his eyes on the mirror. "Slow down when you get to it."

"Why?"

"Just do it."

Drinker did his best in the conditions and kept the huge vehicle straight, slowing down enough for the back end only to clip a couple of the cars.

"Get them back inside," Ryan said, jumping out the door and not giving Drinker a chance to protest. As he ran back to the barricade, he knew that he wouldn't have the time to slide the vehicles into position, especially alone on this icy surface. Instead, he ripped open the door of the black sedan and pulled up the back seats. "You wanna play with fire?" he wheezed to himself, thinking of the explosion that tossed him off the lorry earlier. He dug inside and pulled out the heavy-duty box. Fifteen grenades looked back at him. He took one out and lifted the whole box, sliding it behind the opening of the barricade.

"Dominic. I'm at the northern barricade," he said into the radio.

*"I can see you on the monitor. What are you doing?"*

"Just keep your eyes on it, and let me know when they're coming through. They'll be on foot."

Between the gaps in the barricade, he saw the two vehicles approaching rapidly and not slowing. One by one, he pulled a grenade out, removed the ring and tossed it over the barricade. All within five-second intervals. The first one had already detonated by the time he threw the third, keeping his head low and out of the line of sight as they exploded. As expected, the oncoming vehicles skidded to a halt, slowly and agonisingly, towards the area where Ryan was targeted. One by one, the small explosives sent shrapnel into and under the vehicle's chassis while also kicking up thick clouds of smoke and snow powder. The second vehicle crashed into the front one, and men began to jump out. Ryan took the opportunity of blind confusion and lit one of his flares, standing up and throwing it into the thick white cloud on the other side of the barricade.

He'd hoped the fuel lines had been severed as they drove over the explosions, but if not, the flare would add even more chaos to the mix. He pulled his SIG up and aimed into the cloud, switching to fully auto-matic. He couldn't see who or what he was aiming at, but from the cries, he knew that he had at least hit a few and forced others to take cover behind the armoured cars. As he ran out of bullets, the return fire was ordered, which he'd expected. Once again, he one by one tossed the remaining five grenades into the same area, replaced his empty magazine and threw his final flare into the barricade itself, giving him enough visual cover to begin running home.

He had practised this run multiple times, with his best time coming in at a minute and a half, but he'd never done it in the snow nor with a bloody shoulder and hurting heels while wearing winter gear. The road was straight and clear, with nowhere to hide, and once someone stepped through that smoke and onto his final stretch home, the only thing that would keep Ryan alive was how much distance he had put between them and how good a shot they were.

*"They're walking through now,"* Dominic reported.

Ryan's thighs began to scream, tightening with every heavy pace, and the sharp, cold air invaded his lungs. He swung his head back towards the barricade, and the red cloud had all but dispersed from the ground and began to vanish into the air.

The first figure emerged from the smoke, followed by two more, then more. Ryan tried to count while focusing on his forward momentum.

*A dozen?*

They were armed, holding their weapons close and all taking a kneeling position. Ryan began to duck and weave, making his movements unpredictable. Bullets whizzed by, and he dove to the ground as they zipped overhead, some crashing into the maze wall.

He picked himself up and ran towards the lorry parked outside the maze's eastern wall. The back cargo had been opened and was fortunately empty. A swarm of footprints led inside, but the gate had been left open. *Drinker got them back safe.*

Ryan pulled the radio up. "Dominic. This is the game plan," he huffed. "They'll be in your field of view in a couple of minutes. Let them get to the bridge before you start shooting. They'll either start jumping into the freezing river, towards me, or running away. We'll pick them off together. Got it?"

"You got it, *boss*."

More bullets thudded into the back of the lorry, and Ryan did his best to keep peeking around, letting them know he was still there. He guessed they didn't have any scoped or long-range weaponry but kept his feet hidden behind the tyres should any of them decide to get low and try to take his legs out.

A thundering crack of a rifle almost ripped the sky in half, and the first victim of Dominic's shooting crumbled to the ground. The panic was immediate, and they started to dart forward. Ryan swung and aimed in at two, hitting them both in the lower abdomen. Dominic took another out before they changed course and started to run back. Between the pair, they had dropped nine, and two more were dispatched while attempting to flee. Ryan focused hard on the last one, putting his sights on their lower back and firing three shots, one of which connected in the kidney area.

"All down," Ryan said into the radio, leaving the cover of the lorry and approaching the bodies, of which the final one was crawling to their weapon, only for it to be kicked to the side. Ryan knelt next to the bulky soldier and pulled their head up by the hair. "Speak," he ordered.

"Fuck you." The response was spat at him. A European accent. Heavy, bold, and eastern. "Admiral was right about you." They laughed. "Fucking good boy."

"Well, that's better than nothing." Ryan shrugged, only just realising how much pain he was truly in. "How many more of you are there?"

"More than you can stop."

"You would think that, but two of us just took out twelve of you, so I like our chances. Again, how many of you are there?"

"You think it's just us and those dirty Termites they have? You want to know how many are coming? I'd die before telling you anything."

"We'll see about that," Ryan said, flipping the man over on his stomach and pulling their jacket off. He took out his knife and cut the back of the soldier's T-shirt open, exposing their back. He ran the tip of the blade down their spine and dug it in at the bottom. "What I'm going to do to you I've only seen in TV shows. I don't know if this is possible without killing you, but I guess we'll find out together, hmm?"

From there, Ryan used the knife to pierce the skin all the way up their spine as the screams and begging to stop were almost deafening.

"Okay." Ryan pulled the knife away and held it in front of him. "How many of you are there?"

———

Ryan limped through the cafeteria, white jacket almost fully covered in blood and a distant look in his eyes. One of the onlookers screamed at the sight, causing everyone, including the newer survivors, to turn and stare at the scene before them.

He put his hand up and signalled for silence, removing his parka and slumping it on the nearest table.

Cassy emerged from the kitchen, ready to rush over and hug him before she stopped, noticing something different in his eye.

"They've retreated back to Milton Keynes," Ryan wheezed, sitting on the chair. "They'll be back when they've regrouped."

"What happened?" Cassy asked, looking him and the coat over. "Dominic said you fended off the attack."

"Oh, we did," Ryan cackled. "Just call this... interrogation." He motioned at the blood smears. "Where's the soldier who passed out?"

"Err, he's, err," Cassy stuttered, taken back by Ryan's calmness. "Drinker took him to Medical Room One."

"Okay," he groaned, standing himself up and hobbling to the medical corridor. "Tell Dominic that the top floor is now a four-man job. His team doesn't leave there until further notice." He stopped, seeing Cassy hadn't acknowledged him. "Cassy. Go tell Dominic now!"

He waited for her to take the radio and update Dominic, then gradually made his way to the double doors and pushed through. He leaned against the yellow wall, sliding his damp trainers across the blue tiled floor before stopping outside the open door.

Drinker looked up, shocked at the sight of Ryan. "The fuck happened to you?"

"It's not mine, just the poor bastard who refused to give me information."

"Did you find anything out?"

"Just that thousands will be headed our way eventually, both friend and foe, and we have to decide who we let in." Ryan tossed the jacket on the bedside table and pointed to the soldier in the bed. "Is he out cold?"

"He's conscious." Drinker pointed to the drip out his arm. "Trying to hydrate him, and also gave him some ether to help with the pain."

"Good enough for me. I need a chat with him."

"I don't think now is a good—"

"Maybe not," Ryan interrupted, "but we know that there are people on the way and that they were prepared enough to lay two ambushes. Drinker, I need you out there, keeping order with the new arrivals and helping Dominic set up defence. Can you do that for me?"

Drinker didn't answer immediately; more so, he was taking in Ryan's calmness while also looking like he just stepped out of a slasher movie. "Aye."

"Thank you."

Ryan staggered into Medical Room One, pulling the last metallic splinter from his left shoulder as he landed hard in the armchair, trying to steady his breathing and make sense of what happened.

He leaned forward, spitting blood on the floor. "What you saw..." he winced, talking to the semi-conscious stranger in the gurney, "...it was real. All real."

Back in the cafeteria, orders were yelled out as positions and lookout points were delegated amongst the members of Penbrook Vineyard and the newest batch of survivors.

"We've faced them before," Ryan continued, attempting to cover the fresh gash that ran down his left bicep. "They're called *Termites*." He paused, replaying the image of the swarm that had just tried to ambush them. "That's what they were nicknamed by their captors— Termites—a workforce designed to do nothing but build, work, fight, then die."

A box of ammo clattered across the corridor floor outside their room, and two people rushed to fortify the winery's western fire exit.

"And the speed you saw them run... it wasn't your eyes playing tricks on you. They're strong. I've seen them throw wooden spears through metal barriers." Ryan winced, sitting forward. "This power they possess is the result of a build-up and release of adrenaline, and the only thing that keeps that in check is the consumption of human meat..."

The stranger on the bed tried to open their mouth, and a croak escaped their bloody, bruised lips.

"Don't talk. I'll ask the questions." Ryan sat forward. "Use your eyes. Blink once for yes. Twice for no. Do you understand?"

One blink.

"Good." Ryan exhaled with relief. "Do you know who sent this wave of Termites after you?"

Two blinks.

"Damn. Those soldiers that were chasing us today, were they a part of your survivor's camp in Sheffield?"

Two blinks.

"Were they new additions?"

One blink. The soldier lifted their hand, making a thumb symbol out of it. "Dry..." they gasped harshly. "Dry."

"Dry? What's dry?"

"Drive," they managed before falling limp, and the pained glaze over their eyes was awash with peace.

Ryan reached up to the side of their neck, checking for a pulse. Nothing. He lowered his head, wiping the crusty blood away from his eyes. He saw the final gesture that the soldier had left him. The thumbs up and the word drive.

He looked to his right, where he had tossed his jacket and the mysterious object that was safely in its pocket.

The thumb drive.

## 39

Warm water ran down Ryan's naked body as he stood in the shower with the door wide open, staring back at himself in the bathroom mirror. The blood across his face and in his hair had darkened to a hellish red colour. After months of avoiding his own reflection, he actually liked the warped monster that stared back.

He wasn't scared of what was looking back, nor at what he had done this afternoon. He may have cost five soldiers their lives and performed a Nordic ritual that would disgust any civil human being, but he didn't care.

One of his clean, blond locks dangled down, and he saw Lyndon's face in the mirror. Just another reminder of every family member, friend, and loved one he'd lost to this now-approaching enemy. The sorrow didn't sadden him anymore, but rather, it made him feel alive, like eliminating this enemy was his only destiny.

*This fucking enemy.*

In his own head, he felt like he'd sent a message to the ones he was going to kill. The Termites. Project Zodiac. Connor. Admiral.

"If you think we're even after what I've done, then you are truly more fucked in the head than I ever gave you credit for." He snarled at the imaginary beings in the mirror while wiping the blood from his chin and flicking the crimson droplets to the ever-growing puddle at his feet. "You see, I'm only just getting started."

The monsters vanished, and all he was left with was the stern, psychotic reflection. The whites and green of his eyes tried to break through the spattered blood across his face. The same face that saved nearly a hundred people that afternoon.

*I'll do what I have to.*

He shut the shower door and washed away the final crusty stains while trying to avoid getting too much hot water on his left arm, the newest of his many injuries.

*Get back to focusing on what to do,* he reminded himself as the blood swirled down the drain. *What's on that fucking thumb drive, and who were those men chasing us?*

He turned off the hot water, watching the final droplets come to a halt. Between his newfound pride in hurting people and figuring out what was coming next, he remembered that the very shower he'd just had was from Cassy's water allowance. He opened the door again and caught the newer reflection. Clean. Green eyes prominent. The difference was staggering.

*I don't know who I am anymore.*

He snatched the towel and started drying.

*Get the fuck out of your own head and get to the bottom of this shit.* He pulled his joggers and hoodie on, slipped into his running trainers, and headed downstairs.


Sandra was working overtime in the kitchen, cooking batches of meals double what she had before. Teddy and Johanna helped organise and hand out spare sleeping bags, blankets, and mattresses to the new arrivals. At the same time, Sanjay and Rani took control of maintaining and feeding the animals.

Ryan met Drinker and Cassy at a table and started going over everything.

"Seventy-eight new survivors, plus sixteen from yesterday morning. Craig's okay, just looks like a minor concussion," Drinker reported.

"We have just enough spare clothes in the holding rooms for the newer arrivals to change once a week."

"And food?" Cassy asked.

"This is nothing new for Sandra," Ryan reassured. "She used to feed double this when she was a school lady. According to our rations and inventory meeting yesterday, we can hold out without any fresh crops until next summer."

"Grape water?" she added.

"Enough until March, but the winter and spring rains will top up during that time anyway," Ryan said firmly. "I'm more worried about any rogues coming our way or more survivors."

"Should we get Dominic in on this? He is head of security."

"Yeah," Ryan agreed. "Cassy, radio Dominic and say we'll be up in five minutes."

"Okay." She stood and took the radio, getting some distance between her and the crowded noise.

Ryan and Drinker sat in silence, waiting for her to come back. She held the device close, seeming to be taking longer than normal, concerned. She shot Ryan and Drinker a look of horror. They both stood and ran over.

"Is there another wave coming?" Ryan pressed. "Are we under attack?"

"It's not that." She shook her head, moving her mouth away from the radio and whispering, "The cell door key has been removed from the box upstairs."

"Hannah's cell?" Ryan hushed back, alarmed. "Who's on watch?"

"Callum."

"Has anyone heard from Callum during his shift?"

Cassy shook her head, covering her mouth.

Ryan marched slowly to the stairwell, looking down to the basement entrance, still bolted shut from the outside. He pulled Drinker close. "Go out the front door and see if the second basement has been opened."

"Aye." Drinker took off in a hurry.

Ryan took his pistol out from his back pocket, signalling for Cassy to join him and do the same. He knew he couldn't kill Hannah, but if it came to self-defence, she was fair game.

Only minutes passed before Drinker returned. "Second basement exit is still padlocked."

Ryan held his hand out, asking for the radio. Cassy passed him the device. "Callum. All okay down there?"

No answer.

"Callum?" he asked again, only met by more silence. "Fuck." He motioned for Drinker to join him. "Cassy, lock the door behind us. Don't cause an alarm. Okay?"

She nodded, and Ryan unbolted all three locks, stepping inside with Drinker. To the right, Callum's body lay in a pool of blood, his trousers round by his ankles. The cell door was wide open, with the key still in the lock.

"You might as well come in and lock the fucking cell," Hannah barked angrily. "No point in my trying to escape when this little dickhead didn't mention the other doors were bolted from the outside."

Both marched over with pistols raised, facing into the cell. Hannah sat, washing her mouth out with water. Drinker pushed the door closed, locked it and withdrew the key. Ryan knelt beside Callum, turning his body over. The blood was coming from his crotch, which was missing a certain male appendage. He lifted his gaze further forward, just out of the candlelight, to see the small stump on the cold floor.

"Little shit tasted disgusting too. I thought virgins were supposed to be clean," Hannah complained, spitting back into the bowl. "Some men have no common decency, do they?"

Ryan itched hard not to raise his gun while Drinker stood over the scene, hands on his head.

"I'll do the favour for you two if you want?" she continued. "Though, this time, I promise to go all the way."

"You promised a fifteen-year-old boy sexual favours in return for your escape?" Drinker asked seethingly.

"What would you do in my shoes? It's not like there's any age law these days, is there?"

Ryan took the radio from underneath Gavin and clicked the

receiver. "Dominic. Cassy." He paused, looking down. "She killed him
to try and escape. Callum's dead." Walking away from the door, he
looked up to the dark ceiling, trying to block out the tirade of abuse
Drinker was throwing at Hannah, which seemed to have no effect
on her.

Just another monster living among them.

The basement door was unbolted, and Cassy ran it at full pace,
stopping in front of the cell door, paralysed and frozen.

"If it makes you feel any better, honey," Hannah taunted, "your man
refused when I offered. Now that's what you call loyalty, considering
my blowjobs are, well..." she pointed at Callum's body, "...to die for."

"You shut your fucking mouth!" Ryan snapped, marching to the
cell.

Cassy's trembling stopped, and her right arm swung out towards
the prisoner, pistol aimed and ready.

"Woah, woah, woah." Ryan stopped, arms out, trying to calm her.
"You know we can't do that."

"Oh, this is more like it!" Hannah quipped, standing. "Nice to see
your little girlfriend has more balls than you."

"Shut the fuck up!" Ryan roared again.

"Why? We all know you won't kill me. *I'm your get-out-of-jail-card,*
remember? You won't kill me, even though that's the second teenager
I've murdered here, and I'm pretty sure the first one was a lot closer to
you than this one was. What kind of man are you?" She turned her
attention to Cassy, "And you won't kill me because you're not that
person, even if I told you I'd happily kill your two children, too."

There was a flash. A deafening bang in the confined basement
space. Cassy's arm kicked back from the recoil. Sudden and shocked
cries sounded from up in the cafeteria.

Hannah stood, shocked but alive. No blood.

"Drinker," Ryan said softly while looking over their prisoner, "get
upstairs and calm everyone down, please." He waited until he was
gone, then stood behind Cassy, holding her shoulders. They both
looked into the cell. There were no bullet markings on the wall. No
wounds on Hannah.

Ryan reached down, taking the pistol from Cassy's hand. He

unloaded the clip and stared in. Crimped shells. Blanks. Alessandro's trading weapon was never armed.

*Of course, a fucking weapon supplied by Admiral's men would have blanks in.* Ryan scoffed internally, knowing that they would do anything to hinder the vineyard's defences.

"Well, I guess you do have the balls." Hannah laughed, almost maniacally. "Now get a gun that actually works and do it properly. Come on!"

Ryan led Cassy away to the stairwell. On the surface, she was quiet, as if she were disappointed. He just didn't know if it was aimed at herself or because the gun failed. Once she was on the stairs, he remained in the basement, signalling for her to lock the doors.

"She won't be able to do this again. To anyone," he reassured as the door shut. Left alone in the basement, with the body of a fifteen-year-old and the predator who killed him, Ryan walked back over to the cell door, standing with his hands behind his back.

"Not gonna lie," Hannah snorted as she sat back on the mattress, "she looked more terrified than I did."

"I made you a promise," Ryan said coldly. "Now, I have to honour it."

"What are you going to do? Scare me with Bully Killer talk again? Get the fuck out of here."

Ryan let his hands dangle by his side.

On the left was the cell door key.

On the right, the knife he used not two hours earlier.

"You're the reason Cassy wants to throw away her wings. You're the reason my family is torn apart. You're the reason my daughter isn't talking." He raised the knife and unlocked the cell door. "That tongue of yours is still causing problems. Any final words?"

# 40

The tap sputtered hot water on Ryan's hands as he scrubbed Hannah's blood off. Inside, he felt both at war and at peace. He'd accepted a long time ago what he needed to be, and this side of him had been bearing over like he was afraid to let it out, but now that it was here, he embraced it.

"She's patched up now," Drinker said from behind. "Would've been a lot worse if you'd taken her whole tongue out."

Ryan grabbed an oven cloth, drying his hands while looking at his souvenir in the clear plastic sleeve beside him. He knew Drinker was right, and none of them had the medical expertise to save her should he have removed the whole tongue, but the two inches of flesh next to him would suffice for now. At the very least, she wouldn't be talking to or getting anyone to try and kill her anymore.

After wrapping the tongue and placing it in the walk-in freezer, he pulled on his black denim gilet and met Drinker by the cafeteria doors, looking out into the crammed cafeteria. "Sandra's done well to feed these people so quickly."

"As you said, walk in the park for her," Drinker agreed. "Think she might need some extra hands when it comes to prep."

"We'll have to spread ourselves across the board, then," Ryan noted, rubbing his chin. "We're going to have to produce so many more cleaning compounds, never mind the laundry, too."

"Think we can trust any of the new folks to pitch in?"

"We'll have to see where their heads are at. Who knows what kind of trauma they're processing."

"Or what they think of us right now."

"Let's put a stop to any apprehension now, then." He slapped Drinker on the shoulder and took to the podium. "Everyone!" he shouted at the top of his voice. It took only a few seconds for everyone to turn and give him their attention. Some parents comforted their scared children, and Ryan gave them a moment to settle.

"I know it's been a hell of a few days for you, and you're all in much need of rest and reassurance," he continued. "To start with, this is *The Penbrook Vineyard* that you were being extracted to, and I am Ryan. So, you are in the place you were meant to be. From what I understand, some of you still have family and friends out there trying to make their way to us. If we can secure getting them here, we will do what we can with what we have to make that possible. Once you've all settled and got some rest, we'll be asking you for details of these family members so we can keep track of who's who when it comes to organising living spaces for everyone."

The general expression across the crowd was still one of abject terror, and no amount of calmness from this complete stranger giving them a speech was going to change that.

"As for what happened to you, I can't hide it. We are at war," he announced factually. "Not just my people, but you too. These people that attacked and chased you, they need you. Either to join their fight or to feed them..." He let that sink in while also being aware that not everybody had translated it fully. Whatever the interpretation, he wasn't going to spell out the grim reality in front of children. "... and they're coming. We don't know when, and we don't know exactly how many. For those of you who have surrendered your weapons or have any kind of fighting knowledge, your skills will be invaluable to everyone's survival here. I'm not interested in what you've had to do to get this far. Nobody's hands are clean here. We're keeping our radio channels open to see if we can get any further updates from the military or any other survivors out there."

He knew it was time to finish up. "Get some rest. Your next meal will be served in the evening. Any questions can be directed to any one of our guards watching over you." Ryan pointed around the room.

A quick question was blurted out: "What did you do to that woman downstairs?"

Internally, Ryan smiled, knowing the answer would help keep these new people in check. "I did what I'd do to anyone who even thinks about bringing my people harm."

———

The burning dry wood popped and crackled in the darkness of the evening, spitting embers into the night sky, and the thick plume of smoke and ash rose towards the heavens.

Ryan stood alone, a few metres away from the carefully piled wood and hay, with the two bodies lying across it. The unknown soldier and young Callum. Everyone had their chance to say goodbye to the young man before Ryan carried his body out. It wasn't the boy's fault for what had happened. He had been willing to take on his duty and step up, but Hannah's words were powerful enough to even turn Cassy into a killer, let alone manipulate a hormonal teenager.

*I shouldn't have left him with her,* Ryan had thought multiple times, only for Cassy's reminder to echo in his mind that he was no longer to blame himself for everything. Hannah had done this, all with the intent of dispatching anyone she saw fit.

Ryan said his final farewell, praising the soldier for fulfilling his duty and getting the people to safety, and for Callum for wanting to be a better man.

It hurt that the teenager had died alone, the last surviving member of his family. All gone. Taken in a moment of calculated hatred by the now mute bitch downstairs. Two teenagers she had killed, and Ryan now knew that even if it was a case of mistaken identity in killing Lyndon, Hannah probably would've still taken the chance out of nothing but pure amusement.

*Everything will be better when I set her expiration date.*

The smell of the cremation had hit his nose moments before, and he felt his mind wanting to replay every vision of roasted humans that he'd been forced to endure. He forced himself to stay in the moment and the tragedy of these two lost souls, knowing that he'd do whatever he could to prevent it from happening to anyone else. He may have surprised even himself with the two torturous actions he'd performed today, but that side of him would only be reserved for those who deserved it.

Those people. Admiral's people. They all deserved it. No one would be exempt from that side of him. He'd let Connor live. Let Hannah live. No more. There would be no jurisdiction bullshit from Rennes or anyone inside the European Alliance to prevent it.

Ryan shook off the rising malice and pulled his eyes back to the flames. "Rest now," he said, turning back to the winery.

He closed the fire exit door as he entered, walking back through the medical corridor. He stopped by Medical Room One, which had now been cleaned of all the blood and mucus stains from the unnamed soldier. He reached into his pocket and took out the thumb drive. "What the hell is on this?"

As he stepped into the cafeteria, he was met with a welcomed warmth as the fire burned. There was a stack of dirty bowls and plates on the hot counter, larger than he'd seen for a while. Cassy sat at the table nearest, cradling Alfie while watching over Maisie, who was eating a bowl of dried berries.

"I'll help Sandra clean that up in a bit." Cassy nodded towards the stacks of crockery. "Maisie's eager to help too."

Ryan wasn't surprised, offering a warm smile and kissing the top of Maisie's head before sitting next to Cassy. "How are you feeling?"

"About what?"

"Earlier. Being ready to pull the trigger."

"I don't feel anything," she said, turning and running her hand down Alfie's cheek. "I'd do it again with a loaded weapon if I had to."

He was happy that she would take on the duty if needed, but right now, they needed Hannah alive. "Can I ask you something?"

"What?"

"Can you hold back from doing that until this is all over?"

"You'd let me do it after?"

"Do you think doing it will keep our family safer?"

"After seeing how she tricked Callum, and you might have removed the last weapon she had, I don't trust any second she's alive," she said calmly, peering at Ryan's right hand. "What's that?"

"Oh," Ryan said, holding his palm out. "Something that was of vital importance to get to me, apparently." He held it in front of his eyes. "Even though I can't access what's on it. Maybe I'm supposed to pass it on to someone else?"

Cassy laughed unexpectedly, holding her mouth so she didn't wake Alfie. "Your sister was right about you. You really are a div."

"What do you mean?" Ryan frowned, almost offended.

"The camera system that Harper got to us. What are you watching those cameras on?"

"A fucking laptop!" He stood sharply, kissing her on the lips. "Thank you. Love you. Bye!" He ran towards the stairs, leaving all the new survivors wondering what the strange new leader of theirs was excited about.

By the time he reached the top floor, his limp had come back from his swollen heels. Dominic turned away from the window with a look of confusion on his face. "Everything okay?"

"Yeah," Ryan said with a nod and hobbled to the laptop, plugging the thumb drive in. "How's security detail looking?"

"Just performing final checks on the gates." Dominic pointed out the window to the torch beams that swayed across the outskirts of their grounds. "Nearly done out there?" he asked into the radio.

"*All inner gates are padlocked,*" Teddy reported. "*No footprints leading inside, other than Gate C.*"

"Good. Keep your ears open, too."

"*Got it.*"

Ryan sat, clicking on the thumb drive notification. One video on file. He moved the cursor over and started the import.

Six minutes.

"What's that?" Dominic asked, sitting back in the chair at the front window.

"This is what the first convoy was meant to get to me," Ryan said solemnly. "This is what those soldiers died for today."

"Must've been worth it."

"Hmm," Ryan agreed, watching the timer countdown. Behind the pop-up screen, something caught his attention: the feedback for Camera Two. He bought the video feed up and looked in hard.

There was a figure moving, sitting down in front of a fire.

"Another survivor?" Ryan asked, grabbing Dominic's attention.

"A survivor? Looking for us?" he asked. "Where's that camera?"

"South end of the carriageway." Ryan looked out the window into the darkness, picturing where it was. "Why not just come here if they're so close?"

"What's that in his hand?"

Ryan spotted it, too. A small flash in the person's hand. "Is that a smart radio?"

Something was off about the whole visual. Even at a distance, they could make out the pristine clothing and the man's large frame. Something caused Ryan's heart to stop.

A noise in the distance? Movement? Voices?

It was a flash of light. An illumination. The smart radio vibrated on the table to his left, lighting up with a notification.

"For fuck's sake." Ryan laughed nervously, then paused. "Wait." He reached for it. "We have signal?"

Hastily opening the screen, he was met with a message from a number that hadn't been coded into his contacts.

*Ryan.*

*It's Harper. We got Admiral. The son of a bitch is dead.*

*We've only got this short window to contact you now, but we'll be with you in a couple of days. We've just landed at Brighton Beach.*

Ryan held the smart radio with shaking hands, then watched as the figure seemed to put away their own device. Ryan called the code back, watching on screen as the figure took out their own device and pressed a button.

Call ended.

"Did that person send you that message?" Dominic asked.

"It looks like it," Ryan agreed, staring at the figure on the monitor, "but that sure as shit isn't Harper, and they ain't in Brighton either."

# 41

"Two more nights," General Woodburn said to himself as he rubbed his hands together over the open fire. He looked at his smart radio again, making damn sure the satellite feed had been interrupted once more. Ryan wouldn't be calling back any time soon and would be left in the dark until it was time to reveal himself to the vineyard.

It had never been part of the original plan to let Woodburn go alone, but after some of his men had come within literal metres of the vineyard, a friendly face would be needed to try and keep calmness within the vineyard. One itchy trigger and one paranoid member could result in the death of his friend's daughter, Hannah.

All their units had been ordered to keep clear and head back to their old base of operations, one hundred miles north under the town of Milton Keynes. There was no reason to attack the vineyard just yet, and Woodburn would infiltrate and keep order until Admiral came hunting for them. Was Ryan trusting? Not really. Could he be fooled into letting a friend of a friend inside if it was met with the small promise of false hope? Absolutely.

All he had to do was let Ryan think that Harper was still alive.

His mind briefly drifted to Harper and what could've been if he

had even the slightest amount of spine to accept that not only was
their country destroyed in the name of savage hatred, but also the
multiculturalism and integration of these medieval heathens could not
work in a free and democratic society.

"I truly expected better of you," Woodburn hissed regretfully,
taking a small mouthful of scotch from his hipflask, "but I guess your
loyalty was to ideals and not being a true patriot."

He watched the fire flicker through the night until the sun rose in
the clear sky. February the first didn't bring much in the way of a
warmer climate, and he was just happy that he'd avoided the snow-
storms of a month earlier.

Liberia was its own animal of extremes, but it was a necessary trip.
Harper had to see where it all began, but even that wasn't enough.
Once the file had appeared on Woodburn's desk six months prior, his
head had been turned to Admiral. The misunderstood hero who was
doing the real work to fight back against those who brought the planet
to its knees. It was a no-brainer for Woodburn. Even with Admiral's
limited resources, compared to the European Alliance, he had
managed to get this information to the main source of the petrol and
food supplies from Southern America, showing them to take the fight
to the R.I.C.

The truth was, without this knowledge, China may have never
severed their deal with the R.I.C. and started the newer war. Venezuela
now held a stronger influence against the communist regimes in Chile
and Peru, and the fight was now on to bring down the authoritarianism
that was trying to strangle the world.

"One day at a time," Woodburn reminded himself. "One day at a
time."

The situation was precarious, but he could handle the cold for
another day. He knew half of his Hungarian forces had held off Operation Wolfpack from getting further south and alerting the vineyard
and that some had already rounded up fleeing survivors, but one of his
units had been silent for a day or two. The unit sent to retrieve the
videos of Harper's death.

Their last communication had been the confirmation of retrieving
three thumb drives and burning the evacuation crew that managed to

get a group of survivors south. Woodburn wasn't too concerned, as his men were extremely tough sons of bitches, and had effectively taken out Rennes with ease. The French airport was but a rubble stain on the face of the earth, and apartment blocks rigged with C4 were now ruins in the historic town centre.

"Ironic," he said out loud to himself. "We were framed for bringing down our own buildings, but we've just had to do the same to eliminate the very people who protect our enemies." He reminisced on the horrifying revelation that Admiral had uncovered and how the even brutal truth wasn't enough to turn Harper to their side of this fight.

He opened his pouch of dried meat and took a bite, enough to last him on the two-day wait. It was the first time he'd been alone for years, but it was necessary for the next step of the mission.

"Ryan will have his guard up," Woodburn reminded himself as he tied his pouch back up, watching the sunrise. It had been nearly five hours since he'd sent the false message disguised as Harper. "But he's also way too trusting. Disarm him with hope."

A loud clang came from his left, like someone had thrown a can against a car. Woodburn stood slowly and drew his pistol, walking out onto the road. Another clang came from the opposite side of a heavily organised ring of vehicles. He knew the stack of cars to be the infamous barricade the vineyard deployed to keep vehicles from bursting through. Clever people, but who would be out here at this time, or was it some survivors who had made it to Maidville?

He checked left around the ring of cars, another clang from the opposite side. As he raised his pistol, he felt something cold press against the back of his head.

"Drop it," a female voice demanded.

"Do as she says," came a male voice joining in from further behind. It was Ryan.

"Ryan, I think..."

"I said drop it!" she repeated. Woodburn let his pistol fall to the ground. "Step towards the car with your hands up. Do not turn around." He did as told, thinking of how to explain why he was there. He heard his gun being picked up, the magazine being removed, and the round unchambered.

"Turn around," Ryan demanded.

Woodburn kept his movements slow and unthreatening. Upon his slow reveal, he saw their faces drop.

"General Woodburn?" Ryan asked. "What the fuck are you doing here?"

"I got broken off from our returning team," he lied. "We landed at Brighton but were ambushed."

"Are you okay?" Ryan looked him over. "We got a message from Harper saying you'd be two days."

"That was just as we landed," Woodburn explained. "And yes, I'm okay. Just a bit cold and unarmed." He motioned to the gun. "Did Harper manage to get to you?" he said, carrying on with his charade.

"No. We haven't heard from anyone. We've had a few attacks, so as you can imagine, we're a bit on edge."

"Being attacked? Here? Don't you think I should be armed too?"

"Oh, shit. Yeah. Sorry about that." Ryan blushed, pushing a magazine back in and handing the pistol back over before turning to his fiancée. "Go meet with Team B at the petrol station, then get back home. We'll be just behind." He offered Woodburn a hot flask.

"Okay." The woman nodded. *Cassy?* Woodburn tried to remember her name but didn't care as he unscrewed the top and took a sip, watching her take off and leave the two men alone. *Perfect.* "Tea?"

"I didn't know who was out here. I thought a warm drink could help," Ryan said, handing him some bread, too.

*Way too trusting.* "How did you know I was nearby?"

Ryan slid his backpack off and pulled out a laptop, lifting the monitor and showing four screens. "Harper managed to get this dropped off to us a few weeks ago. Just to add some extra security and take some paranoia off our shoulders. I won't lie, it's helped." He then chuckled innocently.

"Well, that is good," Woodburn said coolly, sipping from the flask and watching Cassy vanish from their view. "Anyone else out here to surprise us?" he asked, screwing the cap back on and placing the container on a car bonnet, gripping his pistol.

"Just us now," Ryan admitted. "Cassy's meeting our second party and heading back. We thought it might be another ambush." He kept his head towards the laptop, pulling out a small device from his pocket and plugging it in.

*The thumb drive! They got it to him.*

"One of your soldiers managed to get this to me—said it was of high importance. I wanted to show Harper, but whatever is on here, you're probably qualified to see it. Might be too *classified* for me," Ryan joked, unaware of what was waiting for him on the pop-up.

"Ryan, don't!" Woodburn ordered, almost pleading. *I'm going to have to kill him now.* Panic surged, and he began to think of ways to either explain what was on the video or how he'd lie to the vineyard about Ryan dying.

*An ambush. Another ambush. They've had a few already. The fiancée heard I'd been ambushed. I can make this work.*

"Don't what?" Ryan asked as he clicked the video icon, turning slowly. His expression changed to shock and betrayal as Woodburn raised his pistol.

The audio filtered out from the video on the thumb drive , cutting through the silence between them. Everything. All out in the open. The recording from Harper's body cam. His final moments.

Ryan's green eyes tinted with sadness as Harper's death was confirmed, and the man responsible was standing in front of him. Woodburn saw Ryan's arms beginning to flinch and raise the shotgun.

*It's either me or him.*

Woodburn stared back, barrel aimed at Ryan's chest, and emptied the magazine.

## 42

T hough he had just stared into the eyes of someone who tried to murder him, and the shots were loud enough to cause his ears to nearly bleed, Ryan happily displayed his devilish grin back at Woodburn.

He raised the shotgun just enough and pulled the trigger, nearly taking off Woodburn's right foot entirely. He waited for the expected cries of agony to finally die down, and after minutes of writhing pain, Woodburn finally looked up at him.

Ryan sat on the trunk of a car with a shotgun in hand. "You can thank one of your old pilots for the blanks," he said, lighting a cigarette. "Now, to the point in hand." He turned the laptop around and displayed the monitor to Woodburn. Harper's body cam footage.

"He was weak!" Woodburn cried, though trying to maintain some form of composure.

"You ate your best friend because you thought he was weak?" Ryan shook his head with utmost disgust, flicking the ash from his cigarette. He then held eye contact. "Harper was a fucking good man. I had to stop Drinker from coming out here and taking you apart piece by piece."

"You don't know what we know," Woodburn snarled. "You allowed the downfall around you. Adam was just as weak as you."

"You don't deserve to call him by his name!" Ryan roared. "You killed your own fucking friend." He stood off the car, eyeing his target over. "You know what, through all this shit that this world has put us through, I've taken many lives, but I've never once thought about selling out my own loved ones because they didn't agree with me."

"Save your fucking morals for your people. We're doing what needs to be done."

"Seeing as you bought it up..." Ryan pumped the shotgun. "What's happened to my people in Rennes?"

Woodburn didn't answer. Instead, he laughed, looking back at Ryan. "Even if I tell you, I know you won't kill me."

"Because?"

"Look at you. You let Connor live. You let the twins live. You let Hannah live."

"I did. You're right, but I still want an answer. What's happened to my friends under your hospitality in Rennes?" Ryan held the gun tight, waiting for an answer while Woodburn delayed. "Are they dead?"

Woodburn nodded.

In the briefest moment, he saw them all. Rich, the unfair affliction he fought. The surviving member of his family.

Mikey and Jen. His best friend and the badass who was his girl-friend were expecting their first child.

Steph. His sister. His guide through life. His guardian angel through their turbulent and unsettling childhood. Losing her husband. Surviving the war. Losing Doc. Losing Lyndon.

All gone. Everything they once were. Taken.

The ground opened around Ryan as he pictured their faces, and everything turned black, like hell was waiting for him. Waiting to take another chunk out of his heart.

"Do you know what kind of bargaining chip you can use me as when Admiral gets here?" Woodburn suggested, breaking Ryan's thoughts.

The question rattled in Ryan's head before it quickly exited out the other ear. The darkness in his peripherals returned, and a red haze peppered across his gaze.

"Yeah, I do," he choked, "but we're running low on cat food."

He aimed the barrel at Woodburn's face and pulled the trigger.

# 43

---

The knife shook violently in Ryan's hand as he carved their names onto the corkboard. Steph. Mikey. Jen. Rich. Callum. Unnamed Soldier. Harper. Six more names on the small memorial at the back of the cafeteria kitchen. Six more lives taken during the Termite War. To anyone on the outside, those names would just be statistics. Nothing more.

His heart wrapped itself in a lead blanket, and his soul wouldn't let him cry. It wasn't that he didn't care, more that if he let himself feel this, he might never recover. The hurt and pain that he'd let himself feel was not more than an inconvenience now and had been dubbed over with a cold, cynical rage that aimed at only one thing.

Killing every single last one of Admiral's men and their fucking Termites.

Ryan removed the knife from the corkboard and took it to the sink, where he washed the blood off. On the induction hobs behind him, two large stock pots simmered away with Woodburn's remains in them. He'd not wasted any organs or skin when turning the former, highly respected general into feline cuisine.

He'd opened the delivery entrance doors to let the stench out, but nothing helped take away what he'd done after nearly two hundred people saw him drag the body through and start hacking on the other side of the hot counter.

His own people looked at him in a newer light, almost a cold respect. Neither condoning nor condemning his actions. They all knew he did what he thought was right.

The newer arrivals looked at him like he was one of the Termites, like he was the monster they should've been running from. In essence, he didn't blame them. Their first experiences of Ryan during his rescue had been less than savoury, but at the end of the day, he had still rescued them.

There were whispers among them of Ryan being a monster, which didn't even scratch the surface of his soul. Other labels of psycho, madman, or his personal favourite... *Blood Ryan.* He'd accepted being a monster long before, and no one new was going to tell him what he would have to do to survive.

*It's not just about killing. There's still more to save,* the faint tether connecting him to sanity reminded. "I know," he spoke to himself. "I know." He dried the knife and slid it into the right chest pocket of his gilet's newest fitting. He moved with assertiveness back through the kitchen and out into the cafeteria, walking through the crowd of people to the podium.

All eyes leered on him. Some with fear, others with disgust.

"Okay," he said factually, holding his hands out, "I get it. First impressions are important, and what you've seen of me so far has gotten some of you feeling like you're trapped with a monster."

"You're damn right," someone whispered.

"Cool." Ryan shrugged. "Here's the thing. I don't fucking care." He stepped around the podium. "None of you are here against your will. You are free to leave, and once you step foot outside our grounds, we'll return your weapons, too." He looked around the room. "It's true. Fucking go ahead if you don't want to be here. My people and I put ourselves out there to get you people to safety, but if you don't want to be safe here... then that's cool. No harm. No foul. No harsh feelings, and also, not my fucking problem. Once you're out there, you're on your own. If you want to face these people who will do worse to you than you've seen me do in the last three days, that's your choice." He pointed towards the exit. "Go ahead. No one is stopping you."

No one moved. No one said anything.

"I would've thought that our intention was to help and save you, including some of your loved ones who very well may be still out there. We will not stop until we've helped as many people as we can, but you better rest assured that I will tear down anyone who brings my people harm. You can either be part of us, or you can fuck off."

Again, no one moved.

"In that case, ladies and gentlemen, welcome to Penbrook. Your first couple of days will be spent in this cafeteria. We're going to have to take information from all of you regarding your families and lost ones, what skills you might have that can help us function as a larger community, and how we can all work together to keep us safe." He stepped back behind the podium. "We're all at war with this enemy, so we need to fight it together."

———

Helicopter blades pounded the silent sky as the flashing lights came to a hovering standstill above the vineyard. The aircraft slowly descended towards the flare outside the front doors. Ryan stood with Drinker in the shadows, weapons by their side as the landing gear touched the ground.

The back ramp lowered with a strained whirr, and a fully armed figure approached, removing their Kevlar helmet. Long blonde hair dangled behind them, and fine blue eyes locked onto the pair.

"Alexi." Drinker nodded with a small smile, approaching and shaking the major's hand.

"Good to see you, my friend," Alexi replied. "Where's Ryan?"

Slowly stepping into the helicopter's spotlight, Penbrook's leader revealed himself. Alexi blinked twice as if he didn't recognise him. Sure, his pale skin and vibrant green eyes were the same, but his light blond dreadlocks were now dyed blood red.

"That's a new look," Alexi remarked, offering his hand.

"Saves me having to wash my hair when I get blood in it," Ryan answered, shaking hands. "What happened in Scotland?"

"I can see you're not in the business of fucking around," Alexi admitted. "Long story short, they knew we were coming. When we approached the east coast of North Uist, they sailed off the west coast, heading south underneath the Hebrides and landing back on the west coast of England, somewhere near Blackpool."

"The survivor camps would've been left with almost no defences," Drinker guessed.

"Exactly." Alexi nodded. "We got sent Harper's body cam footage..." he paused, "... we knew something was up. A short communication window with Sheffield said they were being attacked by some of Woodburn's men. I had to get the footage to you before they tried to intercept it."

"They nearly did," Ryan confirmed. "Got as close as our front gates."

"Did you have to fight them off?"

"Out of the twelve, eleven were gunned down. The twelfth one... I think what happened to him is referred to as a 'Blood Eagle' in your country?"

Alexi's expression didn't change, but the corner of his mouth twitched. "You would've made a hell of a Viking." He extended his hand. "Do you have it?"

"Yeah." Ryan dove his hand into his pocket, pulling out Woodburn's smart radio. "Think you can unlock it?"

"A couple of my guys ran encryption for the first satellites we managed to reconnect to during Rennes first days of reestablishing order. If we can unlock this and gain access to his contacts and whatever programme he was using, it could be a game changer in fighting them."

"Do you know where they are?" Drinker asked.

"We know that the U.S.S Gavato is settled off the west coast of Wales, and that Admiral and his men have made it back to Milton Keynes. They're gearing up. My men can only recon the area before we run out of fuel while looking for any more survivors stranded out there."

"What happens after you run out?"

"We'll head back here and help fortify your town. Then we fight."

"No," Ryan blurted consciously. "Not the town."

"What do you mean?" Alexi asked, confused.

"If we fortify the town, we lead them right to our doorstep."

"What do you suggest then?"

"How many men have you got?"

"Around two hundred between what's left of Operation Wolfpack and the staff at the survivor centres."

"I suggest we fortify the fucking county, then..." Ryan looked to the jet-black sky, his green eyes twinkling with furious excitement, "...let's make Surrey ours and kill any of them who try to enter."

# ACKNOWLEDGMENTS

As always, this part is unedited... so you'll get a true look into just how bad my English is!

A huge thank you and shoutout to the three ladies who make this book readable- my editors. Ericka, CJ, and Abby, it was an honour to work with you all again, and hope to continue this journey with you in the rest of the series.

The core of Team Penbrook! Nas, Lucy, Nadia, and Chava. I couldn't have pushed through and filled in what was missing if it wasn't for your attention to details. I hope the finished version lives up to it.

Dean. You never know how to deliver a bad product, and this cover art has the grip that suits it. Forever grateful for you. I can't wait to see where your future endeavours take you.

Edita. We know where we are now, and what we're doing. At last! My first port of call, and last eyes on this. This is for the doubters we left behind.

Ghost Squad: Chava Kerzel, Ola Tundun, Alex Carraro, Sandra Diamanti, Callum Munro, Dana Symonds, Donna Scuvotti, George Smith, Jenny McG, Nadia Vanders, Franky0258, Harriet Pearce, Shannon Nicole, Mak One Graffiti, Nic Winters, Sarah Zimm, and Vickie McCormick. You all helped with a major plot point in this story... so congratulations... I'm not telling you which part though!

The Critical Drinker, Mauler, and the rest of the guys at Open Bar. Your insights into what levels of story telling work have been invaluable to me.

To all my family, friends, any one who's had an influence on my life, and most importantly... you guys reading this. Thank you.

# ABOUT THE AUTHOR

This is my third time doing this, and I'm still not sure what to write.

I live in Horsham, England. I'm a chef in my full time employment, I also run a new youtube channel: Penbrook's Own.

I'm a huge advocate for mental health awareness, and these books are my own form of therapy.

I'm truly grateful for any and all support, and if I can take your mind off the ever growing stresses of today, then that's all I could wish for.

Printed in the USA
CPSIA information can be obtained
at www.ICGtesting.com
CBHW081919130824
13145CB00009B/129

9 781999 378653